ESSENCE OF RUIN

VOLUME TWO

BY

ALEC LOWNES

Essence of Ruin
Volume Two
Copyright © 2025 Alec Lownes

ISBN (print): 979-8-88993-097-6
ISBN (e-book): 979-8-88993-098-3

Edited by Kirsten Lund
Cover by Huu Ha
Interior Design by Tangcu LLC

Published 2026 by MoonQuill
Arlington, VA

www.moonquill.com

TABLE OF CONTENTS

Chapter 1

Willow stumbled over a root and barely caught herself on the rough staff. She groaned, extricated her tingling foot, and continued on. She'd long ago learned that any pleas for Annabelle to slow or pause would be met with silent indifference at best.

She could just let the woman leave her behind. That was always an option, and one she considered multiple times per day. But flashes of memory would always assert themselves to remind her of why she was traveling roughshod through thick, wild forests with this woman she barely knew.

A broken gate, splinters of stone, and silver and wood clogging the western staging area. Bodies, blood. Her own cracked and charred skin as she swept her fingers in a spell-form towards the rampaging warbeast. It unleashed lightning at the same moment, twirling and mingling with her own spell.

Death, destruction.

But she wasn't fleeing from that chaos—she'd destroyed the creature responsible for it. She was following Annabelle for the promise her erstwhile nurse dangled before her nose like a carrot. The promise of total reintegration between her spirit and body. That Annabelle was certainly leading her towards the perverse mind responsible for the warbeast that attacked Durum was something Willow would have to deal with, but she planned to deal with that only after she'd gained full control of her body.

Willow grunted and vaulted over a hedge of brambles that Annabelle was working through, landing painfully and falling against a tree trunk. She might be able to throw her body around like a ragdoll when she psychokinetically controlled her staff, but the consequences of impacts were even more severe now than they'd been back in the walled city-state of Durum.

Annabelle pushed through the last of the brambles, covered in cuts and stickers, and cast a dirty look at Willow.

"Finished showing off?" Annabelle asked.

Willow tried her best at a sneer, but the pain in her feet and shoulder turned it into a grimace. Annabelle sighed in irritation and looked around for a moment, sizing up factors of which Willow had no concept, then let out a breath.

"We'll camp here for the night," she declared, and shrugged off her pack.

It was a woodsman's pack she found on their way out of the city, while she'd been carrying Willow over one shoulder and keeping a cloaking spell going with the other hand. How she'd done it, Willow had no idea. But they'd gotten far enough away from the carnage of the warbeast attack to pillage an abandoned woodsmen's caravan and disappear into the thick forest.

Willow carried no such pack—Annabelle was at least considerate enough to shoulder that burden for her. Back in her hometown of Bridgewater, Willow was known as the doctor's daughter. Everyone knew her because it was impossible not to notice the sickly thin waif who accompanied her parents at their work. She'd always been wasted, ever since she was an infant. Her parents had told her she'd survived the Wasting.

What they didn't know was that she was the *only one* who ever had.

Willow drove the tip of the staff into the ground with a thread of psychokinesis and began unloading Annabelle's large pack. Small items she could handle, but larger ones required the assistance of what turned out to be the strangest thing about her—the fact that she'd survived the Wasting by intuitively casting psychokinesis on her own body as an infant. Until earlier that year, every bone in her paralyzed body had moved psychokinetically. Willow hadn't even known. Only when Annabelle began healing her spinal cord from the damage of the Wasting had she felt real sensation for the first time.

Willow grabbed the end of the central pole of their hastily constructed tent, and it floated horizontally to the ground. Annabelle threw the large canvas tarp over it, and the rod didn't budge an inch. She began hammering carved stakes into the ground while Willow kept the beam level.

Camp was raised in less than half an hour, with Annabelle laying out the meager cooking supplies they'd managed to scavenge from the woodsmen's caravan: a metal pot, a flint and steel, and a collapsible stand.

"Your turn," Annabelle said.

Willow sighed. She was right. Annabelle had hunted the previous day and provided the main ingredient for their thin stew. It was now Willow's duty to go out and kill something for them to eat.

With a combination of psychokinesis and physical effort, Willow righted herself with the staff Annabelle had hacked from a branch, then scratched the right side of her head. The hair there was barely a stubble from when it had been burned off during the warbeast attack, and it itched terribly. The skin on her right arm, exposed now through the burned woodsman's uniform, was slowly turning a normal color instead of the raw pink it had been after Annabelle regrew it.

"It'll grow back," Annabelle said, and Willow lowered her hand self-consciously.

Annabelle had at first appeared to be one of the nurses at the Sisters of Mercy. But she soon revealed that she had vastly more training than even their best surgeons and hailed from an entirely different city-state as well.

She was hard to gauge. Sometimes she seemed to loathe Willow from the very core of her being. No doubt because Willow was the reason they were going on this trek through the country. Other times, it almost seemed like she pitied Willow. Even rarer, she almost seemed like a friend.

"Yeah," Willow said and tromped off into the woods. It wasn't close to sunset yet, but the forest was dark from the thick canopy overhead. Willow reached into her scarred woodsman's uniform and retrieved a solid ball of light.

It was magelight, or at least nominally magelight. No other magelights took on solid form like this. But then again, no other mages could pump several person-days' worth of essence into their steadfastness layer. She threw the magelight forwards, and it lit softly on the ground, hovering a few inches above the loam of the forest.

Willow sat on the trunk of a toppled tree and slid a knife from the sheath at her side. She worked the blade into the trunk and came up with a sizable splinter of wood, which she began to whittle down. The kill was the worst part, and she wanted to keep her mind off it.

Unfortunately, keeping her mind off the coming task let it wander back to the past. To the beginning of her journey to Durum in the caravan.

The deathworm attacked when they had nearly arrived, and she'd killed it with a swing of her cane, destroying all the flesh on her hands in the process. That should have been the first sign, but she hadn't understood, ignorant of her true nature. Class was the second sign, where her very presence destabilized the professor's spell. He'd noticed, but she hadn't, that something was wrong with her.

Metrology, those bastards. They'd enticed her with knowledge of herself, and like a fool, she'd gone along with everything they'd proposed. She'd almost let herself be killed just to discover her essential attributes. They'd treated her like an animal, and she'd let them. But something had happened in that final, catastrophic testing session. Something that only came to her in her dreams. When she woke on the forest floor, sometimes the silver pendant around her neck, which Carl had inscribed, was uncomfortably warm, like it had just been active. She didn't know what it did, but he'd warned her to wear it always, and she wouldn't disobey him. It was the least she could do after murdering him.

The western staging area, with the home call blaring from the Arcanum above. That crawling thing forcing its way through the warded tunnel. The rubble and bodies. Leopold's corpse, crushed under a block of stone. Lifeless.

Something stirred in the forest, and Willow came back from the edge of a full-on panic attack. Completely motionless, heart still racing, she rolled the splinter she'd carved between her fingers, getting a feel for it as she searched the treeline with wide eyes. The sensation of the splinter sank into her, becoming a part of her body. Or at least that's how she perceived it when her psychokinesis reached out and gripped something.

Was it normal to experience this sensation? Of course it wasn't. It wasn't even normal for her, whose life had been so abnormal even before everything else. But she forced herself to focus outward, on the hunt. Now that her legs had been reconnected to her nervous system, she had plenty of essence to spare for helping with these mundane tasks. The reintegration had come at great pain and cost in distance traveled, but she'd refused to take another step away from Durum until Annabelle had performed the surgery.

A small fox nosed out from between two trees, and she saw the telltale flicker of blue fire on its three tails. Foxfire. Her magelight had attracted a magical creature just as she'd hoped. Willow had always been a big eater, and it turned out there was a reason for that too. Her body was constantly building up unfathomable amounts of essence, and she needed a constant influx of calories to keep up the generation. But out here in the forest, the calories were lacking, so she supplemented with the essence of magical creatures.

The foxfire nosed closer still to the magelight, hoping to take some of the essence for itself. Willow opened her hand, and the splinter shot forwards like an arrow, pinning the foxfire to the ground beside the magelight. It cried once, then grew still.

Willow retrieved the magelight and the dead foxfire before making her way back to the campsite. Annabelle had already conjured water into the pot and was boiling it with a dab of congealed fire essence beneath it on the fold-out stand. Annabelle hadn't gotten the hang of using the flint and steel, so she just cast spells to solve all her problems.

If only it were so simple for Willow.

Willow sat and skinned the small foxfire. Even dead, blue fire darted through its veins. The pelt would make an excellent fire-resistant leather gauntlet if she could sell it. But of course, she couldn't. There was no one to sell it to out here. She sliced muscles off the foxfire and dropped them one by one into the boiling pot. There had to be a better way to sustain themselves while trekking through the wilderness, but neither of them really knew how to camp, so it was boiled meat stew every night.

By the time the foxfire was reduced to a pile of guts and bones, the pot was glowing a soft blue from within, and the smells coming from it were enough to make Willow's grip slip on her knife. She thrust the blade into the fire essence below the pot to clean it, then sheathed it at her side. Annabelle lifted the pot and placed it on the forest floor, where they immediately went at it with spoons.

As she ate, Willow felt her essence artificially replenished by the cooked foxfire. Her body took in the blue fire essence and converted it to neutral essence, refilling what her meager calorie budget couldn't. She was still hungry all the time, but the extra infusion of essence from magical creatures helped. For Annabelle, the extra essence would merely wash through her and be expelled. Even with her spellcasting, she would be at almost full capacity. Willow, on the other hand, was still using psychokinesis to breathe and bend her spine—everything that occurred in her torso and hadn't yet been reconnected to her brain.

They ate in silence as the twilight forest darkened to night. Willow cast her magelight sphere high into the air so as not to attract any other magical creatures looking for a quick meal, and they ate by the yellow magical light.

Willow had just extracted a chewy tendon from her mouth when she dared to broach the subject that was constantly on her mind—the only reason she was following Annabelle at all.

"I'm ready for the last operation," she said.

Annabelle didn't look up at the statement, just continued sitting and chewing chunks of foxfire. Willow waited for a painfully long time, the weight of her demand grinding her conscience down. Then she couldn't wait anymore.

"Did you hear me?"

"I did," Annabelle said, extracting a thin bone from her mouth and throwing it over her shoulder. "We'd lose a day of progress."

"It has to be done sometime," Willow pressed.

"You'll be slower afterwards."

"But I'll get faster again eventually."

Annabelle sighed and dropped her spoon in the empty pot.

"Fine," she said. "We'll start tomorrow. Find someplace secure and get the wards in place."

Willow pushed Annabelle's spoon around in the pot, not believing the other woman had given in with so little argument. "Thank you," she said, feeling guilty about the vast effort she'd just forced Annabelle to commit to. "You don't know what this means."

"*I* know," Annabelle countered. "Do you?"

CHAPTER 2

Willow was sore as hell when she woke on the forest floor, even with the thin bedding roll sparing her the worst of the bruises caused by buried roots and nuts. Despite the aches, it only took remembering her conversation with Annabelle the night before to lift her spirits. She gingerly levered herself upright, fighting a momentary spasm in her arm from her still-awakening brain's inability to separate psychokinetic from physical control, and looked around the rough campsite.

The pot and metal stand stood above the small fire, which Willow had supplemented during the night with actual wood to burn instead of relying purely on essence. The leftover contents of the pot could be faintly scented in the stale air beneath the wards. No doubt they would have been beset in the night multiple times by hungry and curious magical creatures if not for the encompassing wards.

Annabelle turned over and muttered, and when Willow glanced at her sleeping face, she saw lines of worry between the woman's brows. Willow slipped out from under the thin sheet as quietly as she could, taking a route to the pot stand that passed closer than strictly necessary to the nurse.

"Andrew..." she muttered. "I don't... Don't make me... make me go."

Annabelle twitched as if flinching from a blow, and Willow

quickly looked away to cast a thin stream of fire-concepted essence into the bed of ash. Once the fire essence pooled, she pushed the charred stick ends into the center until they took flame and began heating the thin pool of congealed stew.

When she looked back, Annabelle was just sliding out of her bedding, pushing the heel of her hand into her eye.

"How did you sleep?" Willow asked.

She wondered if Annabelle would remember the dream. It hadn't been the first time Annabelle spoke in her sleep, and from what she'd said, Willow thought it likely she suffered from flashback nightmares, just as she did. From what snatches of mumbles she caught, they often concerned a man named Andrew. But whether he was a colleague at the Sisters of Mercy or someone from her life before, she couldn't tell.

"Well enough," Annabelle replied, slowly getting to her feet and stretching the kinks from her back. She surveyed the faintly distorted forest outside the dome of the wards, walking the perimeter once around before placing her hand on the barrier. It wasn't the kind of spell that would repel any physical intrusion—more of an illusion, really. It popped like a soap bubble at her touch, bringing the slightly muted forest into stark relief and filling the formerly stale, silent air with birdsong.

"Where are you going?" Willow called back, suddenly afraid that Annabelle would abandon her on the verge of making her whole.

Annabelle gave an exasperated glance back and trudged off into the underbrush, where Willow faintly caught the sound of her making water.

Alone in the small camp, Willow considered what the very near future would hold for her. Each of the surgeries up to this point had come with excruciating pain as her unconscious mind invoked psychokinetic spells to move now unparalyzed muscles. It had taken days to adjust to the last operation in Durum, which had restored her arms up to the shoulders. And back then, if she really needed to do something, she could don essence-blocking bands to achieve a brief respite from the writhing pain. But they didn't have any of the essence-blockers with them now. Even if they did, Willow doubted they would work on this, the most invasive operation yet.

When Annabelle returned, Willow had spooned out the dregs of the thinned soup into two metal camp bowls. She was now scouring the interior of the pot with a white-hot flame, charring what remained within to just below the softening point of the metal itself.

Without a word of thanks, Annabelle took her metal bowl and gobbled her share of the stew. Willow tried to force her hands not to shake as she took up her own bowl, eating the stew a spoonful at a time. There was almost no essence left in the stew from the foxfire, and the thin liquid merely filled her physical stomach. She could already feel herself becoming ravenous from her body's insatiable need to convert nearly every calorie to essence, even though she wasn't using as much as she used to.

The stew leftovers were unsatisfying, which her stomach announced shortly after finishing, and it was difficult to pack camp with how weak she felt. Annabelle took no mercy on her, as usual, and sped along packing everything into the two dense backpacks, casting exasperated looks at her as Willow struggled to pack just the cooking utensils. Once everything was stuffed inside, they donned the packs and headed west, as indicated by Annabelle's compass.

Willow was sorely tempted to let her psychokinesis take over moving her legs, which were the most recently cured and therefore weakest part of her body, but she forced herself to hold fast. If she didn't exercise her muscles now, they would never grow stronger and never become more efficient than her own psychokinesis. As it was now, she was using up far more energy than she normally did to move around. But once her legs were as strong as any other adult's, she should theoretically see a boost. Whether that would translate to her body requiring fewer calories to fuel its massive essence generation, she didn't know.

They walked in silence for an hour. Willow progressively grew weaker with each step until she stumbled against a tree and caught a flash of movement out of the corner of her eye. Quick as she could, she threw her walking staff with psychokinesis at the movement, which caused the critter to reverse course and head straight towards Annabelle.

Annabelle held out a finger at arm's length, and a thin bolt of static arced from her body to the scurrying animal. It let out a high squeak and crashed to the ground. Annabelle glanced at Willow, then fished around in the underbrush until she retrieved the scorched and smoking body of a furred creature about as large as a small dog.

"Quinc," Annabelle said, looking the body over.

Its fur was light brown, with a blue streak running from the back of its neck all the way down its long, fluffy tail, which was almost like a giant squirrel's. Its back leg twitched, but its head lolled at an unnatural angle. As Willow watched, static arced from the base of its neck to the end of its tail, discharging against a tree trunk.

"Thanks," Willow panted, reaching her hand out towards the underbrush. Her staff rose easily and floated back to her grip. Then she leaned heavily on it as she approached Annabelle.

"They're lightning magical creatures," Annabelle said. "It wouldn't have attacked you. A waste of perfectly good essence."

"Not for me," Willow said, reaching for the quinc.

Annabelle took another look at the scorched fur on the side of the creature, then dropped it in the underbrush, shrugged, and turned away.

"What's wrong with you?" Willow raised her voice and leaned

painfully over to retrieve the body. She worked her fingers into its fur, letting her perception pass into the creature. The same way the staff felt like a part of her body, the quinc began to feel that way as well. Under the fur were sacs along the quinc's back filled with a spongy mix of cells which stored the static it used to defend itself. This was revealed to her as if in a flash of inspiration, though it was only a side effect of partially *becoming* one with the quinc's body. With a gentle squeeze, she discharged the sacs while keeping the valuable essence tissue intact.

Willow closed her eyes, sinking her mind further into the quinc, while the pendant Carl had given her warmed ever so slightly at the effort. She let go carefully, and the body hovered in midair. With a single motion, she stripped the fur off the body and discarded it into the thicket.

When Willow opened her eyes, she caught a look of disgust for a fraction of a second on Annabelle's face before the other woman turned away.

"We're wasting time," Annabelle said.

"I'm wasting away," Willow retorted through gritted teeth. With a whispered concept, she engulfed the small quinc in flame. It immediately began to spit and sizzle, making Willow feel faint with hunger.

"Look," Annabelle barked, turning sharply on her. "We can't keep stopping. Do you have any idea how dangerous it is in these woods?"

It was hard for Willow to take her eyes off the roasting quinc, but she glanced into the canopy above. "It doesn't seem so dangerous to me," she said. "Why did you take us through here if it was?"

"To lose—Listen," she said. "There may be people coming after us, after you, from Durum. After what happened at the gate, I'm sure there are a fair few questions they'd like to ask you. Questions it might not behoove you to answer. Do you understand?"

Willow did. The thought had crossed her mind more than once. What would people, normal people and mages alike, think of her? Would they think she was a monster? A monster that could face a warbeast alone? A warbeast herself? Or a magical creature, like the metrologists had assumed? The truth was, she didn't like to think about what or who might be following them.

The hardest part was that there was very little left for her in Durum. Leopold was dead. And because of her. She was fleeing Durum to save the others from herself, that was true. But it was also true that she couldn't face that place anymore, the place the two of them had shared together. The only way to cut herself off from the spiral of dark thoughts was to remove herself from the situation entirely.

"Yes," she muttered between gritted teeth. She began to walk slowly through the underbrush towards Annabelle, the sizzling quinc still hovering in the air beside her. Annabelle cast a look at the quinc but turned anyway and proceeded to lead the way.

The going was much easier once Willow had food in her stomach and essence in her veins. After being cooked, the little static sacs along the quinc's back were soft and savory, each bursting in her mouth like an overripe plum. For the sacs, there was relatively little tissue to sate her hunger, but they were chock-full of lightning essence, which her body hungrily subsumed and converted to her natural unconcepted essence. The body of the quinc sated her in a much more physical way. After discarding the bones and offal into the underbrush, Willow actually felt relatively good again.

Fifteen minutes later, the thick undergrowth of the forest abruptly gave way, and Willow was surprised to come upon a handful of wooden buildings surrounded by a ring of ankle-high weeds. There were seven large structures as far as Willow could tell, about the size of one of the houses back in Bridgewater, And all single-story. Scattered between these larger homes were smaller buildings, which could only be workshops. In fact, Willow thought she could spy an anvil beneath an overhanging shadow in the closest building.

But there was something wrong with the scene.

Annabelle had crouched down beside her onto the balls of her feet and was rapidly whispering concepts while weaving a complicated spell-form. Willow could tell something was off, but glancing around, she couldn't spot anyone hiding. No quick-ducking faces in the windows, no arrows being fitted into bows. It was silent in the small village.

And there it was: there was no one here. The village was empty. Entirely empty, from what she could tell.

Willow carefully side-stepped over to Annabelle, her staff held out like a ward, until she was close enough that she thought a whisper might carry.

"What is this place?" Willow whispered.

The spell that Annabelle had been weaving shone golden, extending from each of her fingertips like claws. From the taste of essence in the air, the spell was meant to slice and part flesh; something meant for medical purposes, now elongated into a barely defensive weapon.

"I don't know," Annabelle breathed, not looking at Willow but keeping her eyes locked on the abandoned village ahead. She sniffed. "No smoke, but I can smell spoiled meat."

When Willow took an experimental sniff, she could just sense the rank odor under the acrid tang of early fall leaf change. The smell made her hackles go up. Were there bodies in these houses? What did this?

"Keep close to me," Annabelle hissed. "And for the gods' sake, queue up a spell."

Willow clenched her teeth, feeling blood rise to her cheeks. The thought of weaving essence into an offensive spell... it turned her stomach.

"No," she said back, glaring at Annabelle's quick, infuriated glance.

"Child," Annabelle spat, then started slowly forwards.

Willow followed, her staff held closely over her heart. She supposed if worst came to worst, she might be able to whack something to death with it, if the attacking creature was small enough. But if they were up against humans…

Annabelle led the way to the rear of the most outlying structure, a wide house with three shuttered windows in the back. It was constructed of notched-and-fitted logs, chinked with dry moss. Above, there was a shallowly sloped roof made of shingles, each a hand-width and a half wide and slowly growing moss.

"Don't know who builds a house out of wood," Annabelle said derisively, peeking around the corner of the building.

"There were plenty like this in Bridgewater," Willow whispered. "Outside of the cities, log structures are the norm."

"If you're so smart all of a sudden," Annabelle hissed, "then you tell me what we're looking at."

Willow steeled herself and staggered to Annabelle so she could look out past the corner of the house. The other structures were much the same as this one—log walls with low stone foundations and shingles of wood on shallowly sloped roofs. Those roofs wouldn't do to shed any snow, but here under the dense canopy, they would work well enough. Willow looked up at the bright ring of sky visible through the mostly circular gap in the trees, marking the radius of the small settlement.

"This isn't a town," Willow whispered. "Not big enough. Maybe a logging outpost. There's one in the forest near Bridgewater. They trade with further-off towns, lumber for essentials they can't get here. Mostly you get strange people out here, or greedy. People who don't normally fit in with larger towns. People who like to do things their way."

Willow considered why Annabelle would have no knowledge of the norms out here in the sparse forests of the piedmont region. She wondered if things were very different back in Asche. It was a subject she did not want to broach while they were creeping around.

"Right," Annabelle said, turning the corner. She crept along the short side wall of the house, then peeked quickly and turned to the front of the structure.

Willow didn't like it. She felt too exposed with the house to her back and the town laid out all in front. All of the other buildings, and anyone within them, would have a direct line of sight to the pair. Annabelle quickly crouched up to the door and slipped her pointer finger into the gap at the right side of the frame. A puzzled look came over her face, but she pushed the door open and inched inside, until she'd disappeared completely. It only took a second for her spell-clad hand to emerge and impatiently wave Willow forwards.

Willow scurried, bent low, around the front of the house and entered the dark alongside Annabelle, who eased the door closed again. It was pitch black in the house with the shutters closed. Willow heard Annabelle whisper beside her, and a dim light bloomed in Annabelle's hands.

The light was barely enough to illuminate the farthest reaches of the single-room cabin, and what it revealed caused a spike of adrenaline to shoot through Willow's body. It was as if a whirlwind had gone through the home—it had been ransacked. The table, a structure of fitted wooden planks, was turned over a few feet from the door, a blackened notch cut deep into the upper edge. There was a broad axe for hewing beside the overturned table, lying in a vaguely circular puddle.

It wasn't just a puddle, Willow realized. The rotten stench was stronger in the cabin, and she knew at once what it was.

Blood.

Annabelle, standing tall now that they were within the house with the door closed, walked over to the far wall and touched what Willow had assumed to be a long, thin coat peg. She tugged, and the peg came out in one piece. It was whittled to a needle point at the end, which had somehow stayed sharp even though it had clearly been shoved forcefully into the wall.

"Elves," Annabelle whispered, dropping the arrow.

Willow assumed she'd heard wrong and rose with the aid of her staff, looking about the cabin interior with blooming dread. There were puddles of blood on the ground in varying sizes and three drag marks, each leading out the front door. She looked back and saw that the wooden lock had been splintered by brute force.

"I don't understand," Willow barely whispered, trying to keep her rising panic in check. "Who did this? They've left everything. The axe, the crockery. Gods..."

"Not who," Annabelle replied. "But what. This was no human attack. This village fell to magical creatures and elves."

"Elves," Willow breathed. "What are you talking about?"

"Half-breeds," Annabelle said, toeing an iron knife left on the floor. She stooped to pick it up, trying the edge with the ball of her thumb. "They're like magical creatures, but smarter. Dangerous."

"What?" Willow still couldn't believe what she was hearing. "Elves aren't real?" She tried to state it, but it came out as a question.

"Lucky for us," Annabelle continued from beside the largest pool of blood while scraping the tip of her knife through it, as if Willow hadn't said anything at all. "It seems this attack occurred long ago. A month, maybe more. We should be safe here. Safe, at least, compared to out there in the forest."

Safe. Annabelle could only be talking about setting up for her next operation, but Willow wasn't sure now that she wanted to be made so vulnerable in a place of death like this. It felt as though even speaking too loudly might bring whatever—not elves. Surely not elves—back down on the raided village.

But before she could resolve the warring emotions in her heart, Annabelle set her pack down beside the overturned table and glared at her.

"Are you just going to stand here like a sack of shit? Help me right this table. Unless you'd prefer I operate on the floor."

Willow wasn't entirely sure what she preferred at the moment.

CHAPTER 3

The village was dead silent. Even the birds in the trees seemed respectful of the massacre that had occurred here. With a village this size, it was impossible that only adults had been present. Willow didn't want to think of what the scene had been like during the attack.

She slowly crept to the door of another cabin and, staff held before her chest, pushed the cracked wooden panel open with her off hand. Pitch darkness greeted her—this house, like so many of the other buildings, had been entirely closed off with locking, hinging shutters. She supposed the villagers had thought that would help them, and perhaps it did spare them for a few precious minutes or hours. But it hadn't saved them in the end.

Willow hated going from house to house, but she had to make sure there was no one and nothing left in the village before Annabelle began the surgery. The ex-nurse was going all out preparing the interior of the cabin. By the time Willow had finished helping Annabelle scoot the heavier pieces of furniture out of the way of the operating table—which had probably been the dining table not so long before—she had already begun casting layer upon layer of auxiliary spells around the interior. She groaningly explained to Willow that these were standard fare in the Arcanum operating rooms and would be required for such a delicate and overarching operation as the one they were trying to achieve. Then she sent Willow out to inspect the rest of the village.

Willow cast a small magelight and sent it bobbing into the room. Dark blood lay on the floor, long since hardened and cracked, and the interior of this cabin was in a similar state of devastation as the others she'd examined. She nearly turned away before the light hit the back wall, hovering over a shorter, carved bed frame.

The bed of a child.

Willow stumbled out, hyperventilating. Her arms writhed, and she tried to get them under control, but sometimes the best remedy she'd found was to let them go through their attack without forcing anything. Her fingers twitched, and she lost her grip on the staff, which stood upright still, held in place by psychokinesis.

Benny. It was impossible not to see Benny sleeping in that bed. Frightened, huddling in the corner with Margaret while Bryan stood before the door, axe or sword in hand, prepared to give his life to gain his wife and son even a few precious seconds of existence. The door to the cabin swung outward behind her, a hinge rope popped, and it fell completely off the structure. Willow startled away, and the door cracked down the center from an unconscious twist of psychokinesis.

As Willow tried to get herself under control, crouched down on the weedy scraped dirt, she looked across what had been the village square towards the outside of the makeshift operating theater. Bright white light shone from the cracks in the shutters and even through some of the disintegrating moss chinking. Come night, the cabin would be a veritable beacon to magical creatures if Annabelle didn't put a ward around the entire structure. But she was sure that angle had been considered. Although cruel, Annabelle was efficient and calculating.

Practical thoughts eventually banished the panic, and Willow got to her feet once again. The staff slid upright through the dirt to her hand, and she moved on from the scene of devastation. There was nothing alive in that house, human or otherwise. It had been the case for every house she'd visited thus far. The village was entirely abandoned, the stink of blood and death enough to keep even the most desperate of creatures away.

Beside the house was a small workshop, barely ten feet square with a lightly shingled roof that sloped back away from the missing fourth wall, serving as an entrance. In the approaching dusk, not to mention the overarching canopy, there wasn't enough light to see its contents, so Willow sent another magelight bobbing ahead, which illuminated the interior.

It was a small papermaker's workshop. She recognized the frames and suspension tank from the shop in her own hometown, back in Bridgewater. There weren't many hiding spaces to illuminate, and without the chance of stumbling upon something terribly upsetting, Willow decided to enter. There were only a couple of workshops left to inspect, and she had time.

Above, suspended on ropes from the low ceiling, were the frames they'd used to dry the newly formed sheets. The suspension tank was cloudy and smelled stagnant. A few bugs had fallen in, black specks on the frothy water. A fine cotton weave was spread between the wooden frames for pressing and compacting the filtered mash. All in all, she was impressed at how much functionality had been stuffed into so small a workspace.

And in the back corner, under a flat metal plate, was the finished product. Willow lifted the plate and slid free one sheet of wood pulp paper. It was thin and had crisp edges—there must be a straight-line cutter somewhere in here that she hadn't seen. The quality was excellent, just a tad under what had been available in Durum. She wondered where the owner of the workshop had learned the craft, and if they'd come out here as part of the initial expedition into the forest or had been hired later.

But she couldn't keep the thought of that small bed out of her mind, of the life the papermaker had made in the village, and replaced the fine sheet on the stack and covered it with the metal plate. There was no use, of course. The paper would molder and rot soon enough, but it felt wrong to disrespect the product of a life well lived.

Willow was turning to leave when she saw, on a small shelf integrated into the wall of the workshop, a single sheet of paper weighed down under a rounded stone. This one wasn't blank, though, and was filled with writing. Beside it sat a thin charcoal pencil.

She lifted the stone and summoned the bobbing magelight, which washed the paper with yellow luminescence. She saw immediately that it was a correspondence, though to where it had been destined she had no idea. There was no envelope nearby, nor wax seal. She supposed those might be within the house she'd so swiftly abandoned.

She brought the letter closer and began to read.

Steven,

I hope you are doing well. I am writing to request a special supply run. I, more than anyone, am aware of how difficult scheduling a caravan will be in the off-season, but I find it impossible to wait.

The creatures in the wood have grown more hostile of late, and we require stocks of both ammo and new weapons. Additionally, if it is within your power to find a guard willing to leave the city for a life on the frontier, such an addition would be much appreciated. We have already lost two of the woodsmen, and their absence is felt most acutely.

Below I have attached a list of supplies. Owing to the off-schedule request, I am willing to pay up to 20 percent more on the total. I will not haggle with you or our lives through post, and I trust that you will wait to counter-offer until you arrive with our necessities.

Your former business partner,

Cletus

Willow replaced the letter under the smooth stone and looked out towards the rapidly dimming village square. She supposed the supplies Cletus had listed would feed and supply a village of thirty. If so, there had been even more people crammed into each house than she'd imagined in the beginning.

The thought made her sick. He'd never had the chance to send off the letter, and even if he had, the returning caravan would have found nothing but blood and dirt. Things must have escalated quickly from the tone of his letter, and even quicker if he never even sent it off.

Bridgewater had had the occasional magical creature roam the village border, but nothing like this. Was it the forest itself? Was this place more dangerous than the piedmont's hills? Or was there just less cover out there in Bridgewater where an attack against the village could be staged? Or was it the... elves? Willow still had trouble imagining the things that Annabelle had called half-breeds, but from the arrows she'd found lodged in the cabin walls, she supposed they had access to some kind of weaponry. They might be smarter than your standard magical creature, which *might* explain this village's total destruction.

It took barely five minutes to inspect the remaining workshops—all empty of anything living, though entirely stocked with the tools of their respective trades. By the time she headed back across the village square, Annabelle was leaning in the doorway of the cabin, waiting for her. In the dark, the cabin was much more of a beacon than it had been in the shadow of the forest.

"You took long enough," Annabelle remarked as Willow approached.

The light from the open door made Willow squint. "Are you going to do anything about this?" Willow shot back, motioning to the open door and shining chinks in the cabin walls. "We're just asking to be attacked."

Annabelle scoffed. "Suddenly you're the expert," she said. "The light won't attract magical creatures. They'll be scared of it. As for the spells, their essence *will* call them. Now that you've finished dawdling, I can emplace the barrier."

She stepped out past Willow and began casting the complicated ward that Willow had seen her raise every night. Willow paid attention to the concepts and spell-forms, knowing that if anything happened to Annabelle, she'd have to raise the barrier every night. Or risk being mobbed by quincs and salamanders and a whole host of hungry wildlife.

Annabelle took ten minutes to raise the barrier around the perimeter of the cabin—much longer than it took to raise just around their campsite—and when she returned, she looked beat.

"Are you okay?" Willow asked, concern winning over annoyance. Annabelle raised an eyebrow. "I mean… do you have enough left in you to perform the surgery? Or are you going to crap out halfway through?"

"Unlike you, I know my limits," Annabelle retorted and pushed past into the cabin.

Willow followed and had to squint her eyes even further, blinking hard as she closed the door and turned to see the interior.

The cabin was lit with a bright, even light that cast no shadows. It was as if every particle of air in the space was shining with its own power, which Willow supposed might actually be the effect of whatever spell Annabelle had used. The air was warm and had an antiseptic smell, like strong alcohol or, she realized, the interior of the Sisters of Mercy. The logs of the walls and ceiling had been scoured down to bare fresh wood, and most pieces of furniture in the place had been pushed into a far corner, save for the large dining table in the center of the room and a chair beside it.

Annabelle gestured to the table. "Strip to the waist and lie face down," she said, producing a thin pillow, which she laid at the far end.

Willow looked at the table suspiciously, then at Annabelle, and gritted her teeth. Finally, she turned, stripped, and lay down. The table was warm and as smooth as glass, which she realized was the effect of another spell. The makeshift operating theater was absolutely chock-full of essence at the moment.

"I could have helped," Willow said, her voice slightly muffled with her cheek against the surface.

"You?" Annabelle asked, surprised.

"I've got essence to spare. I could have—"

Annabelle let out a surprised bark of laughter. "You wouldn't know the first thing to do, and I don't have time to instruct you. If you don't know, and I'm sure you never even stopped to think about it, I've trained for years to get to where I am. That's your problem, Willow. You never consider others or their motivations. Think next time before you speak, and I might take what you say seriously."

Willow felt her cheeks heat with anger. Any goodwill Annabelle had gained by performing these operations was being steadily eroded by her acerbic personality. Willow estimated she could only take another week of Annabelle's presence before she'd haul off and kill her out of sheer frustration.

Annabelle whispered concepts and stirred the air in multiple spell-forms above Willow's bare back. Willow felt her skin begin to tingle, then fall numb, and her eyebrows creased in confusion.

"Aren't you going to put me to sleep for this?" she asked with not a little panic in her voice.

Annabelle didn't respond right away, finishing up a second spell and drawing it down over Willow's arms, which immediately went numb.

"Not this time," Annabelle said. The hesitation in her voice scared Willow. "For this operation... you're going to have to stay awake. I want to make sure I don't scramble your brain, and for that, you're going to have to remain conscious."

Willow thought she should be breathing hard at this revelation, but her lungs didn't change pace at all, and she realized she didn't have control over them in the slightest. Annabelle had, in effect, cast a magic nullification field on her chest and spine. How she was keeping Willow alive, Willow didn't even want to consider.

"O... Okay," Willow said, having to wait for her lungs to refill to complete the word. In the corner of her eye, she saw Annabelle finish up a third spell, which attached a short essential blade to her forefinger. Willow's eyes widened.

"You won't feel a thing," Annabelle said and began to cut.

Annabelle had lied.

Sure, Willow didn't feel any pain, but there were other sensations, like the feeling of skin parting from muscle, doubling over to rest on her arms as Annabelle flayed her back. Then the never-before-felt sensation of muscle parting from bone as Annabelle exposed Willow's spine. She tried not to think of the quinc and how it had looked as she devoured the essential sacs along its spine. She tried not to imagine herself in its place.

Slowly, very slowly, other sensations began to appear. First a tingling, then a burning. When Willow finally grunted at the beginnings of pain, Annabelle deigned to stop.

"What are you feeling?"

"Something... It hurts," Willow grunted.

Annabelle wove a complicated spell and lowered it onto Willow's back, which numbed much of the pain. Willow had the realization that this rapidly banished sensation had been her nerves firing for the first time. That she had, for the first time in her life, felt something from her back. Willow shuddered at the thought of what she must look like to Annabelle above.

The operation went on for hours. Annabelle only stopped when Willow interrupted with some new sensation and the few times she'd had to cast a spell of wakefulness over herself. It had to be early in the morning, dreadfully early, but Willow wasn't about to fall asleep in the middle of the procedure.

It went on and on until the sun had barely begun to shine through the seam around the door, Annabelle let out a long sigh.

"What's wrong?" Willow asked.

"Nothing. We're finished," she said, her voice heavy with fatigue.

Willow felt her eyes droop as well. Annabelle must have been casting a spell of wakefulness on her too, to stave off unconsciousness. The woman draped a sheet over Willow's back, then staggered to the bed at the far side of the cabin.

"When you wake, don't move," Annabelle warned. "I'll numb you. The pain will be excruciating otherwise."

Willow meant to answer. She could have sworn she'd answered, but darkness overtook her so quickly she wasn't sure at all.

It felt like little more than a blink, but when she opened her eyes again, the sun was shining hard through the crack around the door. Birds were twittering in the trees outside, but she couldn't sense movement in the cabin.

"Annabelle?" Willow asked. When she strained her ears, she could hear deep breathing from just out of her vision. It must be Annabelle, still asleep.

If Annabelle was still asleep, then what had woken her?

The bright line of sun around the door occluded, and Willow's eyes went wide. The wooden door creaked open, revealing the silhouette of a large man whose features were entirely hidden by the glaring sun.

"Well, well, well," he said. "What have we here?"

CHAPTER 4

Willow tried to get up, but the necessity of Annabelle's prohibition on movement became immediately clear. Pain lanced through her spine. Her ribs felt like they were going to bow out and explode, and her lungs and heart began hitching immediately. She would have screamed if her lungs had cooperated. Instead, only a staggered yelping issued from her mouth as she writhed under the white sheet.

It was enough to wake Annabelle. The nurse sprang upright and immediately began weaving a static concept, perhaps for the same lightning attack she'd used to bring down the quinc.

"Uh uh," the burly figure from the door said, stepping into the cabin.

The operating theater spells were still active, which doused the man with even, unshadowed light. He was heavily muscled, with a wild beard and long, greasy hair held back with a leather brace. He wore a dark brown shirt crossed by a bandoleer, on which was mounted a quiver of bolts. He raised a cocked crossbow, bolt and all, and leveled it at Annabelle.

The concepts stopped in her throat.

"There'll be none of that."

His voice was both low and tinged with a strange accent. If Willow could have considered it for a moment, she might have been able to place it. Instead, she continued her staggered yelps, writhing under the white sheet.

"An' you, stop that caterwauling," he spat at Willow. His expression grew hard as the seconds passed, and he moved the crossbow from Annabelle to Willow.

"She can't!" Annabelle yelped, bringing the crossbow right back to her. She flinched, then edged back to the wall. "She can't."

"What d'you mean?" the man asked. Annabelle clammed up, and he gestured with his crossbow. "Out with it."

"She's in pain. I'm a nurse. If I could just—"

"Nuh uh." Another man, skinnier and shorter than the first, entered the room.

This man was holding a short sword and walked right up to Willow, who'd managed to turn almost all the way over on her side. He pressed the flat of the blade on her arm.

"He said *stop it*," the short man said, a paper smile still on his face as he moved the blade up to Willow's neck.

She snuffled in fear, numbness tingling her fingertips. She couldn't breathe; her lungs wouldn't cooperate, and her vision was going black around the edges.

The man lifted up the edge of the white cloth and peered underneath. "Huh," he said, amused, and let it drop.

"Hey Magnus," he said. "Take a look at—"

Willow lost consciousness.

She came to all of a sudden, a gasp of breath causing her lungs to hitch again. She flopped like a fish on the table—arms useless and legs as well. In a far-off part of her mind, she registered the presence of the sheet on top of her and flushed in anger at the man who'd lifted it just a moment ago, but she was helpless to stop him even now.

"Shhh, shhh," Annabelle hushed into her ear. "Willow, you need to calm down."

Willow yelped in reply but couldn't get her lungs working well enough to force out a complete word. The pain was beyond anything she'd ever experienced. It was all-encompassing. Her entire world. It blinded her with its urgency.

"If I could just—" Annabelle began.

"Nope," the voice of the second man replied. "You start casting anything, you'll get my blade through your neck lickety-split. Shut her up some other way."

Annabelle lowered her face into Willow's rapidly closing field of view. The edges were going dark again, and she felt that numbness. She had seconds left.

"Stop trying to breathe," Annabelle implored. "Just let it happen. You have reflexes that'll keep you alive. You've wound them into your... body all your life. Now let them work."

Willow opened her mouth to ask how—to ask why this was happening. To beg for death. Instead, she passed out again.

* * *

When Willow awoke for the third time, Annabelle was there waiting for her. The sun hadn't changed position outside the front door and still shone painfully into her eyes. She realized she must be passing out for only seconds at a time before her body began breathing all on its own again.

"Willow," Annabelle implored.

Willow closed her eyes and tried as hard as she could not to breathe. To pay no attention to her lungs, to her ribs. They burned like fire, or like she was being pummeled to death with a particularly nasty piece of wood. It was impossible to ignore, but she tried anyway. After everything, couldn't she do this?

She took a breath. Her body breathed for her, the way it had her entire life, except not at all like that. This time, it was her actual body performing the motions, and she felt a disturbing fatigue set up along her ribs, as if she'd been running for a mile or more. Was she even strong enough to breathe on her own? Please, gods, let her be.

She only got one more breath in before her mind slipped, and she fell back into the loop of struggling to breathe and being unable to let go. Her vision went black again as she cast an imploring stare at Annabelle.

Do something, she mouthed, then was out.

* * *

Awake again.

Willow immediately relaxed her entire body. Her cheeks went slack, eyes drooping closed, scrabbling fingers lying smooth. With her half-lidded eyes, she saw the two bandits sitting in chairs against the far wall watching the spectacle. The large one, Magnus, was chewing a strip of jerky. From his wet munching, Willow caught the unmistakable scent of fire essence.

Foxfire essence.

"That's—" Willow said, then immediately convulsed.

The small one chuckled. "This never gets old," he said, and reached into a pack at his feet.

No, not *a* pack. *Her* pack.

She bristled at the violation but tried to relax her body, nonetheless. Her vision grew dark at the borders, but she began to breathe, which cleared up the creeping numbness and tunnel vision.

"That's right," Annabelle soothed. "That's the way." She leaned closer, inspecting Willow's neck, and whispered in her ear. "Now would be a really good time for you to stop pissing around and blow these fuckers up."

Willow jerked in surprise, which sent another spasm through her lungs. It took her another minute to clear it up, growing even closer to passing out once again. However, she managed to keep hold of consciousness this time, but barely.

It was all Willow could do to keep breathing. All she could do to lie completely still and not twitch her muscles with psychokinesis, thus setting up the feedback loop which sent them into writhing seizures. How could Annabelle expect this of her?

No, she realized when she looked into Annabelle's eyes. She didn't expect Willow to recover and eviscerate the bandits. Annabelle hoped she would—she *wished* she would. She was desperate.

She was afraid.

Which made Willow afraid. For the first time since awakening, she put together their situation a point at a time. They'd been awakened by bandits, who'd probably found them in the night from the shining cabin interior and waited until they'd gone to sleep before barging in. The bandits were stealing their food, which meant they might not have much of their own. Which also meant that she and Annabelle effectively had no traveling packs.

It was, all things considered, about the worst situation she'd ever found herself in, including the warbeast barreling down the warded tunnel back in Durum.

She had to do something.

Willow tried to reach out. Tried to seep her awareness into the table she lay on, skin to wood, and make it a part of her body. If she could familiarize herself with it, see it the same way as her staff or axe, then she could rip a couple splinters off the long edge and jam them through the two bandits before they even knew what hit them.

The instant she obtained the slightest perception of the wood, everything went to shit. Her psychokinesis took over breathing, which warred with her body's reflex, and sent her into a stuttering, writhing seizure. Annabelle held her down, pressing hard into her back, which didn't help matters.

This time, the black closed in even faster, and Willow was out like a magelight.

* * *

"—the hell did you do to her?" the thin bandit asked.

Willow opened her eyes slowly, keeping her body completely still. Magnus was gone. The door to the cabin was open, evening light shining through, and the thin bandit had Annabelle backed up against the wall with his short sword at her throat. He was smiling, like he was about to open a present.

"I didn't—didn't—" Annabelle stuttered, and a thin line of blood trickled down her neck.

"Sick," Willow whispered, making the short bandit's head spin around.

He smiled even wider and turned, removing the blade from Annabelle's neck. She immediately put her hand to the shallow cut and winced.

"She's awake!" the thin bandit announced and made his way across the room towards Willow, sword bobbing like a baton in front of him. "Now I can ask the real questions. Such as: what the fuck has this woman done to you?"

"Sick," Willow breathed. "I'm sick."

"Yeah, no shit," the bandit said, trailing the cold tip of the sword down Willow's spine.

She realized the sheet was entirely off her, exposing her back to the cabin. Willow closed her eyes hard and tried not to gasp. "Anyone would be sick after this. Looks like she skinned you like a boar. 'S that what you did, sweetheart?"

"I operated," Annabelle said. "Willow is sick. Very sick."

"No sort of operation I know, and I've done plenty myself," the thin bandit said, giving a wicked smile that revealed a missing canine on the left side of his mouth. "Looks to me like you got opened up, missy. Flayed like a fish, skinned like a deer. I wonder why it can't be fixed with a simple healing spell. I know you can do one, missy. You tried to cast before."

"There are some things," Annabelle said, "that can't be healed with simple magic. Some cures which have to be administered at the root."

The bandit chuckled. "I'd like to see it," he said, turning back to Annabelle.

She blanched. "The operation's over. It's finished already," Annabelle said, her lips growing white as chalk. "She just has to recover."

"I said," the bandit repeated slowly. "I want to see it. If I have to open her up myself…"

He pressed the point of the sword into the base of Willow's neck. She was sweating buckets on the table—which a flyaway part of her mind found amusing, as it was late fall and cool outside. The blade's edge was coming precariously close to breaking skin, and it was all she could do to keep her mind off her lungs. She wouldn't dare to try seeping her consciousness into the table again, not with the sword so close.

"Please," Annabelle pleaded.

Just then, there was a dull thud from outside the cabin. Willow, unable to look at much else, had been tracking the setting of the sun. It was twilight outside, which piqued her anxiety somewhat, though she couldn't quite put her mind on why with everything else that was happening.

"Magnus?" the thin bandit called. "That you out there?" When no one answered for a beat, he took a different tack. "Whoever's out there has to the count of three to buzz off, you hear?"

Nothing but a shifting against the cabin wall and a thud, perhaps a clumsy step. The thin bandit took the sword from Willow's neck and made his way to the unsecured door. But before he crossed the distance, the door creaked slowly open.

The bright operating light caught Magnus full-on. The thin

bandit, who had been readying his sword for a low thrust, lowered the blade and let out a sigh.

"Why didn't you answer, you big clod?" he asked. "This one here was just about to show me something really..."

He trailed off, brow wrinkling in confusion. Willow could see it too—something was off. Magnus was still in the door, half illuminated by the operating light, but his expression was vacant, jaw slack, eyes wide. It was like he was sleepwalking.

"Hey," the short bandit barked. "What's wrong with you?"

Magnus took a clumsy step through the door, and immediately Willow knew something was terribly wrong. He was wearing a hood, no, a white-furred skin, which ran from the top of his head down his back, and stuck to his arms and legs. He hadn't had it before, not that Willow saw, which explained the overwhelming scent of blood if he'd just skinned it. In fact, she spotted a thin trickle coming down from where the skin touched his hairline.

Annabelle, who'd been pushed up against the wall beside the door, gasped with her eyes wide in fear. She took a step away along the wall.

"Answer me, gods dammit!" The thin bandit broke out of his cautious stance and crossed the cabin. He reared back as if he were going to deliver an open-handed slap across Magnus's face, but the queerest thing happened first.

A crunch came from Magnus, and as Willow watched, his eyes bugged out and his face pinched slightly together. His left cheek jutted out while the right one sank in, and his face distorted as the skin hood enveloped it completely. When the hood closed, two yellow-pupilled eyes opened at the front.

The thin bandit staggered, but Magnus—or the thing that had been Magnus but certainly wasn't anymore—swung a haymaker that caught the thin bandit in the side of the head with a sickening crunch.

Two of the Magnus-thing's fingers were clearly broken, jutting off at strange angles, but the thin bandit had collapsed like a sack of rocks onto the floor, bleeding from the ear.

As Willow watched the altercation in horror, Annabelle rushed to her side and began painfully hauling her off the table and onto her thin back. Willow couldn't help but react instinctively to being yanked so hard, which caused her muscles to lock up again, though she bit down on her scream. The Magnus-thing had lain down on top of the thin bandit, and there was even more crunching coming from beneath the short, white fur.

Annabelle managed to shift Willow onto her back, though Willow could feel the unsteadiness of the nurse's feet under her. Willow didn't weigh much, but Annabelle was no strongman. Willow caught sight of their packs, directly behind the crunching, bleeding, writhing mass on the floor. Unsurprisingly, Annabelle didn't even attempt to go for them, only snagging the white sheet that lay on Willow's legs before hobbling past the mass and out through the door.

There were sounds in the coming dark now, oh yes. Strange sounds which Willow had never heard before, and she understood what had happened. When the bandits had come upon them in the morning, they'd popped the ward around the cabin. Unfortunately, they weren't well versed in magic. They hadn't realized that the numerous spells Annabelle had cast the previous night to turn the cabin into a makeshift operating theater would attract all sorts of magical creatures—hungry to devour the essence and whatever happened to be nearby. When Magnus had left, sometime while Willow was passed out, he must've run into something he couldn't handle.

Annabelle staggered away from the cabin, across the town square, and just into the treeline when a loud *caw* from overhead caused her to stumble, dropping Willow. Willow bit down hard on her lips, unable to stop the scream from erupting in her throat.

"Shit, shit," Annabelle whispered, glancing up and all around. "Okay."

She began to mutter the familiar warding spell, weaving her fingers quickly to form the gossamer plates which linked together into the illusory bubble. It wouldn't help against anything that had already seen or caught scent of them, Willow knew, but it should keep them hidden. Whether it would work so close to what was about to become a feeding frenzy was still to be discovered.

By the time Annabelle finished, Willow had gotten her muscles back under control—that is, she had successfully relaxed them again, even with the additional torture of roots digging into her ribs and spine. Annabelle went immediately from casting the ward and into a spell whose concepts included those of dreamless sleep.

"Wait," Willow whispered.

Annabelle sighed and dispelled the gathering spell-form. "What?" she snapped. "I'm going to put you to sleep so you can't give us away with your caterwauling."

"What..." Willow waited for breath to fill her lungs again. "What was that?"

Annabelle glanced back at the village. The light from inside the cabin was clear even from their vantage point in the trees, and dark shadows slowly moved towards the source.

"A skinbear," Annabelle said. "Ambush predator. They slither around up in the trees and wait for something to walk on past, then they drop. They don't have any bones of their own, so they use the body, while they've got it, to ambulate and seek more food."

"How awful," Willow whispered.

Annabelle didn't wait for permission but began weaving the sleep spell again. Willow hoped that she would wake in the morning and not have fallen prey to some ambulating horror from the deep forest.

LEOPOLD'S INTERLUDE 1

Leopold felt like he was dying as he urged himself on. Every step sent excruciating bolts of pain through his hips and up his spine, but he endured it. Willow had endured so much worse over the years. He could hold out until they found her.

The forest was so dense that the canopy nearly blotted out the sun overhead. Huge towering oaks crowded around the artifacts of civilizations past. Poured stone, metal rods, even shards of glass had been sucked up into the trees to be consumed over slow centuries. If you felled one of these beasts, there was no telling what you'd find within.

He stumbled over a root, and an arm shot out to catch him before he toppled all the way over. Leopold regained his footing and looked at Bryan, who'd been fast enough to halt his fall.

"Thanks," Leopold said, adjusting a spare pair of glasses on his nose.

Bryan smiled in reply and kept on walking. The company wasn't waiting around for them, and they'd been told specifically that if they fell behind they'd be picked up on the return journey. Leopold wondered how much of this was bluster and how much was the truth, but he didn't want to test the hardened mission commander.

The man was named Rolf, and Bryan had managed a few words to Leopold about him while they were digging a latrine away from the main company. He was the highest-ranked soldier in the city, but he never appeared on the wall for duty. Rumor had it he was reserved for special missions that required secrecy and stealth. Without the threat of open war between the city-states, there wasn't much higher a soldier could climb. Bryan was satisfied with his position, but Rolf hadn't been.

After the attack on the city, Leopold hadn't been conscious at the Sisters of Mercy for more than an hour before Dean Weatherby himself made an appearance by his bedside. He'd asked about Leopold's condition, performed his own cursory exam with a glowing ball of essence that gave him the ability to see through cloth and flesh, and pronounced the surgeons' task satisfactory. Leopold would walk again, with practice.

But there was another matter, and the dean requested a curtain to be drawn around the bed before he warded the cloth itself with a sealing spell. He asked about Willow and if Leopold had really seen her at the gate. Leopold said that he had and that he came to right before she cast the lance of flame, which had apparently obliterated the advancing warbeast.

And then the dean had asked him the hardest question of all.

Willow was missing. Did he know anything about that? Could he explain why she'd been able to do what she'd done? It wasn't until he told Leopold that there had been another woman, a nurse, with Willow right before the Monstruwacans' lens blanked out that Leopold even considered saying what he knew. Willow was missing, again, but it appeared this time as if she'd been kidnapped.

On their march, the dean was up towards the front of the column of twenty men, wrapped in a traveling cloak and walking with a staff. He looked like one of those traveling mages from the storybooks Leopold's father brought him when he'd deigned to visit their backwater town before scurrying back to the city. Those plates with the mages in their pointy hats commanding lightning and fire had always inspired him. They'd eventually inspired him to attend the Arcanum—where he might have destroyed any hope for Willow's future because he'd told the dean everything. From Willow's essential attributes to her special training sessions with Professor Brandeweiss, to her unintentional murder of said professor. The dean had listened stoically to all of this, even the impossible parts. At the end, he rose, thanked Leopold, and made to leave their small, curtained enclosure. But before he swept the curtain aside, almost as an afterthought, he said he was putting together a company of men to track Willow down wherever she'd gone and offered Leopold a place in that company.

As if he could say no. It took two days for them to gear up and set out, and in that time Leopold had pushed himself past what he previously considered his upper bounds on pain. The surgeons had had to reconstruct much of the bone and flesh around his upper thighs, as they had been crushed by a tumbling block from the initial bombardment of the city, and they warned that it would take a while before his nervous system fully reintegrated. They really wanted him to stay for a week if possible, but he wouldn't hear of it. He had two days, and two days was all it took for him to start walking again.

Bryan was picked for the company, which at first surprised Leopold. He was a wall guard when he wasn't guarding caravans, and the man had little experience with this sort of mission. But Leopold caught on rather quickly that the dean had surreptitiously assembled Willow's closest friends into this company, and they were heading straight for her. It was Bryan who had housed Willow with his family for months after she single-handedly saved their caravan from a freak deathworm attack. What the dean would use this concentration of her allies for was anybody's guess.

The forest was getting darker, and soon enough, Rolf called the company to a halt. He ordered them to set camp and dig latrines.

Bryan and Leopold went off to pitch their tents a little further away from the rest of the guards.

They worked in silence, Bryan finishing much faster than Leopold, who wasn't used to the ropes, staves, and canvas envelopes. Then the guard helped him execute the correct knots to ensure the tent wouldn't fall over on him again like it had their first night.

"Let's see if you've got the weatherproofing down right, shall we?" Bryan said and crawled into Leopold's tent. Leopold looked on in confusion as he currently held the weatherproofing canvas in his hands, but he followed Bryan inside anyway.

Inside, Bryan slung the roll that contained his sword off his back and laid it down on the dirt floor.

"Bryan—" Leopold began, but Bryan held his finger to his lips and gestured Leopold forwards. As he unfurled the wrapping, it became clear that there was more than just a sword in the bundle.

An iron rod topped with a screw-on wooden handle fell out beside the sheathed sword. The last time he'd seen this metal cane, he'd been at the mercy of an approaching deathworm, and Willow was hauling back to smack it, probably to distract it from eating him. What happened instead was that the cane sliced entirely through the deathworm and sailed off into the night. Willow had looked at her hands in horror afterwards, thrown up, and passed out. That one attack had nearly stripped both of her hands of all their skin and muscle.

Leopold moved in closer until his mouth was right beside Bryan's ear. He could still hear the commotion of raising camp outside, but he didn't want anyone else to hear what he was about to say.

"I thought it was lost," Leopold whispered.

"I saved it," Bryan said. "I thought it was inscribed. I... took it to a dealer. I thought I would get myself a new weapon."

Leopold knew in an out-of-body way that he should be furious with the man for stealing Willow's cane, but he just couldn't summon up the anger. Not towards Bryan, who'd housed Willow for so long in repayment for their lives and who'd paid for her surgery upon entering Durum without a second thought. If he felt like he needed a new weapon to keep himself safe for his wife and son, then who was Leopold to cast blame?

"But it wasn't enchanted," Leopold said, and Bryan nodded. Leopold put his hand on the guard's shoulder. "Thank you."

Bryan didn't need to mention the work he'd had done on the cane—after passing through a deathworm, it was a miracle it was still in one piece. He'd restored it for Willow. Perhaps he even meant to give it to her before she'd disappeared from their lives after killing Professor Brandeweiss, but had never had the chance.

"She might need it, when we find her," Leopold said. "I don't know if she's got a... a..."

Tears came hot and fast down Leopold's face, and he covered his eyes with his hand. Gods, he couldn't even think about what Willow must be going through. She was both the most powerful being any of them had ever known... and the weakest person alive at the same time. Was she going along with the nurse Annabelle willingly? Or was she being coerced? Their brief reunion at the western gate before the attack hadn't been enough for him to know if she was still running from the guilt of what she'd done.

And always, there was that other voice—a whisper in the back of his mind. A feeling about the dean, about this Rolf, and the company of men they'd set out with to rescue Willow.

It didn't seem like a rescue party.

Leopold wiped his eyes and took a shuddering breath. Bryan nodded, rewrapped his bundle, and backed out of the tent. Leopold still had the weatherproof canvas tarp to unroll, but he felt exhausted. His hips were killing him, his legs were shooting phantom pain, and all he wanted was to lie down on the hard ground and go to sleep.

No, he had to keep moving. Willow was moving. Willow was always moving. Always pushing past her limits, always breaking through the boundaries of the possible, even if she didn't know them as such. She'd worked through an impossible essential resistance as a result of her psychokinetic body, building up a city's worth of essence volume and a regeneration rate that would make a wall-mounted essence cannon blush. And she'd done it all hoping beyond hope that someday she'd be able to have a normal life.

He could give her that—he wanted to. The month he'd spent searching for her in the city had shown him that. He loved her, and he thought she loved him too. He would give her everything he could, everything he had to give. If he could only find her again.

She was so strong.

Had she already moved beyond him?

CHAPTER 5

Surprisingly to Willow, she *did* wake up in the morning. She was lying on her back—her top covered again with the white sheet, Annabelle sleeping close beside her. Without moving her head more than a degree or two, Willow surveyed the nurse's face. In sleep, she appeared to be fighting her own demons, her brow knitted in anger or fear, Willow wasn't sure which. Annabelle muttered in her sleep.

"Don't want... Not Durum..." were a few of the phrases Willow managed to make out in the ten minutes she listened. She lay perfectly still, not wanting to give herself another seizure, until Annabelle muttered again.

"Carl... dead..."

Willow gasped, which sent spasms rippling down her ribcage and caused her to yelp in pain. Annabelle shot up, her hands ready in a spell-form, and quickly sought an enemy. The forest, apart from Willow, was quiet, and the view slightly distorted through the intact ward. Nothing had broken the circle in the night, and nothing had broken it now.

Annabelle sighed and rubbed her brow. Willow writhed and tried to relax, but it took a minute to remember the way, which brought her dangerously close to passing out again. Eventually, though, she was able to return to lying peacefully on her back, breaths automatic and slow.

"This isn't going to work," Annabelle said, looking back through the trees.

Willow rolled her eyes as far around as she dared and caught sight of the edge of the clearing that housed the abandoned village.

"What?" was all she managed as a question.

"The village," Annabelle said. "I was counting on... Dammit. Somewhere safe. There's no way we can stay there now. If the skinbear isn't still in the cabin, then something else will be. Gods do we have the worst luck."

"Then what?" Willow managed to whisper. She didn't want to voice her main fear: that Annabelle would abandon her in the forest because she was too risky to bring along. That they didn't have enough food for one of them—not even two of them.

Annabelle sighed, then looked the other way, west, as far as Willow could tell.

"We have to keep going," she said. "This village can't be too far from the forest's edge. We'll make it there, then... something. We'll figure something out."

With that, she went to work. The ward bubble popped, but Willow noticed that Annabelle didn't dare to hunt so close to the village. She took the sheet, wrapped Willow front to back with it, then seamed it with a quick spell, creating a makeshift shirt. After which, she left Willow mostly alone while she snapped branches from neighboring trees and fastened them together with magic to form a litter.

Willow gritted her teeth at what she knew was to come. Annabelle hauled her onto the litter without any warning, and Willow did her best to bite back her screams, though a couple of yelps broke loose. She couldn't get her breathing under control fast enough and proceeded to pass out, but only for a few seconds. When she came to, Annabelle was sitting next to her, considering her.

"I should just knock you out," Annabelle said. "It'd be easier."

"No," Willow managed to breathe when her lungs finally exhaled. "I don't want... to be asleep."

Annabelle pressed her lips tightly together. "That," she said, "and it's not so good to be kept sedated for so long. There are... complications."

Well, Willow certainly didn't like the sound of that.

"I'll... be quiet," she promised, to herself and Annabelle at the same time.

She couldn't stand being weak again, not after she'd gained so much. She had to get better. And the only way to do that was through being awake and learning to use her nerves and muscles to move her torso and spine, instead of the magic which had done so for all her life. If she slept, she'd never learn it.

"Sure," Annabelle said, disbelieving, then moved to the back of the litter. She wove a spell of levitation and quickly cast it on the bed of branches.

The litter quite literally fell apart. Both the levitation spell and the spell sticking all the branches together spun off at the same time, leaving the litter merely a slumping pile of branches with Willow atop—like a pyre ready to be lit. Willow couldn't see Annabelle's face, but she could imagine rage, exhaustion, and annoyance in equal measure. She didn't particularly want to see Annabelle's reaction.

Annabelle huffed. "Gods!" she moaned. "Why can't you just... It's your gods damned spells."

"I know," Willow said back, trying to keep the shame out of her voice. "You used too many."

"I know what I did, you child," Annabelle snapped, then began weaving the spell for sticking the branches together again. Once that was done, the branches aligned themselves to become the litter once more.

"Should have been Carl," Annabelle muttered from behind Willow's head as she hauled on the litter. The whole contraption moved half a foot on the forest floor before Annabelle had to stop and regain her grip.

It was going to be very, very slow going.

Two hours after setting out—Annabelle huffing and sweating at the front of the litter, and Willow trying her best to cede control of her torso over to her nervous system instead of her psychokinetic spells—they finally broke through the border of the forest. At the pace they'd been going, Willow thought the village might have been only half a mile from the border, which made a sort of sense, since they took part in caravan trading.

When the dappled light changed to full-on sun, Annabelle panted and threw the bow of the litter down, staggering a few steps forwards before collapsing to her knees. Willow craned her neck around to see where they'd ended up, only eliciting a faint twinge before she consciously tamped down on her psychokinesis.

It was a broad, rolling land, beset on all sides by small groves of tall trees. Low hills that rose and fell like a frozen sea hid the majority of the vista. The grass was medium length but matted underfoot. It was a large natural glade, and she had no idea how long it might go on.

Willow's stomach made its presence known with a long growl, and she turned her head to take in the other half of the scenery. Her spirits fell.

"It's a desert," Willow said, raising her voice loud enough that she hoped Annabelle could hear past the front of the litter. "No animal would live here, magical or otherwise. And we don't have any reserves."

"Don't you think I know that?" snapped Annabelle from out of sight, then Willow heard her take a deep breath. "We'll just have to stay here at the forest's edge to hunt. Build up enough of a surplus to get us across to the next stand of trees. Though they look small. I'm not sure there's much living in those small ones over there."

"And maybe by then..." Willow trailed off. She didn't want to say what she hoped, for risk of sounding ridiculous and of letting herself seem even more fragile to Annabelle.

"Maybe then you'll be able to move your ass," Annabelle finished for her. Not the way she would've said it, but it got the point across.

Willow nodded slowly.

"Well, until then." Annabelle hauled the litter around until it faced the trees, giving Willow an expansive view of the deserted rolling plain.

"W-What are you doing?" Willow said, panicked.

"What does it look like? Using you as bait, of course. How else are we supposed to get any food around here?"

"No, no!" Willow shouted, then stifled a yelp as her ribcage seized up.

"Just try not to do any magic," Annabelle added sardonically. "Or you'll attract something even I might not be able to blast off."

"Shit, fuck," Willow gasped.

She tried to roll herself sideways off the litter, but that action was met with a fresh wave of writhing that seized her lungs up to the point of nearly blacking out. By the time she regained sense, Annabelle had already pulled her back past the treeline.

"You don't have to do this," Willow pleaded once Annabelle stopped hauling the litter. The woman walked around the assembly of branches, looking up into the trees and nodding. "We could figure something else out! I could make a magelight!"

"I doubt it," Annabelle said. "And even if you succeeded, I'd always counted on you handling anything that was too big for me. But now you're less than useless, so you'll have to be bait."

"Wait!" Willow yelled, then snapped her lips shut.

In the falling dusk, she realized her voice was much too loud in the lightly swaying trees. Annabelle had already started in on the warding spell, rippling the air between the two of them as she set up camp between Willow and the treeline. Willow watched helplessly as Annabelle became more and more distorted, her voice tapering off to less than a whisper. The smeared, blurred figure in the ward sat down.

Willow hoped that she was paying attention, and that she'd be able to handle whatever came out of the forest to feast on Willow's wildly contorting essence.

How could things have come to this? She tried to think, keeping her mind off the rapidly darkening forest and the faint natural sounds therein. Annabelle and Carl had been tasked with bringing Willow, once she'd been tested, to their mentor in Asche. Annabelle had been healing Willow, not of her own charitable nature, Willow was sure, but because their mentor would expect her to be healed upon arrival. If Carl had still been alive, they could have traversed through a portal, which apparently was a window in space connecting two places, though Willow had never seen magic like that before. She wondered if it was something he knew because he, like Annabelle, came originally from Asche.

A low bush just past Willow's feet rustled lightly. She held her breath, which only elicited another battle of control over her lungs, causing a fair amount of snuffling. She tried to reset, letting herself breathe automatically, slowly, as she watched the bush.

A smooth, broad head emerged from the base of the bush, perhaps two handspans wide and barely visible from what shafts of moonlight penetrated to the forest floor. The creature carefully waddled out and swung its head around, beady eyes taking in what it could.

It was a salamander, unmistakable from its larger size and slick, amphibian skin. The whole creature was perhaps three feet long and slithered along on thick, powerful legs. Its head was outsized, wider than she'd expected, with a lipless mouth that ran the entire length from side to side. It waddled forwards, past her feet, and alongside her leg.

"Annabelle," Willow whispered. The salamander paused, swinging its head around, then continued to walk past her hip, beside her nearly paralyzed arms. "Annabelle!"

The salamander didn't pause that time, and it chilled Willow to think why. Did it think she was a wounded creature, the way she'd tricked other magical creatures using her magelight? Was it not afraid of her voice?

It sidled up to her shoulder, then worked its entire body around. It gazed at her with those beady eyes, and she saw its skin was mottled orange and dark brown. Not just a salamander then, but a hellbender.

It opened its mouth, and short flames erupted from its mottled skin, lighting up the small clearing. Its mouth wasn't just wide but ringed with powerful muscles and inset with short, sharp teeth. A red flame gurgled deep in its throat as it turned its maw towards her neck.

Willow opened her mouth to scream.

A thunderclap beside her ear blasted forest litter into her eyes and mouth, causing her to choke and writhe again. She tried to use the moment to its best advantage by rolling off the litter away from the hellbender, but no such luck. Her arms would barely obey her, connected as they were to her healing spine.

Choking and spitting, Willow blinked rapidly to see the danger, but all was dark. Then, a soft yellow light grew from behind her, and she heard hard footsteps.

"Hmm." Annabelle turned the blackened corpse of the hellbender beside Willow's head over with her shoe. "I might have overdone it."

"What?" Willow asked, only hearing murmurs from her right ear. "What?"

"Oh damn," Annabelle sighed, forcing Willow's head to the left.

Willow felt hot blood trickle down into her hairline and knew her eardrum had been blown out again.

"Definitely overdid it," Annabelle said as she positioned herself to hold Willow's head to the side with her knee.

She wove a healing spell, whispering overpowered concepts to get through Willow's still impossibly complex network of psychokinesis.

Willow stared into the darkness, scanning the treeline for any more approaching magical creatures.

Somehow, she fell asleep from exhaustion before Annabelle even brought the spell down on her head.

* * *

Willow woke slowly, noting a dull morning light suffusing the treetops. Had she slept all through the night? It was a miracle she was still alive, given that she was still on the litter inside the treeline.

"Annabelle?" Willow called, darting a glance around the low bushes and dead branches, but nothing moved. A faint sound came from behind her, and she'd finally worked her head around to see what it was when Annabelle popped the warding bubble.

She looked a mess. There were dark circles under her bloodshot eyes, and her face had the haggard, drawn-out look of someone who'd forced themselves to stay up all night with magic. Willow realized she didn't know when the last time Annabelle had slept was. Had she gotten any sleep at all when they'd fled the village?

With the popped warding came the intoxicating smell of roasted meat, and Willow forced her head even further around. Annabelle wasn't cooking, but the charred hellbender sat beside her, which had clearly been inside the bubble. Willow couldn't see any other prey.

"Was there nothing else?" Willow asked.

Annabelle shook her head slowly with an expression of faint hatred on her weathered face. "Must've scared the rest off," Annabelle grumbled, shaking her head again.

"But we have the hellbender," Willow said hopefully. "Right?"

Annabelle sighed and slowly got to her feet. Within a few minutes, she'd sliced the hellbender down its length and flayed most of the skin off. The meat within was overdone, but evenly cooked. Willow supposed that's what happened when you got hit with lightning.

Luckily, Annabelle was feeling generous, because she fed Willow without attempting to force her to feed herself. The hellbender was surprisingly lean for its size, most of which was taken up by cooked offal. Annabelle scrunched her face in disgust and threw the salamander skeleton and all of the organs into a nearby bush. She was about to do the same with the skin when Willow started.

"Wait!" Willow yelped. She could smell the skin, and it smelled like... like... Well, it smelled like essence. Fire essence.

Annabelle looked down at the bunched skin and barely hid her disgust as she ripped shreds off and fed them to Willow. The skin, paradoxically, was much more filling than the little meat had been. She could feel its essence coursing down through her stomach and out, mingling with the neutral essence in her blood. With the skin entirely consumed, she even felt satisfied.

Annabelle scrubbed her hands with leaves and immediately began hauling the litter towards the treeline.

"Where are we going now?" Willow asked, glad to be leaving the always dangerous forest.

"Out onto the plain," Annabelle said. "At least long enough for me to get some sleep. We'll try again tonight for more food."

Willow didn't like the sound of that, but she couldn't argue with leaving the forest for the moment. It took a solid thirty minutes for Annabelle to drag her to the treeline, then ten more to slide her over the matted grass to a safe distance before she put up a small ward and immediately collapsed.

Having slept through the night, Willow, unfortunately, had absolutely nothing to do while Annabelle was unconscious. With just a view of the treeline, there was little to look at either. Out of boredom, she began trying to move her muscles on purpose, attempting to attenuate the psychokinesis that had allowed her to breathe all her life.

It was slow going, but she had hours. And hours. And hours. Breathe in. Breathe out. It was agonizingly boring, and painful some of the time. She began to occupy herself by inching her torso further and further to the side, off the litter, using her head and neck alone. In that way, she finally got a half view of the plains behind her.

They were utterly beautiful in the midday sun. A brisk wind rippled the matted grass in visible waves. Staring at that grass was almost enough to help her relax, but she couldn't quite find the way to true peace with the forest so close by, even with the warding in place. Especially after the salamander attack last night. There could be anything waiting in the shadow of the trees.

With an eye on the trees and another on the rippling piedmont, Willow progressively gained control over her lungs—at least to the point where, if she fully concentrated, she could regulate her breathing on her own. She could take and hold a breath when she wished it, instead of letting her body place the process on automatic. When she was distracted, the process didn't go as smoothly.

Which was exactly what happened when she saw a spot of dark brown crest one of the rolling hills at the very limit of her eyesight. Her breath hitched, her muscles seized, and she forced herself to calm down while gritting her teeth against the pain. By the time she'd regained control over her breathing, the spot of brown had elongated.

It wasn't a magical creature, or at least not one that she'd seen before. It didn't have the look of a deathworm, though it appeared to be segmented into five distinct partitions. That brought hope to her heart, but she couldn't do anything to fan that flame until she'd seen more. And that required waiting. Long waiting.

The mysterious object neared only slightly as it wound its way up and down the piedmont hills. It was clearly on a track that wouldn't bring it much closer to where they were encamped by the time it crossed the field and disappeared into the trees to the north. Willow knew, if it was what she hoped it was, that she had to choose her moment carefully. Too soon or too late and she would be passed by unnoticed. But if she confirmed her hopes when it was at its closest...

The object stopped growing closer and began to recede as it turned due west and directly away. Willow couldn't be entirely sure, but the slight breeze had delivered what may have been the lowing of an ox. That, combined with the look of the thing, gave her about even chances that it was a caravan crossing the hills.

Annabelle would never approve. But if she was honest with herself, Willow knew there was no way they were going to hunt and accumulate enough food for the nurse to drag Willow all the way across the treeless hills. Their only hope was either Willow gaining mobility—which didn't look like it was going to happen anytime soon—or catching a ride.

Willow concentrated on releasing all control of her lungs. And when they rose and fell automatically again, she directed essence down her arm and to her right hand. There was no way she would be able to perform a complex spell-form, but complex wasn't what she was aiming for. She channeled concepts of fire and water, a weak layer of enclosure, and a strong vertical movement. The spell capsule writhed in her hand with warring water and fire essences, red and blue swirls beneath the thin golden barrier. She splayed her fingers—the only movement she could get out of her arms at the moment—and the capsule rocketed high into the sky.

She immediately lost track of the capsule. There wouldn't be time for another try, not at the rate the probable caravan was receding. Even this had been a long shot with little chance of success.

A sphere of bright white cloud bloomed overhead, rippling the thin wisps of cirrus strung across the cold vault of heaven. Willow was shocked at the size of the new cloud, which brought another worry immediately forwards.

"Oh shit!" she gasped, right before the crack of the steam explosion pounded her eardrums.

Annabelle's warded bubble popped immediately, and the nurse shot straight up, fingers curled in a spell-form. She looked quickly around, then up. "What in the fuck did you just do?" she demanded.

Willow barely heard her over the ringing in her ears. When Annabelle looked at Willow, half-turned in the litter, she was smiling.

"They're coming around," Willow grinned.

Annabelle followed her gaze out to the hills, where she saw a caravan making a tight turn about two miles away.

"You child," she sighed.

CHAPTER 6

The caravan ride wasn't smooth, but it was worlds better than being dragged on the pine litter by Annabelle—even if Willow had effectively been reduced to an interesting curio. She sat on a bench beside a veritable mountain of crates, the stretched canvas awning of the wagon supporting her back. Annabelle eyed her with barely suppressed annoyance as Willow willed herself to stay upright.

Then the wagon hit a large stone, which was too much for Willow to adjust for. She began tipping over, Annabelle making no move to catch her. Instead, an elderly woman gently wrapped her arms around Willow and tilted her over until she was lying out on the bench.

"There, there," the woman cooed.

Her name was Bonnie, and she was a trader and co-owner of the caravan, along with her husband Lester, who sat up front driving the wagon. She slid a roll of fabric under Willow's head and put a hand on her shoulder, holding her against the bench to prevent her from rolling off. Bonnie seemed to enjoy taking care of Willow, who certainly felt as though she could use some extra TLC, especially after being alone with Annabelle and her barely restrained scorn for so long.

"Almost three minutes, I reckon," Bonnie said and smiled up at Annabelle. "She's getting better all the time."

Annabelle looked out the back of the wagon. The treeline they'd emerged from was long gone. They'd been riding with the Clairmonts for nigh on three days now, skirting the edges of forests and staying in the hills, though how Lester knew which route to take, Willow had no idea. Perhaps it was because they'd taken this run along the frontier towns so many times before that it had become second nature. Whether through boredom or charity, they'd seemed mighty excited to catch Willow's signal.

"Well, I think it's just great," Bonnie said, without regard to Annabelle's silence. They didn't get along well, Willow had noticed, although she suspected that was in large part due to Annabelle's silence and aloofness.

Once she was able to get her breathing more under control, Willow had been happy enough to engage Bonnie in conversation. The older woman was, after all, keeping them company back here instead of sitting up with her husband.

"Soon I'll be able to beat the caravan," Willow boasted from the bench.

"How about we take things one step at a time?" Bonnie said with a smile.

She'd been intensely curious about what was wrong with Willow that caused her to be nearly paralyzed. Annabelle had vehemently denied that Willow had been injured. And in the few gasping words Willow had been able to produce on that first day, she backed up the story. Bonnie had been tactfully respectful of their obvious inclination not to discuss it. That lasted right up until she'd seen the fresh scars from Annabelle's surgery while helping wash Willow after they'd stopped that first night. The probing questions had been well worth feeling clean again for the first time in over a month.

What Bonnie hadn't expected was for Willow to regain so much control over her body as the long days progressed. Willow herself hadn't even known she would improve so quickly. However, having the time to practice in the back of the wagon instead of being used for bait or dragged on a litter was probably part of the equation.

Willow reached up with both hands, and Bonnie took them in hers. She rhythmically squeezed the old woman's callused, strong hands, and Bonnie squeezed back. Pain rippled in her upper arms, but she had to practice or she would never get better. They did the hand exercises for ten minutes before Bonnie switched seats and sat at Willow's other end, taking a leg in her lap.

"You're a miracle worker," Willow gasped through the pain as Bonnie resisted her weak attempt at pushing against her. Bonnie first pumped Willow's left knee all the way to her chest, then let it straighten out again, a total of thirty times before moving on to her right leg.

"Does these old bones good," Bonnie said. "Keeps me limber too. Learned it in Glint."

"That's where we're headed?" Willow asked in surprise, recognizing the strange name from their first day's conversation.

Bonnie nodded.

"Took in with a healer while we plied our trade, loaded up with goods for the go-around. Thought it would be good if Lester was ever thrown. Hells, thought I might be able to coach him through it if I was thrown, though I don't know if I'd be able to get through his thick skull."

"I heard that, woman!" Lester shouted with mock rage through the parted canvas tarp at the front of the wagon.

"S'true," Bonnie shot back, then her face softened again while looking at Willow. "There was a boy, must've been fourteen if he was a day, got thrown from a horse couple weeks back. The healer was working his arms and legs just like that. He could squeeze a little with his hands, but nothing past here," she gestured right beneath her prodigious bosom.

"My parents did the same," Willow admitted. "Old Kurtis. Fell off the bridge when he was drunk. It was a miracle Jamie got him out of the river, but he could never walk again after that."

"Your parents're healers?" Bonnie asked, surprised. "What happened to him?"

"He died," Willow muttered. "Got sick, pneumonia. Probably from the river, but it didn't help he couldn't walk it off. It took two weeks for him to die."

Bonnie gave a single, curt nod, then grasped Willow's lower leg and bent her foot back. Willow pushed against her hand, moving it inch by inch away, though she knew that Bonnie wasn't putting nearly her full strength into the task. Part of the therapy was meeting the patient where they were without straining what little muscle control they had. Fortunately, the exercises seemed to be working for Willow.

It hadn't been hard to lie to Bonnie and Lester that first day, though Willow didn't know if she'd be able to tell a falsehood so convincing now that she knew them personally. Annabelle and her ad-libbed explanation—extracted by a furious Bonnie that night at the campfire after she'd carried Willow all the way back from the wash basin—was that Willow had been sent to seek treatment for a wasting disease in Durum and that they were refugees after the warbeast attack. Bonnie and Lester hadn't known about the attack, and after quizzing them about the details, grew silent and contemplative. Willow assumed there were many they knew in the walled city.

Bonnie finished with the first leg and started in on the second. "Not many out here who could heal a broken back. Could you, with magic?" she asked Annabelle.

Annabelle shrugged noncommittally.

"It's complicated," Willow supplied, wishing Annabelle would at least make more of an effort to appear like a normal nurse instead of a high-strung and glorified babysitter for Willow. "At the Sisters of Mercy, there were surgeons who could do just about anything, but only so many hours in the day. With a city that large… there were many people who were left untreated who could have been saved."

"I suppose it takes a lot to learn," Bonnie said, finishing with Willow's foot and holding her hands out.

Willow reached forwards, and Bonnie helped pull her upright. Placing her hands on the bench to either side, Willow engaged her core as much as she dared without going all the way over into a fit.

"It's not as hard as you'd think," Annabelle offered from across the wagon. "There's a lot of spells you have to learn, a lot of techniques, and the anatomy is monstrous. But it's no worse than what any mage takes on at the Arcanum. What's stopping so many is the administration. They want to curry high prices and prestige, and there's no better way than capping supply. So only a few students get admitted to the school a year, and those that do are set up for a life of overwork."

Willow was fascinated by Annabelle's spontaneous offering. She'd so seldom offered her own opinion on any matter while they were together, instead always taking the opportunity to subtly, or not so subtly, insult Willow for either her naivety or physical frailty. It was interesting to hear the bitterness in her voice.

"Is it not the case for nurses?" Bonnie asked. "If you can do what you did for Willow…"

"It's not the case for nurses," Annabelle confirmed. "They take on as many as they can. After all, it's their job to provide support staff for the physician mages. But nurses are seldom schooled in more than setting up the operating theater, sterilizing instruments, and sending message spells. Everything else they learn involves the merely physical acts of care and support."

"And you still did all that?" Bonnie pressed, looking at Willow's hunched back. Willow's abs were beginning to cramp, and she shifted her weight to her arms to keep her balance up.

"I had… extracurricular tutoring," Annabelle admitted.

Willow decided that that was nearly the understatement of the year. What she'd really had was a full medical magic education in Asche before coming over to Durum to infiltrate the Sisters of Mercy.

"You do what you have to," Bonnie said, as if she had any inkling of what Annabelle had meant by what she'd said. "Most folk assume Lester does the tallies and keeps track of stock. They never look me twice in the eye in some of those forest villages. But they don't know that Lester's trash with numbers."

"Woman, I'll trash you!" Lester called back, amusement clear in his voice.

Bonnie waved him away. "Where I grew up, they didn't teach girls to read. Only after I got out did I pick it up, little by little."

"Where are you from?" Willow managed to gasp. It was hard listening to the conversation and keeping her mind cool enough to keep her psychokinesis from taking over.

"A little backwater you've never heard of," Bonnie said, a smile in her voice. "I skipped town when I was fourteen and never looked back. Took up as a barmaid in a tavern about three days' trek to the north. I had to learn to read. The owner made me do his books, the lazy drunk. That's where I met Lester."

"Aye," Lester called back. "You had flowers in your hair."

"And you were jealously guarding a pitcher," Bonnie said. "He was quite the man in the day."

"Still am!" Lester said. Bonnie shook her head in amusement.

"Was he a trader then?" Willow asked just as her elbow buckled, her bicep writhing in a control battle. Bonnie caught her before she collapsed into a wooden support rib and laid her down on her side on the bench.

"He was," she said. "I skipped town only after knowing him a week. I thought, if nothing else, I'd see what this world had to offer.

Well, I've seen that and more. Never would've thought I'd be old and still riding in a wagon, though."

"You've never had it so good," Lester said.

Now that Willow was lying down again, Bonnie lifting her legs back onto the bench, she sensed something. A strange feeling, very faint but slightly familiar. A scent? Like when they cooked a magical creature? Not the meat alone, which smelled different from creature to creature, but something else. The essence, perhaps, but not at the same time. This sensation didn't have a particular concept to it, unlike the fire of the foxfire or the salamander. It was plain and unconcepted. Like neutral essence.

A pit dropped in Willow's stomach as she heard Lester suck air between his teeth from the front seat. The wagon began to turn.

"What's that?" Bonnie asked.

"Not rightly sure," Lester said. "Could be a ghost."

"The Blackbolt's?" Bonnie asked. Lester grunted. "It's drifted then," she said.

"What's happening?" Willow asked.

"Nothing to worry yourself about," Bonnie soothed, smoothing her hair. "There's a ghost, perhaps, up ahead. It won't approach as long as we stay far enough away. It usually haunts the plain around Blackbolt, a little town to the north, but it's drifted. We'll give it a wide berth."

"An essence shadow," Willow whispered.

"What's that?" Bonnie leaned down.

"At the Arcanum... they call them essence shadows," Willow said, remembering her last foray into the metrology department.

The students had, unbeknownst to her, constructed a device that would drain all of the essence out of her body to finally get a measurement on her essential capacity. They told her they'd fibbed to the department to get the equipment, that they were doing research on a captured essence shadow.

"They're what's left of mages," Willow continued. "When they die quickly, all the unreleased essence gets knotted into a shape that's like what the mage used to be. But they're not really a ghost, just a shadow."

"Whatever it is…" Lester trailed off from ahead. "I think it's getting closer."

Bonnie got up from Willow's side, but not before pointing at Annabelle. Annabelle crossed the wagon without an uttered retort and put a hand on Willow's shoulder to keep her from rolling. Meanwhile, Bonnie passed her prodigious bulk through the split canvas separating the front seat from the canvas-covered back.

"Turn south," Bonnie said, then cursed under her breath. "You're right, it's coming right for us."

"Damn those motherless curs in Glint for loading us down so," Lester said, snapping the reins twice. The caravan turned tighter, but Willow knew from experience that the train couldn't turn too tight or they'd risk overturning one of the rear wagons and snapping the connecting axle. The train picked up some speed too, but not much.

As the wagon train turned, Willow caught sight of the shadow in the distance. It was perhaps two miles away, barely visible as a yellow shimmer on the crest of a hill against the cold blue sky. She sensed it more than she saw it, that strange feeling of neutral essence. That made sense if this was in fact what remained of a mage, since a human's essence had no natural concept, unlike a magical creature's.

It was clear from Lester's cursing and Bonnie's goading that he was trying to get the oxen to go faster, but from the annoyed grunts up front, she didn't think they'd be up for the job. She was surprised they were going so fast already with the other four wagons laden as they were.

After a short, muttered conversation up front, the caravan began to slow on Lester's verbal command to the oxen. Bonnie came through the slit canvas again and opened a wooden chest strapped to the wagon bed right behind Lester's seat. She rummaged around for only a moment, straightening again with a wooden mallet in her meaty hand.

"What's happening?" Willow couldn't help asking. Although the sight of the shadow had been blocked by the rest of the train behind them, the sensation of it had been growing. If she had to guess, she thought it might be gaining on them.

"Gonna unhitch the train," Bonnie said, walking steadily towards the back of the wagon despite its rolling and bouncing. "It'll let us go faster. And get us away from whatever the ghost's chasing."

"Chasing?" Annabelle suddenly perked up. "What do you mean?"

"Sometimes magical creatures will get fixated on an item in the caravan. Usually it's something we picked up in a town, sold by someone who didn't know what they were selling. Magical artifacts and the like. You can't stop anywhere near the forests at night without special chests to hide them, or the sprites will swarm you. It seems like something in the wagons has caught its attention, though I can't think what. Everything we got came from bulk orders. If it catches up to us, it'll drain the essence from whatever it is back there before we have a chance of selling it. If it touches you, it'll give you bad memories. And they're bad luck."

Willow got a sinking feeling the longer Bonnie talked. It wasn't something in the wagons that was attracting the shadow, but someone. Specifically, her. She was so good at attracting magical creatures that Annabelle had seen fit to use her as bait. Willow hadn't figured on roaming magical creatures becoming attracted to her. Then again, she hadn't figured on a great many things happening that did.

The caravan came to a stop, and Bonnie leaped out, more gracefully than Willow had expected. She began wailing on what could only be the linchpin holding the connecting rod between wagons, seeking to loosen the fastening enough to disconnect and take off. But taking off wouldn't do a damn bit of good, Willow realized. They'd still be carrying what attracted the essence shadow.

She was endangering them, just like she'd endangered Durum. If she needed any more certainty, she got it from the way Annabelle was looking down at her.

"Help me up," Willow said.

Annabelle darted a quick look towards Bonnie, still wailing away on the pin, before levering Willow into a seated position. Willow twisted her body around, judging the ten feet to the edge of the wagon and how certain she was that she wouldn't collapse if she jumped down onto the ground from that height.

"Catch me at the bottom," Willow said.

"I'm not your servant, child," Annabelle shot back but scurried out of the wagon all the same. She lit down on the opposite side of the connecting axle, facing Bonnie.

"Get back inside," Bonnie said. "I've almost got—"

Willow staggered to the edge of the wagon, and the sight of her stole the words from Bonnie's mouth.

"What're you doing!?" she cried. "Get back inside, the both of you."

Annabelle reached for and swept Willow lightly down, more careful than Willow had expected her to be. She gained her feet and stumbled only once, but her core didn't seize up. Not yet.

"Can you walk it?" Annabelle whispered into Willow's ear. Willow could hear the fear there, and the fear set a memory to playing in her mind. Of Annabelle propping her up before the smashed silver-chained gate of Durum, facing the oncoming warbeast. Annabelle was scared stiff.

"Yes," Willow said, though she wasn't at all confident that that was true. She could hear Bonnie struggling to leap the axle behind them as she turned back to Annabelle. "Keep them away," she begged.

Annabelle set her mouth and nodded. Willow took her first tentative steps in four days.

"Stay back," Annabelle said from behind her.

A gasp from Bonnie told Willow that she'd finally made the hurdle, and there was a short tussle, but she refused to look. She focused all her attention on putting one foot in front of the other, on not seizing up and falling over—ready prey for the shadow. A second set of footsteps came quickly around the side of the wagon from the front. Lester. She heard him pull up short and gasp in fear.

"Sweet Iesu," he whispered.

CHAPTER 7

Willow had been so intent on her steps, her gaze directed downwards, that she hadn't been paying attention to the sensation of essence which had been building to her front. She set her feet and slowly looked up, fear curdling her insides.

The essence shadow had stopped barely ten feet away, parallel to the train of wagons. Up close, it had the vague form of a human, though the neutral essence that made up its body whipped and gusted in the nearly still air as if it were caught in a hurricane. The violence of the essence drifts was particularly disturbing to Willow.

She didn't know what to do. It was looking at her and she knew it. It was studying her. Was it... could it be scared of her too? It had come thinking it would find a tasty snack in the form of an artifact and had instead found a living mage. Or did it not think? According to the metrologists, the shadows weren't conscious at all. Instead, they were just drifts of essence patterned on the nervous impulses of particularly powerful dead mages. But something about the shadow made her doubt that. The way it considered her, maybe.

Its mouth was open, howling silently as the ethereal wind tore at its form. Hands scrabbled at the air around it, as if fighting to get out of a box, but all of this produced not a speck of sound. The shadow was completely mute in its anguish.

"Willow!" Bonnie shouted. "Willow, get back!"

Willow couldn't help it—she was afraid of the shadow. Of what it was that she didn't understand and of the mystery of the thing. She staggered back, eyes wide, and that must've been enough for the shadow. Enough to convince the manifestation that she wasn't a threat but was instead a snack. It shot forwards. Willow put her arm out to stop it, and it flowed around and up her arm, slamming full-on into her body with the force of a particularly nasty storm gust.

It felt like warm rain. Warm rain pattering down on her face. It was dark. She was in a muddy field.

She was on the piedmont again, beside the wagon train. Bonnie was running towards her, fighting against Lester and Annabelle's restraining arms. Screaming at her. The essence shadow gusted over her vision again, and she lost all connection with the here and now.

Lying down in the mud. Thundering footsteps. Rain in her eyes. Not able to breathe. Not able to catch her breath.

Back on the piedmont, Willow had fallen to her knees. She felt woozy. The shadow was taking her essence, but it was nothing like what had happened in metrology or with the deathworm. It was barely sipping, where on those other occasions, what had been taken was more like a torrent than a drip. She wasn't weak from the drain. She knew, somehow, that it was the memories. Yes, they were memories. And her vision clouded over as the world listed to the side, and she fell into memory once more.

* * *

Clara ran through the hot, wet dark as huge, roiling storm clouds occluded the sun. Cast into being either by her side or the mages from Asheville, the clouds made the battlefield a rolling quagmire. The rain was scalding in the pitch dark, though she knew that, on the other side of the portal, it was nearly noon back in Durham. A hundred mages ran with her, all under her command.

Before them was the enormous portal cast by the mages of Asheville. It was intended to penetrate Durham's defenses and open directly behind the colossal city walls, which were nearly finished. But the portal had bounced due to an unforeseen layer on the protective city-spell—one the mages of Asheville hadn't detected—which now repelled portals from outside. The portal instead opened just on the outskirts of Greensboro, and only quick work by the on-duty sergeant mage had kept it from closing altogether.

This was it. This was the chance that they'd been waiting for. After decades of open war, Asheville had made a fatal blunder, opening a portal from within their own city. Durham's mages would use that mistake to strangle them. Clara would make it so.

When Durham's portal opened on the rolling hills, their randomly selected battleground, Asheville's warbeast was already through—a monstrosity with the head of a lion and a snake for a tail. Durham's portal, casting a diluted beam of noonday sun on the mire behind her, was large enough to admit entrance to their own ultimate warbeast—the squid-hound. The dog, twenty feet tall at the shoulder, whose back bristled with hooked tentacles, had shot through and immediately out onto the battlefield.

Only when Durham detected interference in the warbeast battle from Asheville's mages did Clara order her own contingent through.

She'd brought a hundred, because a hundred were all that could be summoned on a minute's notice. Clara herself had been off duty, doing a little cleaning before Winston came home with Isabel. But when her pocket watch clanged with the alert, she'd immediately donned her robe and dashed across the square to the gates of the College of Mages.

Now, with only her officer's robe for protection against magical attack, she was leading the contingent across the slick mud, slipping and falling with the rest. They were headed to meet the mages from Asheville in battle—and to keep them from interfering with the squid-hound.

Hot rain lashed her face, soaking her robe, as spells began firing between the two lines of rapidly approaching mages. She recognized the lances of fire from her allies, launched by artifact staffs called dragonborn. She'd just had time to snatch up her own staff—made of three separate staves twisted together in a spiral, an artifact of a much rarer variety—before word came down that her contingent was needed on the field.

The lines clashed in a chest-thumping impact. Clara locked onto a mage in a red robe ten feet away and shouted three concepts while twisting her off hand into the much-practiced spell-form. Small spears of ice formed around her wrist and shot into the man's calf, which instantly caused him to stumble and splash down into the mud. Grabbing the last spear of ice, she quickly kneeled and stabbed the man through the neck before coming upright and searching around for the clashing warbeasts.

With the immediate carnage, it was hard to spot them, though they were each thirty feet tall and she could feel their reverberating steps through the ground. A mage from her side, in control of a levitating sword, sliced it across and easily bisected a mage from Asheville. The newly dead mage was revealed to be a young woman when her hood fell back as she toppled to the ground, surprise evident on her face. Volleys of fire, lightning, and frost crossed the battlefield in quick bursts, finding their targets with devastating effect or flying wild into the sky, illuminating the roiling storm from within.

An inhuman howl of pain made Clara spin around. The warbeasts had gotten behind her somehow and were just fifty feet off. The howl had come from the squid-hound, who'd suffered a vicious bite to the back from the venomous snake-tail of the chimera. They were locked together by the squid-hound's hooked tentacles, but the chimera was doing a good job of keeping the hound's snapping jaws away from its prodigious mane.

Their warbeast was overmatched. It was only a matter of time before it was destroyed completely, and then the chimera would turn on Durham's mages.

"To me!" Clara called out. "Formation six!"

Twelve mages immediately dashed back from the battle line, which had moved twenty feet further from the entangled warbeasts, and she felt a moment of pride for her hard-drilled contingent. Twelve was enough for the group cast. She needed to separate the two warbeasts. The staff in her hand was rare, a staff of Greater Restraint, and meant exclusively for battling warbeasts. When she hurled it, it would lock onto the nearest warbeast and form a cage of luminiferous aether impenetrable from within.

And there was the catch. It might lock onto their warbeast, and then it would be worse than not using it at all. She had to get the beasts separated.

The twelve mages had formed into a tight hexagon with her at the center. She felt their aether ebb and flow as they cycled, chanting the concepts of formation six by memory.

"Driving wind! Unbearable force! Repulsion!"

It was a spell meant to break an enemy line, to scatter them apart for a straight dive through their ranks. It should work just as well against the two warbeasts, though she'd never heard of it being tested against the aether-infused creatures. She knew they were, to some extent, resistant to aether concepted differently than their own, but she'd seen the power of formation six in drills. She couldn't believe it wouldn't at least separate the two.

The aether surged and began rotating, falling in from the edges of the formation to the center. To her. The essence of the twelve mages would be momentarily transferred to her to direct, and her guiding mind would give the spell cohesion that wouldn't exist if they had all cast the spells separately. That would give the resulting group cast a power unmatched by a group even twice as large working individually.

Disaster struck.

A lance of flame erupted through the edge of the formation, catching Clara in the chest and blasting her off her feet. The formation scattered, each individual mage unsheathing their artifact weapons and firing back at the enemy who'd targeted the group cast. It was beautiful machinery to behold.

Hot rain pelted Clara's face. She was full to bursting with the spell, but she was lying on the ground and couldn't even see the warbeasts anymore through the press of bodies. She suspected they were behind her again, duking it out. Where was her staff? It wasn't in her hand.

She tried to catch her breath, but she couldn't. Clara inclined her head and saw a cloud of steam gently rising from her chest. There was nothing left on the right side of her chest. Not charred skin, not her aether-infused robe. Only a gaping hole and oozing blood, steaming into the hot rain.

Clara felt bile rise in her throat, but when she coughed, it was blood that sprayed out. The team sent to disrupt their group cast was better equipped than her twelve mages were able to handle. There was no one left to evacuate her, even if she could've been saved. She didn't think she could.

Isabel. She thought of her daughter and realized that she wouldn't know what happened to her mother. Not right away. Winston would return with her to an empty house, expecting Clara there to meet them. They'd find out later about the attack, about how she'd run out to lead her troops, even though she'd been on leave. That she'd taken this risk. Would he understand? Or would he think she was selfish?

She would never see them again. With the weight of twelve

mage's aether humming in her body, she fell back in the mud and closed her eyes against the hot, driving rain.

There, eight hundred years ago, she died. Almost all of her died.

* * *

Willow opened her eyes, not to the roiling dark clouds of the battlefield, but to the cold dark blue of a clear fall sky. She blinked, but the sky didn't disappear, and the battle didn't resume. She looked down, and there was no hole in her chest.

The wagon train was there, as were Annabelle, Bonnie, and Lester. Annabelle and Lester were no longer restraining Bonnie, and all three were staring open-mouthed at Willow.

No, at a spot just above Willow, because she was almost lying on the ground, but not quite. She was propped up on something, and she turned her head to look.

Clara. It had to be her because, for a moment, it was as if Willow were looking into a shining mirror. But that was only the memory, even now blowing away like a dream upon waking. The bright woman sitting behind her, Willow's head on her lap, didn't look anything like Willow. She had high cheekbones and a kind smile. Her long hair flowed around an ornate caster's robe, which looked like a museum piece, embroidered as it was with crests and coats of arms. Willow could barely see the colors of the coat. The essence shadow of Clara was slightly translucent and glowing yellow.

Willow tried to jerk away, but her abs gave out on her and began to writhe immediately. She squirmed and gasped, and Clara's hand reached down to her spasming muscles. She touched Willow, and the pain fled, along with the seizure. She'd siphoned some small part of Willow's psychokinesis or disrupted it with her own essence.

But Willow was spent from even those few seconds and the walk to intercept the shadow before. She had no choice but to rest her head in Clara's lap. The dead woman was looking down at her with a small smile.

"Are you really her?" Willow asked. "I remembered... a battle."

"Yes," the shadow said, in the voice Willow remembered, and for a moment recognized as her own. "I died. But not. I couldn't move on."

"Where?" Willow asked, the question clawing at her. If there was a time to ask, it would be now. "Move on to where?"

Clara looked up into the blue sky, and Willow followed her gaze but found nothing there. Whatever Clara saw, it made her smile.

"It's waiting for me," Clara whispered. "The white gateway. Can you see it?"

Willow shook her head.

"You will, one day," Clara said. "Everyone must. But you..." The smile fled from Clara's face. There was pity there now, and something else. Pride? "Willow Tremont," Clara whispered.

"How do you know my name?" Willow asked.

"I have seen it in the future," the shadow of Clara said. "Past the gate. You are the best of us, Willow. But much will be asked of you. Know now that I see with sight beyond sight, and that your time will come."

"I'd sort of prefer if it didn't come right away," Willow said. "You can... see the future?"

"Everything that has been or ever will be," Clara said. "But I grow weary of this world and seek to pass on. Isabel and Winston have already gone through a dozen times. I yearn to reunite with them. Sometime, someplace, before the end when all are made one."

"What does it mean?" Willow asked, wonder in her voice.

There was something about Clara's voice, or perhaps the memories in her head, that led Willow to realize Clara was also speaking in deep awe. Clara knew something about what happened after death, even more than what had happened to her as a shadow.

"You'll find out. Someday," Clara said with a small smile. "For now, I must go. Thank you, Willow, for giving me enough to restore my sanity. Thank you for giving me this chance."

Before Willow could say anything, her head gently lowered to the ground as Clara stood up above her. Willow just barely managed to turn over and get to her knees before Clara began to ascend. As she and the others watched, Clara rose to a point fifty feet above and simply vanished. There was no sound. There was no flash of light. Only silence. And the absence of what once was.

Heavy footsteps came from behind her, and Willow felt hands on her shoulders. She looked and saw Bonnie kneeling beside her, her face still upturned and searching the sky for the essence shadow.

"Come on," she whispered, pulling Willow up from the ground. "Let's get inside the wagon. Don't know when it'll come back."

"I don't think she's coming back," Willow said, but let herself be led anyway.

CHAPTER 8

Willow thought that the experience with the essence shadow Clara would warn Bonnie and Lester away. She half-expected them to decide before nightfall to drop Willow and Annabelle off in the piedmont. Willow wouldn't have blamed them. What had happened with the essence shadow was because of the way she was. The essence shadow wouldn't have been attracted to the caravan if it wasn't for her, and it wouldn't have had enough essence to drink and return to sanity if she hadn't had so much extra.

This she explained around the fire that night, tired of lying. Tired of being cagey. She didn't speak of Durum or what happened there, couldn't touch those lies, but she resolved not to lie to Bonnie and Lester anymore going forwards.

And... they just listened.

They raptly leaned forwards, drinking up her retelling of Clara's memory, of the battle that took place here over eight hundred years ago, and the monstrous forces both sides had brought to bear. They listened like schoolchildren around a puppet theater, eyes wide. And when Willow explained about her disability, about her essence and how it had attracted magical creatures before, they absorbed every word without judgment. They listened as if it held no bearing on what would happen next.

But the next day, they didn't abandon her. They loaded up the lead wagon again and set off, Willow riding beside Bonnie. Willow was startled when Bonnie reached over to grab her hand, but she was just doing the physical therapy exercises.

How had they heard everything she had to say and just accepted it? How had they accepted her?

But, she reflected, it hadn't been the first time. Bryan and Margaret had also taken her into their home with open arms. But that had been before Willow realized what she was. How dangerous she was. When she'd known, after she killed Professor Brandeweiss, she'd removed herself from their home. But it was to their protestations, wasn't it? They'd wanted her there. But they hadn't known what kind of danger she posed to them.

The two ideas warred with each other in Willow's mind. The knowledge of her threat, of the danger she brought to everyone around her by her very presence. And she set it against the acceptance they all seemed to have of her. Would that acceptance turn sour if they found out what she truly was? And what kind of danger she put them in?

As she went over it again and again in her head while repeating the physical exercises with Bonnie, she came to the same conclusion each time. No, they wouldn't have thrown her out. Why had she been so sure before? Was it Bridgewater? Was it growing up treated by everyone in the town like a leper? Like she had some kind of contagious disease? Maybe Bridgewater was the outlier here, as strange as that was to imagine.

And she struggled with that knowledge for most of a day while the caravan rolled steadily west. What did she owe these people who let her in? Who accepted her? There was danger, but only a small danger now that she'd left Durum. Without a warbeast coming, seeking her scent, maybe she didn't have to run anymore. Maybe she could counter the negative effects of her presence and stop feeling so damned worthless all the time.

Maybe.

The wagons slowed to a stop, which was strange as the sky was still mostly light, without the first touches of orange sunset on the bottoms of the clouds. Willow, currently practicing sitting up by herself, turned to look through the slit canvas at Lester.

"What is it?" Bonnie called from beside her.

"Damn," was all Lester had to say. Bonnie gently patted Willow on the back and stepped around her, through the slit canvas to the front of the wagon.

"Is that—"

"Yep," was all Lester said.

Willow heard a heavy sigh from Bonnie. Her curiosity was getting the better of her. Though she caught Annabelle's sharp shake of the head, she gently levered herself off the bench and drew the canvas aside.

There was a river about a half mile off. Past the river, maybe five miles onwards, nestled in the slightly larger rolling hills, were several traces of smoke ascending to the sky.

"Is that Glint?" Willow asked. Bonnie startled, then helped Willow onto the seat while still standing beside Lester.

"It is, aye," Lester replied. "Much good that does us."

"Why?" Willow asked.

Bonnie pointed towards the river, which was probably two hundred feet wide. Where she pointed, Willow spied a tangle of timber leading to a line of poles rising from the riverbed, which met another tangle on the other side, though this wreck was more intact. Intact enough to show what it had once been.

"A bridge," Willow realized. "The bridge is out?"

"Looks like it," Lester said. "Next crossing's... what?"

"Fifteen miles north," Bonnie answered and grimaced.

"Is that long?" Willow asked. She thought they might be able to make that in a day, if they didn't run into any high strangeness.

"Not long, but I don't like it," Bonnie said. "Bridge is one of the old ones. One of the ruins, outside a ruined city. I don't trust it as far as I can throw it."

"And even you wouldn't be able to throw it far," Lester said solemnly.

Bonnie clucked her tongue in agreement.

"Well," Lester sighed. "No point in starting out today. Too close to sunset. We'll circle the wagons closer to the river and think on it. If I remember, there's a crossing maybe twenty miles south."

"Probably washed out as well," Bonnie said.

"Maybe," Lester said as he snapped the reins. The oxen gave an annoyed low and trundled forwards.

They made camp about a hundred feet from the banks of the river. But only after Lester gave the sky a good scan and Bonnie concurred that there shouldn't be any surge from the river during the night. Willow couldn't imagine a surge that would reach them up on the small hill they'd chosen. But then again, the bridge hadn't withstood whatever had come down the river either, as it had presumably been built to.

Bonnie loaded dried meat, carrots, and potatoes into a pot while Lester worked at cutting slivers for the fire. Annabelle had once, in one of her more cooperative moments, offered to light the fire with magic, which he'd readily accepted. Afterwards, though, he'd commented on a strange taste in the food, which Willow knew had been the fire essence leeching through the pot. He hadn't asked her to repeat the procedure since, which left Willow and Annabelle unoccupied while they watched.

Willow, sitting on a blanket in the grass, began the laborious task of getting to her knees, then leaning over, then rising up. She managed it without a hitch, which made her proud. She then walked over to

Annabelle, who was leaning against the lead wagon and suspiciously watching a handful of dark towers to the north—probably the ruins Bonnie and Lester had spoken of.

"I want to go down to the river," Willow said. Annabelle glanced at her, then went back to watching. "I would appreciate it if you went with me," Willow spelled out. Annabelle didn't so much as look at her.

"I could fall in," Willow suggested.

Annabelle sighed and levered herself off the wagon. "I could stop you," she said, locking eyes with Willow.

"I'd rather you didn't," Willow said, then walked away, keeping a somewhat normal pace in the pressed grass.

As she'd hoped, Annabelle began walking behind her, suddenly leery of her charge falling into the rushing water and disappearing. How much Willow was Annabelle's charge, or would be, anymore, she wasn't quite sure. It was one of the things that she was figuring out.

By the time they reached the river's muddy edge, there was a bright fire back at the wagons and the sky had gone purple and orange. The tips of the dark spires in the distance still held the light, shining like beacons. Annabelle, Bonnie, and Lester seemed wary of the ruins, but to Willow, they were mostly an afterthought. In Bridgewater, there were a few ruins scattered here and there, and they never seemed anything other than broken down. She wondered why the three were so suspicious of the structures.

Mud sucked at Willow's boots, and she fought to keep her balance, as well as control over her body, as she tromped towards the water's edge. The grass for twenty paces on either side of the river had been uprooted, leaving a slow-draining quagmire. Probably the result of the flash flood that had torn through the piedmont hills. Whatever else the flood had been, it had been unprecedented in its destruction.

The remains of the bridge were a testament to that, their thick piles still standing proud of the rushing water.

Willow anchored her feet in the mud with a half-twist and let out a breath. She swayed forwards, and Annabelle caught her arm in a vice grip. When Willow looked, the expression on Annabelle's face was equal parts annoyance and disgust. Well, if Willow had her walking stick, she wouldn't need Annabelle's help so much. She fantasized briefly of a day where she wouldn't need the persnickety nurse. When that time came, Willow wasn't planning to stick around. What Annabelle did without her charge and mission, she didn't care.

"Had your fill?" Annabelle asked and sniffed the air, wrinkling her nose. The denuded slope reeked of rotting grass and dead things under the ground. "Let's get back to—"

Willow had put out her hand, fingers spread, towards the torrent. She closed her eyes and breathed out. A wash of water splashed at her feet, as if an invisible, clumsy limb had brushed the surface.

"What are you doing?" Annabelle hissed, yanking Willow's arm. "Come on."

Willow squeezed her eyes tighter and tried to imagine the mud at her feet and the river rushing over the mud. She could feel Annabelle's boots, sunk ankle-deep, beside hers. Annabelle set her feet to yank Willow again, and the mud shifted precariously underfoot. She slipped and landed hard on her ass. Willow didn't know if she'd done that herself or not.

The water stirred, splashing out a foot into the torrent. Then it stirred again. Willow screwed her face up and sank her consciousness deep into the mud, into the water. The water rushing, the mud yielding. Unyielding.

In a straight line between her and the opposite bank, the water leaped as if it had hit an immovable obstacle. The river surged up and over, crashing down on the other side in a frothing rapid. It was an impossible sight, but the river kept rising as if, out of the mud, a great root or limb were emerging. The river doubled back on itself, whirling in an eddy before spilling back over the other side, sheeting down mud made as hard as rock.

When Willow came back to herself, she found her breathing ragged and a sheen of sweat over her face. Her outstretched arm was trembling, and her knees felt weak. Before she pitched forwards into the river, she took a quick stumble back. The mud was solid under her feet, sucking her boots no longer.

Annabelle yanked her arm again, and with her assistance, they climbed the washed-out slope of the river. Willow didn't turn until they'd reached the top, and by then it was almost too late to see anything.

The sun had vanished behind the ruined city to the north, but in what little illumination was left from the faintly glowing bruise-purple clouds above, Willow saw a miracle. The river to her right was a good ten feet higher than it had been before, and the height difference was busy propagating north towards the ruins. To the left, the river crashed and frothed in newly formed rapids, eventually evening out to what she suspected was its normal level.

Directly before her, though, was something unbelievable. There was a tunnel going under the river, hardened mud on the right and coursing water on the left. The floor of the tunnel was dry, hard mud, with the moisture driven out until it was as solid as hardpan. The width and height of the tunnel were enough for a wagon train to fit through—just barely.

"Okay," Willow said, weary from what she'd done.

It wasn't a spell, not exactly. She hadn't shaped essence beyond what her body did on a regular basis with her psychokinesis. What she'd done, though, was imbue the mud with that power, extending herself through the shifting bed of the river. She'd compressed the river bottom into near-stone and formed it into a shape that would allow passage.

Annabelle looked like she was currently at war between grudging awe and annoyance. Willow knew where she'd come down in that war, in the end, and before Annabelle could chastise her again, she turned and set off back to the camp. A campfire burned beside the lead wagon, and the shifting shadows showed where Bonnie and Lester were milling about, their voices sweetly bickering on the wind. It was a good hundred or more feet away, but Willow wouldn't let Annabelle help her, though her body would certainly not turn down any help offered at that moment.

No, Willow had done something herself. Something amazing. The days when she relied on the recalcitrant nurse were coming to an end. She knew that, felt that in her bones. What help she needed now, she could provide herself. Or, perhaps, even others might deign to help her. She'd let crushingly low self-esteem force her into Annabelle's hands, and the woman had done nothing but knock her down again and again.

Not anymore.

Bonnie didn't ask why Willow was sweating like a hog when she came into the circle of firelight. She just offered her a bowl of soup and helped her down onto a woven blanket they'd set on the ground. When Annabelle emerged, Willow noticed Bonnie offered no such help.

LEOPOLD'S INTERLUDE 2

The first attack came in the middle of the day.

The column was marching through the green-tinted and shadowy foliage when suddenly one of the guards at the front cried out. Leopold was in the back with Bryan, and they saw the man fall, but not what had caused the cry. Other guards caught the injured man, and one hollered, "Medic!"

Dean Weatherby sprinted back from the head of the column, lugging his seven-foot staff with him, and dropped to his knees in the center of the guards around the injured man.

Rolf shouted, "Form up!" and everyone who wasn't Leopold, Bryan, Dean Weatherby, or the injured man took their places in a circle facing outward.

Leopold had been pushed close enough by that time to see what it was that had felled the guard. A solid five inches of wood sprouted from the man's collarbone like a small tree limb, no thicker around than Leopold's thumb. But he could see, from where blood was beginning to well around the injury, that there was even more embedded in the man's chest. It had nicked the man's boiled leather chest piece, but Leopold didn't even consider that the shaft had come as an attack from afar.

"Leopold!" Dean Weatherby shouted, and Leopold broke his stare off the shaft. The dean motioned him down, and Leopold fell to his knees. "Put your weight here, on his chest," the dean said, gesturing to the chest piece. "Hold him down. I'm going to remove the shaft."

"Uh huh," Leopold said, still not completely sure what he was looking at.

He pressed down on the man's chest, which elicited a groan and caused the man's eyes to roll back in his head. The dean gripped the shaft firmly and yanked it out in one swift motion. Leopold was quite unprepared for the amount of blood that gushed from the wound.

"Stay sharp, Leopold," the dean said at his momentary waver, and began building a complicated layered spell which Leopold barely caught the concepts for. Something about blockage, something about reconstruction. Something about returning.

The dean slid the spell over his hand like a glove and pressed down on the puncture wound, which Leopold was realizing had been from an arrow. The half-bloody bolt on the ground didn't have any fletching, but it had an unmistakable pointed tip. As the dean pressed down on the puncture, the blood which had run under the man's chestplate pulled back into his body. The man screamed through clenched teeth as his lifeblood drew back into him, and by the time the dean pulled his hand away, the puncture wound was gone.

Dean Weatherby let out a sigh and sat back on his heels. "Gods! I haven't performed first aid in decades."

"I've never seen a spell like that," Leopold said.

"You will, if you go into the mobile mage corps," the dean said. Leopold had heard of the corps before—groups of mages who were sent to natural disasters outside the city walls. He supposed a spell like that would be terribly useful in such situations.

"You've healed him, then," Leopold said, but the dean shook his head.

"Now the real battle begins. Sometimes the patient pulls through without flinching, but most times the body must fight to regain its humoral balance. We'll have to scourge the body of a buildup of phlegm every few hours. Even then, the black bile may overcome him."

Luckily, the guard had passed out while he was being healed, so he wouldn't have to hear this terrible prognosis. Rolf circled around the wounded man, then bent down to whisper into Dean Weatherby's ear.

"I suspected as much," the dean said. "We must keep moving. We can't lose the track."

The second attack came not from the treetops, but from the ground.

Two guards were now assigned to carry the third on a stretcher constructed from branches and rolled canvas, while Dean Weatherby administered treatment every few hours. The man sweated terribly and called out in his delirium, but for at least a few minutes after the treatment, he seemed more peaceful.

Near the front of the column, something rustled the leaves, and one of the guards was suddenly jerked into the air while his leg gave a wet snap. The guard began to scream. It took only a moment's work for the dean to slice the rope overhead while three others waited below to catch the unlucky guard. The dean similarly healed the guard, but at least with a broken bone, the guard was back on his feet in a matter of minutes. The arrowed guard still hadn't come completely conscious again after the attack.

When they set up camp for the night, Rolf ordered an increased shift to take watch around the tents. Leopold sat in the open flap of his tent, thinking over the events of the day and fingering the solid sphere of essence in his cloak pocket. Willow had given it to him two months before, and it still hadn't decayed. He was lucky, he supposed—it contained a supremely powerful store of fire-concepted essence. He was wondering, as he slid his fingers over the surface, if he'd need to use it in self-defense. That's when he saw the dean silently slip out from the circle of guards and into the darkness of the forest.

"What in the seven hells?" Leopold muttered and looked around, but none of the guards sent up the alarm at the dean's disappearance. Leopold gained his feet and left the circle in the same direction— none of the guards stopped him either.

It wasn't hard to track the dean through the forest, not with the man's seven-foot inscribed staff shining a yellow light. Leopold had no such staff, and though every step pained him, he crouched as low as he could and followed in the man's wake. What could the dean be doing out here in the night?

Dean Weatherby stopped and turned his head around. "I suppose you might as well come out, Leopold," he said. "No use in creeping around, especially where we're going."

"Damn," Leopold whispered, then stood up and entered the circle of light.

"I didn't want to involve you," the dean said. "But we've got no choice now. You're going to see things tonight that are considered vital state secrets, and you are not to repeat them to anybody without my explicit permission, upon threat of imprisonment. Do you understand?"

Leopold swallowed and nodded. What had he gotten himself into?

"Where... um, are we going?"

"Not far," Dean Weatherby said, and turned to continue on. "I suspect they'll find us before we find them."

Who the *them* Dean Weatherby was referring to was revealed shortly after, when they'd traveled not five hundred feet from the encampment. Not far by most standards, but far enough for the sounds of cooking and sight of the fire to disappear entirely. As Dean Weatherby stepped forwards, his circle of light illuminated a face in the darkness ahead.

Leopold startled at the sudden and completely silent arrival, then looked around on pure reflex. The circle of light illuminated several other faces just like the first, all green so as to blend into the trees. They surrounded them, somehow even behind them.

"I have come to treat with the elves of this forest," Dean Weatherby said. "Do you represent them?"

"We represent only ourselves, human," the first face hissed, and the *elf* stepped out of the shadows.

If the term had given Leopold any romantic notions of the impossible, mythic creatures, those were quickly dispelled by the form that made itself visible. Six-legged like some kind of insect, the creature was covered completely by green chitin. Even its face was just a mask of chitin, proved by the semi-transparency of the creature's sharp cheekbones. Its chin looked wicked enough to cut wood, and the hollows of its cheeks were multisegmented. Its arms, though, were strangely human.

"You have attacked our caravan and injured two of our party," the dean said, nonplussed by this non-answer. "Why?"

"You intrude in our domain," the elf said.

"I left several offerings—"

"And you hunt one of our own."

At this, the dean stopped, his eyebrows quirking up in a look of confusion. They weren't looking for an elf, were they? They were looking for Willow.

"We track two human women who came through here not a handful of days ago," Dean Weatherby said. "Are they still alive?"

"The human is still alive. The other was in great pain."

"The other," Leopold interjected, "did she have long, dark hair? Was she thin, like you?"

The eyes in that insectile face swiveled to fix Leopold, and for a moment, he regretted that he'd spoken at all. But if they were talking about Willow, he had to know. He stepped forwards.

"Did she have a limp?"

"She was dragged on a bed of branches," the elf hissed. "She is changing."

"Changing? How?"

"She becomes one of us. Even now we can feel her breath through the trees. She is the greatest of us, our queen."

"We mean her no harm," the dean interrupted. "We are only trying to find her, to bring her the aid she requires."

"With iron and sinew? I think not," the elf said, and a slight creaking caused Leopold to turn towards an elf at their side. It had silently produced a bow, which it was drawing that very moment, the arrow sighted on Leopold's chest.

"D-Dean?" Leopold said, and the dean grabbed his arm and pulled him close.

The staff began to glow even brighter, exposing the arachnid shapes of the elves surrounding them. All sighted arrows at the pair. Leopold doubted if the light alone would deflect the missiles.

Leopold reached into his pocket and gripped the sphere. The elf's eyes immediately snapped down to fix on his hand, as if it could see through the cloak. Leopold debated with himself if he should pull the sphere free or activate it while it was still within his pocket.

The elf gave a short hiss, and the rest of the creatures lowered their bows. A layer of sweat broke out instantaneously over Leopold's skin, and he felt cold and clammy. At that moment, he wanted nothing more than to be back in his tent, leaving the guards to do this kind of dangerous stuff. Why had he even gone with the dean?

"You are her paramour," the elf whispered.

Leopold gripped the sphere, frozen to the spot, but he nodded slightly.

"We did not know. Please, forgive your humble servant," the elf said, bowing low at the waist. Creaking sounds from all around them revealed the others bowing as well. Dean Weatherby looked incredibly confused as to what was happening. Leopold wasn't quite sure what it was either, but he wouldn't look a gift horse in the mouth.

"You will pass unharmed through this forest," the elf hissed. "We will make clear the queen's path to you."

"Gratitude," Dean Weatherby said, jerking Leopold's arm back the way they'd come.

Leopold backed away from the elf, who wouldn't take its eyes from him even as it bowed. They passed through the circle of insectoid creatures and back into the seemingly uninhabited woods. They looked over their shoulders until they could hear the first sounds of food preparation from the encampment.

"Do you have any idea what just happened there?" Dean Weatherby asked.

Leopold looked at the man and saw his eyes piercing into his own. His thoughts went to the sphere of Willow's essence, but he decided to play dumb. "Willow and I were involved," Leopold said. "I know you know, but I don't know how they could tell."

"That's just what I'm wondering myself," Dean Weatherby said, looking Leopold up and down. Apparently deciding that there was nothing left to puzzle out, he turned towards the camp.

"Wait, Dean Weatherby," Leopold said. "What... I mean, those things—"

The dean sighed. "Elves. Magical creatures of intelligence."

"Such a thing should be impossible, shouldn't it?" Leopold asked.

"They're half-breeds. The forest people had looser morals than we can even conceive of, and the elves are the result. Deadly in the forest, their existence is kept a tightly controlled secret in the walled cities."

"But why? What's the harm in knowing?"

"You can't imagine even one reason why a foolhardy hunter or mage would want to capture an elf or other half-breed and draw the species' ire?"

"Oh," Leopold said and felt disgusted at the idea.

CHAPTER 9

The next morning, Willow awoke sore all over, as if she'd been running through the night. It only took a few seconds to realize that her muscles were battling her psychokinesis, which had reasserted itself during the night, though not to the extent of causing them to seize up. With a focusing breath, she forced her psychokinesis to retreat, running out of her bones and tendons. The pain vanished immediately.

Bonnie was already up, as she had been every morning for the entire trip, and was packing their small camp back up in the lead wagon. Willow looked around but found Lester and the oxen missing. Before she could ask, Bonnie caught her panicked stare.

"He's just gone down to the river," she explained. "Fetch them a drink and fill the skins. Then I suspect we'll be off. South, I reckon. We'll reach the next bridge by sundown."

Willow tightened her lips and nodded. What she'd done at the river felt more like a dream than reality. Could it be that? Just a dream? At that moment, she wished it were. There was no telling how they might react.

Unfortunately, one look at Lester's face as he returned with the pack of oxen was enough to dissuade her of that notion. She'd helped Bonnie pack the blankets while Annabelle sat in the back of the lead wagon with a thick blanket pulled tight around her shoulders. She looked miserable, but Willow couldn't bring herself to care much for the other woman's comfort. Not when she had her own problems.

Bonnie turned at Lester's approach and gave him a double-take.

"What's wrong?"

Lester opened his mouth, gaped for a few seconds, then closed it again, shaking his head.

"Did something happen?"

"Must've," Lester coughed, then gestured over his shoulder with his chin. "Don't think we'll need to go south anymore."

"What d'you mean?"

"You'll see in a moment, I reckon."

It took half an hour for Lester and Bonnie to hook the oxen together in sets of two and string those harnesses up to the wagons before they were off. From the height of a wagon wheel, Willow could see that the river did look different, even at that distance. To the north, it was much wider than the stream to the south, and there was a suspicious hump in the middle.

Lester clicked his tongue, and the oxen began ambling towards the river—and the strange hump. As they approached, Willow kept her balance at the slit in the front canvas of the lead wagon, trying to catch sight of what she hoped had only been a dream.

The river water jumped up and sheeted down, catching the early morning light and scattering it like a cut jewel. A nearly circular tube ran under the roaring river. Even from twenty feet away, the air took on the distinctly heavy tang of incoming rain.

The roar of the jumping water was too deafening to hear much by. Bonnie and Lester leaned together to shout into each other's ears. Willow heard Lester ask a question, though not what about, and Bonnie turned to look at Willow.

She tried not to flinch, tried not to look guilty or suspicious. This wasn't magic, as far as a mage would be able to tell. Something had shaped the earth here that couldn't be explained by spellcraft, but would Bonnie and Lester know the difference?

Bonnie yelled back, and Willow caught the word *mage* in the shout. Lester nodded, then urged the oxen on. The beasts were strangely comfortable with entering the tunnel—or if they were spooked, they didn't show it. In a single file, the three wagons crept into the tunnel. The mud under-wheel was so hard that it didn't dimple with their passage.

It took five minutes to cross the length of the tunnel of water, and by the time Willow saw sunlight on the other side, she was well ready for the experience to be over. What had she been thinking? There was no way she could guarantee that the tunnel was safe. She wasn't aware of anything similar ever being done before. What if the rushing river had weakened the mud embankment during the night? What if the tunnel had cracked and come crashing down around them while they passed through it? It was a miracle it had held until the morning.

She breathed a sigh of relief when the last wagon passed out of the tunnel and up the muddy slope. Glint was much closer now. From what she saw, there were nearly two dozen low buildings, only a couple of which had second stories, so it appeared to be a medium-sized town, like her own Bridgewater. The cooking fires of the night before were gone, though a thick plume of smoke issued from somewhere past the first row of buildings at the front of the town. Perhaps a charcoal firing or a blacksmith using raw wood instead of coal. There was something intensely familiar about the sight of the town that crushed Willow's heart with homesickness.

Three men on horses departed the town and galloped towards the small caravan. Willow noticed Lester grip the reigns tighter, his lip jerking with tension. Bonnie squinted from beside him.

"I say that's Gerald," Bonnie said. "And his brother Lars to the right?"

Lester squinted, then seemed to relax, leaning back against the wooden backrest. "I'd say so," he said. "Though what do you expect they're doing out here?"

"No clue," Bonnie said. "Mayhaps we're about to find out."

The three horsemen cantered to a stop about a hundred feet up. It wasn't until the caravan was fifty feet away that Willow saw the leader speak to the two others, and they all slung back the heavy crossbows they'd been holding. She hadn't realized that they'd been in the horsemen's sights until that moment, and the past danger caused her back to prickle with anxiety.

The leader, Gerald, if Bonnie was right, galloped up to the right of the lead wagon, and the other two took station on the left.

"Lester, Bonnie," Gerald said, tipping a wide-brimmed hat. The man had a coarse dark beard and short-cut hair. Powerful muscles flexed under a linen shirt covered by a vest holding a quiver of crossbow bolts. A back sling held the weapon itself. "Who's this?"

"Gerald, this is Willow. In the back is her nurse, Annabelle. We found them on the outskirts of the Great Eastern Forest. They'd been robbed."

Gerald quickly sized Willow up—during which she managed to keep her composure and not collapse under the strain—before tipping his hat to her. "I'm sorry to hear that," he said. "It's a might dangerous in that forest, and not just for the bandits."

"What's going on, Gerald?" Bonnie asked.

Willow realized then that he'd shown them the courtesy of cantering his horse alongside them rather than making the oxen stop the train. Bonnie and Lester must have been well recognized indeed to receive such treatment from the guards.

"Strange days," Gerald said. "Strange days. 'Bout a week ago, something big and nasty came out of the west. A big, mean slug, looked like. Water gushed out of the thing, and the awfullest stink. And that was before it hit the river. The damn thing swelled up like a bladder. By the time it crawled out of there, well…" He grimaced.

"We saw the bridge," Lester said. "It's a damn shame."

"Damn shame," Gerald agreed. "Took out Dixon's bridge too, the son of a bitch. You wouldn't believe the wave that thing made when it slopped out."

"Dixon's, too?" Lester gaped. "How far to the nearest crossing?"

"Well, there's the ruins," Gerald pointed with his chin to the north. "Then fifty miles south at Turnhold. Haven't heard word yet if theirs made it. Speaking of which, you mind telling me how you're here?"

"Willow here's a mage from the Arcanum at Durum," Bonnie said, something like pride in her voice. "If you want to see something you've never seen before, just mosey on down to the river and take a gander. Don't know how much longer it'll last. Willow?"

Willow shook her head, trembling from the stress of standing at the back of the bench for so long. Lester seemed to notice right away and took her hand, leading her up onto a large crate and over the bench until she sat between him and Bonnie.

"No way to tell," Willow said. "I've… never done something like that before."

"Shit," Gerald said. "Can you do it again? We've been isolated ever since that thing crossed the river. You think you could put the bridge back?"

"No. I don't know. Maybe," Willow said. "I don't… I don't know."

"How about you show your manners, Gerald Lebouf?" Bonnie scolded. "She's been through a lot. You just take a look and make your report, and then you can ask your questions. But not until after she's put up."

"Yes… Yes, ma'am," Gerald said.

It was funny to Willow to see the big man so chastised, and apparently she wasn't the only one. His two companions—one of whom was his brother if Bonnie was to be believed—had carefully sculpted expressions of non-interest, though their eyes turned up at the corners with suppressed mirth.

"Now go on," Bonnie waved him back. "She'll be at Frank's. I'm sure Constable Rigby will be wanting to hear all about what you're going to say."

Gerald nodded, then tipped his hat a final time before setting off at a gallop. The other two guards followed to either side as they hammered across the flattish plain between rolling hills, back towards the river and the wonder she'd left behind.

Bonnie patted Willow's knee. "Don't pay them no mind," she said. "You've gotta be rough to safekeep a whole town. Lord knows Gerald's got a good heart, though his manners could use some work. Not much trouble comes by Glint, though that wasn't always the case. When the river ran bright with nuggets, they'd get a couple of raids a year. You could say they haven't quite settled into the town they've become. Haven't quite forgotten what they once were."

"What are they becoming?" Willow asked, curious.

"Poachers," Annabelle said from behind. Willow turned around to see the woman's head sticking through the slit canvas, eyeing the town quickly approaching. "They poach the magical creatures in the mountains to the west."

Bonnie nodded.

"It's nothing worse than what we did," Willow reminded Annabelle, who scowled back at her and then disappeared into the covered wagon.

"I don't know what happened... back in Durum," Bonnie said, seeming strangely at a loss for words. "And you don't have to talk about it. I can tell it pains you. But Glint, it's nothing like that sort of place. You don't have to worry here."

Willow nodded and tried to believe her.

CHAPTER 10

Glint was both like and unlike Bridgewater. Alike in that it was a small town situated under a large sky, hemmed in by the mountains to the west and the river to the east. Bridgewater had been surrounded by stands of pine forest, though the land hadn't been as hilly.

They were different in small, subtle ways, which Willow couldn't quite put her finger on as they rolled the caravan down the hardpan main road. Every man and woman who passed the lead wagon nodded and greeted Bonnie and Lester—it was clear they were a welcome and frequent sight in the town. Some called up asking about their wares, to which Bonnie invariably replied to come see them in the morning. A young woman, mid-twenties, swung up onto the seat beside them and had a quick, muttered conversation with Lester. Lester nodded, and the woman jumped and took off down the road.

"We've got a usual place set up for the caravan," Lester said to Willow by way of explanation. "A little bare spot, used to be the panner's, but that burned down going on three years now. It's clear and flat enough for us to park the wagons and fence the oxen. That's where we'll hold court," he said with a smile.

"Is it a big event, you coming here?" Willow asked.

She remembered when her father made his way back to Bridgewater in a buggy. He was no caravaneer, but he *was* a traveling merchant who often brought interesting or odd findings back to the town. For a week after his return, they'd get visits at the oddest hours, townsfolk interested in seeing what he'd had to offer. Of course, the most interesting things he'd shared with Willow and her mother first.

"No way to likely tell," Bonnie cut in. "As we only see Glint when we're here." She touched her finger alongside her nose, and Willow couldn't help but laugh.

"You'll have to tell us how they act when we're gone," Lester said.

Willow almost spoke up to correct him, but Bonnie caught her eye with a meaningful glance, which made Willow think. Would she be moving on before them? Could she just stay?

Willow kept her mouth shut, sensing the brooding silence coming from Annabelle in the back of the wagon as they ambled down the main street. They finally stopped at a wide, two-story building with a facade painted in white and rust-red. The sign announcing it only had one word: Frank's.

A thin, reedy man in his late fifties came out the front door with a smile on his face and approached Bonnie's side of the wagon.

"Didn't think you'd get past the river," he said, and reached up to take her hand, pressing her fingers between his own. "You go north, or south?"

"Neither," Bonnie said, which brought a look of confusion to the man's face. She nodded to Willow sitting beside her. "Frank, this is Willow Tremont."

"Howdy do?" he said, tipping his head.

"And back there's Annabelle, don't rightly know her last name, who's Willow's nurse. They need a place to stay."

"You're in luck. The Benson brothers just vacated the premises, and the room above the store's unoccupied. Give me a couple hours and it'll be fit to be seen."

"We don't have any money," Willow started, but Bonnie shushed her with a pat on the knee.

"I don't reckon you'll need it. You run those boys out?" Bonnie turned back to Frank.

"Out of town," Frank said, and his grin soured. "They done stole Mc-Master's horse. A man can let a lot of horseshit—sorry, miss—go, but not that. I didn't think the constable would string them up, but he told them if they ever showed their faces again, he would. They got out pretty quick."

Bonnie chinned forwards. "To the mountains?"

"I'd like to say so," Frank said. "Though I couldn't bear to watch. If they're smart, they'll set up in one of the small camps out yonder, make a living out there. May God have mercy if they try stealing from any of those folk, though. They won't live to see the sunrise."

Bonnie shook her head, then looked over her shoulder and sighed. "I reckon you'd better get a start on that room. Our guests might be occupied for a while yet."

Willow turned to follow Bonnie's gaze and saw Gerald walking quickly down the street, a thin plume of yellow dust rising behind him. He didn't have the crossbow out front, which was good, though she saw the limbs of the killing machine dangling behind his back.

"Bonnie, Lester," he touched his hat. "McMaster would like to have a word with your mage here."

"I thought he would," Bonnie said.

Willow felt her stomach drop with what this could possibly mean.

Gerald took Willow and Annabelle the way they'd come, back up the main street. Willow walked with the help of a tall, thin staff, which Bonnie had cajoled Frank into giving her. She still wasn't sure whether or not it was a loan or if Bonnie'd just browbeat the man into giving up one of his products.

With the staff, walking became much easier. Her feet ached less, her legs were well shy of cramping, and her back didn't have to take all the weight of her torso and head, which would force it dangerously close to seizing up. Willow actually made good time, though she suspected Gerald walked slower for her sake. Annabelle followed behind, and Willow could nearly feel the suspicion radiating off the woman. She wondered, not for the first time, if Annabelle would resort to violence if someone tried to impede them on their westward journey.

And what would Annabelle do if Willow herself refused to continue?

Gerald led them to a wide wooden building off the right side of the main road. Its front porch was raised a few feet off the ground by way of a series of wide steps. Wooden boards supported an overhanging roof, which she could imagine providing shade in the glaring summer sun. Gerald waited at the front door while Willow made her way up the stairs—Annabelle offering no assistance as she came up behind—and he led the way in.

The interior of the building was dark compared to the outside, though warmer. There were oil lamps ensconced on the walls, but their wicks were cold. Instead, a series of small windows, which apparently ringed the structure, provided light into the interior of the large building.

It took a moment for Willow's eyes to adjust, but by the time Gerald had led them a few steps further in, she spotted a collection of paintings on the walls. The oldest were so dark with soot they were nearly unrecognizable, but the newest were a string of portraits of men in flawless dress—some donning hats, some without. Gerald caught her inquisitive glance.

"The mayor's house," he supplied. "The appointment's for twenty years. These are the old mayors. I remember Duddy here from when I was a lad, but none of these others. Eustace McMasters has been mayor since I was ten, and he's coming to the end of his term."

"Twenty years is a long time," Willow remarked.

"Used to be life, when this was a company town. But the gold ran out and…" he shrugged. "Things change."

He led them to a room with a closed door and gave a knock. A muffled voice issued from within. Turning the knob, Gerald swept into a room brightly lit by south-facing, multi-paned windows.

A short man was sitting at a small desk to the left of the room, and he nearly jumped up at their entrance. Willow looked around for the honored mayor, and by the time she'd clocked the absence of other occupants, the short man had crossed to her side.

"The mage?" the short man said privately to Gerald, who nodded towards Willow. The short man put on a smile and approached, hand held out in greeting. "You must be Willow Tremont," he said, apparently as happy as a clam.

Willow just barely managed to plaster a smile across her own face before her hand was in his, being shaken—vigorously but gently.

"Yes, I am," she said, then took a closer look at the energetic little man. "Mayor McMasters?"

"Eustace," he corrected and turned to Annabelle.

"Annabelle," she said, and Eustace took her hand just as vigorously.

Willow saw the flicker of a smile on her lips for just a moment, which was more than she'd expected. For a brief instant, Willow considered how much Annabelle had gone through at her side and how little recognition she'd gotten for it. Then Willow remembered how Annabelle treated her during the entire journey out and decided not to care.

"Well, I can't begin to describe how excited we are at your arrival," Eustace said. "Especially after what Gerald reported from the river."

"And what did Gerald report?" Willow asked cautiously. She had very little clue if her small project was still standing, or what shape it would be in if it was.

"The most incredible thing," Eustace said. "If I didn't trust Gerald with my very life, I wouldn't have believed it for a second. The water is arching?" he asked Gerald, who nodded. "Arching over, leaving a dry path *under* the river. Incredible. Your work, I take it?"

Willow felt put on the spot. It was the first time she'd been forced to own up to it since she'd worked the mud last night, and her lips felt too dry to speak for a moment. She cleared her throat.

"Yes," she said, trying to put much more confidence in her voice than she felt. "Yes, I made it."

"Incredible!" Eustace continued, his voice dripping with excitement. "My father, Bill McMasters, rest his soul, once told me of a traveling mage who came through and raised a gold deposit five miles to the north. He said the river ran with gold for months. The panners caught so much they could hardly believe it. Now, this did lead to the gold crash, which proceeded into the slump we're currently in. No one's panned so much as a tenth-ounce nugget in the last two years. But still!"

Willow hesitated. "I can't say I've brought much better. When I made the tunnel... I didn't think of what it might do. The flooding towards the north—"

"Think nothing of it," he said. "Nothing north of here 'sides those ruins, and no one there 'cept outlaws. It would be a mercy to wash that place clean, though I don't think a little rise like that would make much of a difference."

"The tunnel," Willow started, unable to restrain herself any longer— thoughts of Durum's wall in her head, of real buildings built with real spells, instead of the magic she'd performed. "I don't know how sound it is. There's every chance it might collapse in the next few hours or days."

"Let it never be said that Eustace McMasters sits on his heels," Eustace said, waggling a finger above his head. "I thought, why, if this fails and we haven't made good of it, I'll be run out of town. I've already sent a crew through with a short wagon to begin laying boards atop the piles. If, or when, your tunnel fails, we'll be well disposed to continue the bridge's reconstruction, I'll have you know."

"Oh," Willow said, surprised by the level of forethought admitted by this energetic man. "Well, that's good."

"But where are my manners?" Eustace nearly shouted. "I had Gerald escort you here and nearly got lost in shop talk. Welcome! Welcome you both to Glint! We would be well pleased to host your stay for however long you require. Which... by the by, how long would that be?"

Willow opened her mouth, but before she had a chance to answer, Annabelle cut in.

"One night, then we'll resupply and continue west," she said.

"West?" Eustace asked. "Do you plan to poach the mountains?"

"We're headed for a small settlement in the mountains," Annabelle said, sidestepping the question.

"We don't have any money," Willow hissed. "Not anymore."

"Well, of course, any fare you require will be provided," Eustace answered expansively. "You've already helped us so much, it truly is the least we can offer. If I could entice you into a longer stay, perhaps..."

"No," Annabelle cut him off. "We must be going."

But Eustace wasn't looking at her. He was looking at Willow, and she realized he didn't care half as much as he pretended about what Annabelle had to say. He was focused on Willow—whom he perceived to be the only mage in the room.

"I..." Willow began, at a loss for words. "Perhaps."

His smile was genuine and, if possible, even more excited than it had been before.

Chapter 11

There weren't many things to unpack in the bedroom above Frank's general store. After hearing from Eustace about the removal of any kind of fee, Annabelle went straight to Frank's counter to assemble a list of supplies that would take them over the mountains the rest of the way to Asche. While Frank attempted to haggle her out of some of her choices—he'd clearly been told to give them whatever they wanted but was finding the order difficult to his mercantile interests—Willow slowly stalked out of the store and onto the hardpan main road.

She carried the oversized shirt Bonnie had gifted her in the caravan and was wearing instead a set of tight pants and shirt, meant to give freedom of movement when traversing the mountains to the west. The shoulders were padded for a heavy pack, as Frank had explained, which she was grateful for.

Before he'd begun focusing on Annabelle's insistent queries, he produced a long robe from the back room. The fabric was thick and closed at the throat, complete with a hood. It hung to her heels—she spotted at once where it had been hemmed in the last couple of hours—and the weighty material was heavily embroidered.

It was more than Willow could accept.

"No, no," Willow said, trying to hand it back to Frank. But the man smiled, his head shaking slowly on his thin, bony neck. "I can't accept this."

"A mage needs a cloak. At least that's what the stories say. I won't have you seen leaving my store, knowing I could have made you right after you'd lost so much on the journey out."

Willow's lip trembled, and she had to bite it to keep from crying. Annabelle rolled her eyes from behind Frank and continued perusing a set of hanging axes.

"Thank you," Willow whispered, not daring to raise her voice, lest she embarrass herself by sobbing.

Frank smiled, if possible, even wider, and helped her into the cloak. The embroidery on the back—stars and lines linking constellations—was tightly worked into the fabric, and she suspected it wouldn't snag on any branches they might pass through.

He settled the mantle on her shoulders, gave a twitch to the fabric here and there, then stepped back.

"Now you're a mage fit to be seen leaving Frank's," he said with a smile. Willow didn't trust herself to speak, so she nodded and left by the front door.

To say she drew stares as she staggered down the street with her staff and robe would be an understatement, though no one approached her as they had done with Bonnie and Lester. She realized she was an unknown element. There was no way for her to understand where she stood with the town, not unless she spoke with the caravaneers. She made her way as quickly as she could down the main road, under the cold sun and past wood-sided houses, to the formerly empty lot Bonnie had indicated.

Bonnie and Lester were hard at work setting out their wares. A small crowd had gathered, gabbing and watching them unload trunks from the back of two wagons. They were arranging their goods on a series of tables Willow didn't remember seeing in the caravan—although she hadn't been in the rearmost two carts.

The thin crowd parted and a hush settled, alerting Bonnie, who was at the front unloading pinned rolls of fabric from a trunk onto a table. She looked back and beamed at Willow. She still wasn't used to getting this reaction from anyone besides her parents and Leopold. It was making her a little uncomfortable, but not in a way that spoke of danger. More in a way that meant she'd have to do some soul-searching later on.

Bonnie waved Willow over. She crossed the short gap between the crowd and the table, where Bonnie wrapped her in a hug as massive as it was gentle on her frame.

"You just look incredible," Bonnie said, holding her out and looking her up and down. "Like you walked out of a storybook. I bet Frank made you take the robe, didn't he?"

"He did," Willow confirmed, ducking her head into the robe as much as she could, feeling the eyes of everyone in the crowd on her. "I kind of wish he didn't."

"Nonsense," Bonnie said, then gestured her around to the back of the third wagon where Lester was grunting. They rounded the back to see him sweating and straining as he hauled against a wooden crate.

"I told you the crate was too much," Bonnie called.

"Quit your nagging, woman, and—" He cut off when he looked up, eyes widening. "Well, look what Frank did. I bet he feels mighty pleased, as he should."

"Come on down here, packmule," Bonnie waved. Lester let the leading edge of the crate slam into the wooden boards of the wagon bed. Then he hobbled over and hung his legs off the back edge.

"What can we help you with, Willow?" Lester asked, mopping his brow with a handkerchief.

Willow suddenly remembered the shirt tucked under her arm,

beneath the cloak, and gave it to Bonnie. "Thank you so much for this," Willow said. "I was in no right state when you came upon—"

"I'll hear none of that," Bonnie scolded, but with a smile. "And you're right about that. You were in no right shape, especially for how sick you were."

"The bandits..." Willow began, but she stopped when Bonnie and Lester exchanged a look. "What? What is it?"

"It's not just the bandits, Willow," Lester said, his voice lowered. "If you didn't swear by it, I wouldn't believe for a second that that Annabelle was a nurse."

"She is! Of course she is," Willow protested. Spy too, but she saw no reason to burden Lester and Bonnie with that history.

Bonnie held up her hands. "As you've said many times, but I wonder. She don't have no bedside manner, that's for certain."

"I'm not arguing with you there," Willow agreed.

"The way she had you lying at the edge of the forest," Lester thought out loud.

"She's done things to me that the greatest surgeons in Durum couldn't dream of," Willow said. She didn't know what they were getting at, but she suddenly felt defensive of Annabelle, which was a very strange sensation.

"Aye. I saw what she did," Bonnie growled.

Willow flashed back to Bonnie's quick intake of breath when she'd begun washing Willow's back—to the sudden rage that had to be quelled carefully, lest she brain Annabelle with the frying pan.

"And you've never seen anything like it," Willow said, pressing the point. "Only she could've done that."

"I agree with you there," Bonnie relented. "But have you ever asked *why*?"

Only too many times, but there was no way for the kindly old woman to know that. She didn't know about Carl, about the secret messages Annabelle and he exchanged with their mysterious mentor, and to whom Annabelle was transporting her.

"She made me whole," Willow said, clenching her fist around the staff. All to a purpose, she well knew.

Lester sighed. "We think she's trying to use you," he said.

"I know," Willow said, finally admitting it to herself. Though she'd known on some level all she was good to Annabelle for was this meeting with her mentor, she'd partitioned off that information in her head, not letting herself see the whole picture.

How had Bonnie and Lester caught on? And they weren't letting her put off facing it any longer! She'd had vague intimations of abandoning Annabelle, especially during the nurse's more annoying episodes, and these two were forcing those thoughts front and center. Why was she staying with the nurse, playing at continuing the journey with her?

What would she even do if she left?

"You know where you're going, though you don't say," Bonnie broke in. "You're a right terrible liar. You say you're going into the mountains, and I don't doubt that, but I'd wager you're goin' deeper. And let me tell you, going very far into the mountains, I wouldn't advise. Not without a hunting party."

"I can take care of us," Willow said, though she wasn't quite sure if that was true. "I can do things..."

"Oh, of that we have no doubt." Lester chinned back the way they'd come through the river tunnel. "But have you stopped and asked yourself *if* you should? What is it *you* want, Willow?"

"No," Bonnie said gently, taking her by the shoulders. "What is it you want, Mage Willow? That's what they call you folk when you graduate, isn't it?"

The tears came, and she had no idea why. She quickly tried to wipe her face, and the cloak came away all wet.

"I never graduated," she said. "I never had the chance."

"I'd say you've been through enough to leave that behind," Bonnie said, and looked at Lester. He nodded, and she folded Willow into a comfortable hug.

Hoofbeats split the muttering of the crowd on the other side of the wagons, and Lester left for a moment, then returned. "I daresay Gerald's here for you," he said. "Would you like me to tell him to go away?"

"No," Willow said, sniffing. "No, I'll see him." And she started out, but Lester gently caught her shoulder. She turned in surprise.

"Don't forget," he said, eyes boring into hers. "What you are to these people. It's plain to see you've never thought much of yourself. I don't need to be a mind reader to catch it, but to these people, you're one step short of a god. It's been decades since the last mage came through. Just... think about that. Think about what they see in you. Try to believe it about yourself."

Willow set her jaw and nodded, then walked around the wagon back—and there was Gerald, sitting on horseback among the milling, gossiping crowd. He caught her eye and flicked his head that way.

Willow crossed the thin crowd again, and this time tried to catch the eyes of the people she passed. In their stares weren't disgust or pity, as there had been in Bridgewater, nor fear, as she'd assumed from those in Durum who knew what she'd done to Carl. No, it was something different.

Awe.

She was stunned by it, and perhaps that look still lingered on her face when she approached the shoulder of Gerald's horse.

"She's a beaut, isn't she?" he said, patting the horse on the neck. "Fastest in Glint, that I can tell you."

"She is," Willow said. The horse regarded her for a moment with a depthless black eye, then snorted.

"If you'd be so inclined," Gerald began. "Eustace thinks it might be a good idea, after you voiced reservations about the... well, what you'd done to the river, to go out and see it again? Maybe you can give us a clue as to what's happening there? How long it might last?"

"Sure, yeah," Willow said, not knowing how to reply to an official summons. "Should I follow you out, or..."

"Oh no, you'll ride behind," Gerald said, and gestured to her. "If I may?"

"Be gentle, please," Willow said in a small voice, which brought a look of surprise to Gerald's face before he nodded.

"Sure thing."

He pulled her up until she was able to get her foot in a stirrup and swing her other leg over. The whole process was much less intense than she'd suspected it would be. Was it because he was taking care? Or because she'd changed? It was impossible to tell.

Gerald clicked his tongue, and the tall, chestnut brown horse began to canter away from the crowd, who'd been watching the two of them with unrestrained curiosity. Willow found riding double to be much less painful than she expected. Still, she thought Gerald might be pushing himself as far forwards as possible and didn't envy him the effect it would have on a man's anatomy.

It was a ten-minute ride out to the river. But from the moment they left the last building of Glint behind, she spotted dark figures collected around the base of the tunnel. As they drew near, those figures resolved to several oxcarts carrying lengths of wood and a whole group milling around, talking. One caught their approach and gestured to the others. Willow wondered if it was her snapping, billowing cloak that caused such excitement.

All in all, there were a dozen men clustered around the roaring tunnel of water with their horses and carts. Those carts were piled high with cut wood of various shapes and sizes—some pilings were thick enough around to sink into the riverbed; others were straight, flat boards that would undoubtedly make up the body of the bridge itself. Willow didn't know the first thing about architectural magic, but she'd seen enough bridges in her time to know the beginnings of one.

The men clustered around in a half-circle while Gerald stayed the chestnut horse and patted her neck. He helped Willow down, then disembarked himself, leading the horse over to a cart to tie up. Willow was left in the uncomfortable position of being at the center of the group and the focus of everyone's attention.

"Um..." Willow trailed off, not knowing what she should do next.

"Leonard!" Gerald barked, and a tall, wiry man stepped forwards from the front of the group. Gerald walked right up to him. "What is all this material doing on this side of the river? I thought Eustace ordered you to set up half the supplies on the opposite shore."

"Giving order's all well and good," Leonard said in a thick accent. "But we ain't never seen—" He darted a look at Willow. "What I means to say is, the horses is too spooked to go through. Under the water."

"Well I've brought the mage responsible," Gerald gestured to Willow. "This is Willow. She erected this tunnel yesterday, and she'll give it a look over now. I trust you'll accept her blessing?"

Heads nodded in the group, eyes not daring to look away from her. Willow felt the weight of all that expectation and looked at Gerald. His mouth was in a tight line, and he jerked his head forwards.

The message was clear: *do your thing.*

Willow had to admit that the staff and robe, ruffling in the breeze, struck one hell of an impression, and she was thankful all over again to Frank for the ensemble. Perhaps he'd known how much help she'd need for this job, for her role here. How severely her own self-esteem had taken a beating—not just recently, but during her whole life. He was one man here who saw her as not just a mage, but as a person with foibles and all.

The semicircle parted reverently, and she walked through—not so much a stagger as before, but more with a slight limp—towards the roaring, gusting wet air. The tunnel looked even more majestic at high noon, with the sunlight glimmering off its upper curved surface. The falling water seemed to be having some kind of an effect on the air around it, because the wind just couldn't keep still. She was pelted with a fine spray of river water and had to squint as she passed beneath the lip of the tunnel.

The sunlight was filtered through the roaring water overhead, giving the hard-packed mud of the tunnel floor a shifting, dappled appearance. Only the slight familiarity that still remained from her previous interaction with the mud convinced her that the floor itself wasn't rippling. This kind of effect might not warn off an ox, but she had a bad feeling that horses carrying carts wouldn't do too well under the short stretch.

Willow knelt down and pressed her off hand against the hardpan floor, palm to fingers. Her awareness expanded, eager to reinhabit what she subconsciously considered to have once been a part of her body. It spread to the edges much quicker than she'd been able to that night with Annabelle, and what she found disturbed her.

The ramp she'd constructed out of pressed, hardened mud was rapidly disintegrating. Already what she estimated as half of the jump had been worn away. It hadn't affected the course of the river overhead yet, but there was significantly less reinforcement behind the leading edge to prevent a total collapse. If this much damage had been wrought in the last day, she suspected the tunnel might not last another day, or even to the end of this one. What she surmised was that once one part of the ramp broke through, the rest would follow shortly, stranding anyone working on the other side of the river and killing anyone traveling under it.

With grim determination, she walked back through the tunnel to the waiting band of workers, who'd edged as close as they dared to watch her do little more than press her hand to the ground. They backed away again as she gained the slope of the river, and Gerald met her at the top.

"So?"

Willow shook her head. "They were right to fear. What I've done's been worn away. I give it a few hours before something essential collapses and the whole thing caves in. I'm sorry."

Gerald grimaced and looked up and downstream. "It'll be a terrible flood when all this water crashes through," he said. "The wave might go all the way to the next town."

Willow nodded, feeling beaten.

"And there's no chance of accelerating the bridge back across the river if the tunnel collapses," he added.

Willow bit her lip.

"Is there nothing you can do? I'll be honest with you. The last mage came through here so long ago it's beyond many of our years. If you say no, no one will blame you. No one will think twice, including me. But—" And at this, he laid a gentle hand on her shoulder. She looked up at him from where she'd been intently studying her shoes. "I've heard stories. We've all heard stories. And this? What you've done so far, it's a miracle. I suspect you have a few more surprises in you. Don't be afraid."

Don't be afraid.

What did he know about fear? What did he know about magic? About that force that could wound much easier than it could heal. About essence, overwhelming essence that threatened to explode outward at any moment, wounding and killing everyone around you. What did he know about being a living, breathing bomb?

She'd killed already, and she opened her mouth to reiterate the impossibility of the task when a thought stopped her.

The magelights.

The little magelights were all contained in their own shields. Shields that had lasted months, that might as well be permanent, when everyone else's magelights dissipated within minutes or hours. Quite to her surprise, Willow realized she already knew how to solve this problem. She'd done it a hundred times before. It wasn't like what Annabelle was asking her to do, to weave essence offensively. To create death. This was something much simpler.

"Okay," Willow whispered, just loud enough for Gerald to hear.

She turned around and faced the roaring mouth of the tunnel, which seemed at that moment to be a great sucking vortex. An effect that would soon collapse if it wasn't supported from within.

Willow let go of her staff, but the length of wood didn't fall, continuing to stand upright beside her. This elicited a shocked murmur from the gathered workers, and Willow chided herself for her momentary stupidity. She'd revealed her impossible magic, her innate psychokinesis, and so unthinkingly.

But no one called out. No one clamped brass manacles on her wrists and tried to drain her power. She wasn't in Durum anymore. She wasn't a freak. Not here. Far from it.

She was a mage.

Or as close to one as the people of Glint could remember.

With a rising wave of calm certainty buoying her up, she stretched out her hands and whispered the familiar concepts of the shielding layer of her magelights. She pumped essence into the spell, shaping the essential barrier with her mind and hands. Then came strength and steadfastness, followed by extra layers of containment meant to fight against the natural inclination of a spell to evaporate over time. She threaded the spell through the tunnel and expanded it until it scraped the raging water, then widened it even further. Gasps and whispers came from behind her at the sight of the writhing, moving tunnel of light, which was now manipulating the shape of the gushing water.

Willow expanded the shield horizontally until it took on the shape of an almond, or an eye. The hardened mud underneath compressed, then shifted as she lowered the completed shape even further into the earth. With this lower seating and smoother shape, she hoped that, when the day did come that the barrier failed, the resulting wave of water would be much lessened.

Finally, as a precaution against that inevitable day, she installed several beacons along the interior of the tunnel. With a quick twist of logic and essence, they would strobe with fiery red light when the essential barrier was close to failing. She couldn't tell how long away that day may be, but for the sake of Glint, she hoped it would be at least a few weeks into the future. Whenever it was, they wouldn't be caught unawares when the time came.

With a great exhale, she lowered her hands, her work done. Mud streaked the water coursing over the saddle-shaped tunnel, which flared at beginning and end, keeping the river contained to the bed it crossed. The silt was from the disintegrating mud ramps she'd disturbed upon seating the new magical tunnel. They would soon collapse entirely, though she didn't think any change in the river's course would result from the destruction of the tiny ramps.

Willow took up her staff again and turned back to the gathered workers. Their eyes were, to a man, round and shocked at what they'd witnessed. They alternated between staring at the tunnel and staring at her. Willow looked at Gerald, but he gestured to her with a rolling hand. *Go on,* he seemed to say.

Willow cleared her throat. "Um, excuse me," she said, which had a larger effect than she'd expected. Every pair of eyes locked onto her, and she saw in not a few faces true reverence bordering on religious fervor. With so many eyes on her, she felt the compulsion to tug the cloak up over her collarbone, but she forced it away.

"The tunnel is secure," she said. "I've replaced the physical effect with a magical tunnel, which will not permit any water to pass while it stands. Within the tunnel walls, I've installed a series of strobing warning lights that will alert all to the imminent collapse of the effect. As to when that might be, I cannot say. What I've done here is… unorthodox, to say the least. Mages do not often construct artifacts out of pure essence as I have, and its longevity is probably best measured using tools I currently do not have access to. But, for at least a few weeks, I presume this tunnel will stand. And you will know long in advance before it collapses."

Their gaping expressions didn't change much at the explanation, and Willow uncertainly looked to Gerald. Gerald suppressed a slight smile and strode up beside her.

"You heard the mage," he said. "The tunnel's been fixed. Now I expect you all to perform the task for which you've been paid. If Willow here says the tunnel might only last a few weeks, then that means double time. We need to get this bridge built, and pronto."

He clapped, which seemed to snap them out of their daze. The group moved off in various directions, getting the carts ready to travel through the newly constructed essence tunnel under the river. Looking over her shoulder, Willow was proud to see that, now that the water wasn't jumping over earthen ramps, the optical effect of the shadows was much lessened. She assumed the horses would appreciate that.

Gerald wrapped an arm around her shoulders.

"I know that can't have been easy for you," he muttered as they walked towards the chestnut mare. "But Glint thanks you. I thank you, for what you've done here today. You truly are a miracle worker."

"I..." she started to deflect, then stopped herself. "Okay," she said. "Thank you."

At her request, Gerald dropped Willow off at Bonnie and Lester's instead of Frank's. She honestly couldn't say what she'd do in the small room—and she assumed Annabelle would be hard at work procuring the various paraphernalia they'd need to enter the dangerous mountains.

What she really needed was to talk to the two caravaneers.

The small lot they'd led the wagons to was entirely changed by the time Gerald helped her off the chestnut mare. Townsfolk milled about under awnings cleverly comprised of the removed canvas wagon covers. Under the awnings were tables and stands of various goods and knick-knacks, though many of the tables were turned over towards more serious purchases, such as seed, fabric, and folds of leather. A table at the end bore steel weapons, from swords to war axes.

There were so many townsfolk around the five stalls that, for a moment, Willow achieved the impossible and blended into the crowd. As she came up behind them, no one parted before her or stared at her. That sort of attention had always been paid to her back in Bridgewater and Durum, but for entirely different reasons. There, it had been her wan appearance. Here, it was something different. Something that was, perhaps, welcome.

Lester, haggling with a wide-shouldered man stroking the cutting edge of an axe with his thumb, caught sight of Willow first and waved her over. The man turned, mid-haggle, with a disbelieving expression on his face, and his eyes immediately widened. He stepped back as Willow sheepishly approached the table.

"Now, Tom, I know for a fact that, if you don't believe me, you'll believe our mage Willow here. Will you not?"

"Uh, sure," the man said, looking cornered.

Willow could tell from Lester's voice that he was in a mode she'd never seen him in before: the auctioneer and salesman. He was hellbent on making a sale, and everything in his demeanor reflected the fact.

"Willow, were we not accosted by the ghost of Blackbolt on the route here? And was this axe not in the very caravan the ghost passed by?"

"That is true," Willow said, unsure where Lester was going with this shtick.

"Then, though it may look unassuming, you can be assured that this axe survived a direct encounter with the ghost of Blackbolt. And not only that, was present when our very own mage Willow here dispelled the beast."

The man's eyes somehow got even wider. "You destroyed the ghost of Blackbolt?"

"I..." Willow began, then caught Lester's subtle nod and cleared her throat. "Yes, the ghost is no more."

The man opened his mouth to either comment or question, then shut it again. He looked down at the axe once more, then nodded to himself. "Alright, Lester," he said. "You've got yourself a deal."

They exchanged three silver for the axe, and the man left, holding the axe strangely reverently, not taking his eyes off the leather head cover. Willow walked over to Lester behind the table.

"You've been telling stories about me," she accused.

"'Course I have!" Lester laughed. "You're the most interestin' thing that's happened to Glint in going on thirty years."

"Did being so near the ghost actually affect the axe?"

"You'd be the one to know, not me," Lester said.

"I couldn't sense anything," she said.

"Then no."

"But you lied to that man!"

"Willow," Lester fixed her with a serious look. "I never said one untruth about that axe. Tom was in need of a new axe since his was lost in a fight with a sprite, and I had an axe to sell him. What he wasn't in the market for today was an heirloom. He has that now, and an axe, all in the same bundle. How many do you think he'll tell that story to tonight at the tavern? Ten, twenty? I'd be surprised if the whole town doesn't know by the morn."

"Was the ghost really so dangerous?"

"Dangerous? No, though everyone's heard of it. It's a strange thing, and people like to know about strange stuff around them. To know it's gone... well, it's a service you weren't paid for, and won't likely be. But I can leverage it, young Willow. And you can too."

"Me? But how would I—"

Lester gestured to the left, and when Willow looked, she saw Bonnie talking up a roll of hard leather. As Willow looked, Bonnie gestured over to her and smiled. The prospective buyer followed her gesticulation, and their eyes widened when they saw her. Willow quickly turned back to Lester.

"Your story," he continued. "This is it, Willow. This is your story, this is your life. We're telling it from as close to the beginning as we can, but you'll have to tell the rest in time. In a town like this, people like to know what they're getting into. We're paving the way, so to speak. By the morrow, you'll be a legend here, whether you decide to stay or go. If you stay, you'll be as welcome as if you were born here, which few can claim who was born elsewheres."

"I... don't know what to say," Willow said, feeling lost in the tumult of having her emotions whiplashed again and again.

"You don't have to say a thing," Lester said quietly. "Leave that up to us. But Bonnie's wantin' a word, and she'll curse me blue if I keep you any longer. Go on now."

Willow turned back to see that Bonnie had gotten rid of her customer, and the roll of leather as well, and was gesturing her over. Willow walked behind the tables until she was beside the large woman, who looked her up and down.

"You look beat," Bonnie said succinctly.

"I've been riding on a horse," Willow supplied.

Bonnie nodded, as if that's what she'd suspected all along.

"And I fixed the tunnel. It should hold longer now. Though how long, I can't tell. I put in some stuff to warn them when it's about to go. It's the best I could do."

"Well, that sounds like it deserves some celebration," Bonnie said with a smile.

"I'd rather not," Willow said. "I'd like to have a lie down, but..." She couldn't imagine getting comfortable in the small room at the top of Frank's, knowing Annabelle might come in and berate her at any moment for wasting precious time. At this stage, Willow wasn't so sure that they *should* be rushing. What could staying for a few days hurt? Or perhaps even longer.

"Tarp's off, but you can lay down back there in the third wagon, I reckon," Bonnie said. "It's cleared off enough anyway."

"Thanks, Bonnie." Willow managed a weary smile. She felt the strain of both riding to the river and back on horseback, and of creating and molding the tunnel, in every bone of her body. She staggered back to the wagon, hidden behind the first two, and crawled in. Sure enough, there was just enough room to lie down between two rows of trunks.

The robe was voluminous enough that she didn't even need a rug to lay on, and she was out in a handful of seconds.

CHAPTER 12

It's dark. The dark of true dark, not even a star in the sky. Willow doesn't remember seeing such darkness ever in her life. There's a hot wind blowing, blasting in from her back.

She turns and sees two red eyes in the dark. Something hisses in the black, and it rushes towards her. Willow gasps and falls backwards, pinwheeling her arms, but she doesn't hit ground. She falls and falls, deeper and deeper into the darkness—the red-eyed thing jumping over the edge of the cliff after her, flashing teeth snarling as she plummets down.

Willow woke with a scream and thrashed for a second against a hand on her shoulder. Her psychokinesis lashed out, embedding itself in the cart, in the trunks around her, and they rattled and jumped as Willow's muscles writhed. She moaned in pain and forced herself still, opening her eyes.

Bonnie was at the side of the cart, mouth open in surprise, eyes flashing around between the trunks that had rattled and jumped on Willow's wakening. Then her eyes were all for Willow, and Willow forced her arms and legs to quiet, the psychokinesis gradually dispelling on an ethereal wind.

"Willow?" she asked.

"I'm okay," she said. "Just scared me, is all."

Bonnie nodded. "Gerald's here. I told him you were sleeping, but he insisted."

It took Willow a second to put the name with a face, then she nodded slowly and pushed herself up. Her arms were sore from the cramp that had run through them, but other than that, nothing seemed to have been damaged by her abrupt waking.

But what a strange dream. She'd never had one like it before. It felt almost... real. Like something was really stalking her in the dream. She'd been more scared than she'd ever been in the forest, even with the bandits.

Willow groaned softly, then sat all the way up and slid out of the wagon. Sure enough, she could see Gerald's feet on the other side of the first two wagons, which had been set front-to-back to hide the third. Bonnie gave her a concerned look, and Willow tried to disarm her with a shaky smile.

With her robe donned and staff in hand, she rounded the corner of the wagons to find Gerald. While she'd been sleeping, the sun had mostly set, leaving an orange-red spray of color against the undersides of the towering clouds overhead. In thirty minutes or less, it would be full dark.

"You wanted to see me?" Willow asked.

Gerald turned quickly and cleared his throat. "Yes. I wanted to discuss some things with you. They're of a sensitive nature."

He looked around the stalls, which were just as lively as they'd been earlier in the day, then nodded towards the road. Willow followed as he led the way. They walked for a dozen or so feet before he began to speak.

"How do I find you, Willow?"

"Asleep," Willow said shortly.

"I suppose I meant to ask how you fared after raising the tunnel."

"Oh," Willow said and looked within to check her reserves. She felt surprisingly topped up, and she had to remind herself that—even though she'd woven a difficult and powerful piece of magic—she also hadn't been using psychokinesis to move her body all day.

Overall, it appeared that she'd had more than enough essence generation capacity for the task.

"I find myself well. Not as tired as I had imagined, certainly."

"Incredible," Gerald whispered, and when Willow looked up at him in curiosity, he quickly continued. "After the river, I took it upon myself to ask around the oldest of us to see if they remembered anything of the last mage who came through here. Most didn't, but there were some who were old enough to watch the working. They'd said that after the mage raised the gold, he'd had to rest for three days before he could travel on again."

"Well, I don't know if what I've done is comparable to that," Willow parried the compliment. "And I'm... a little strange for a mage."

"Strange isn't the word I'd use. Powerful, maybe. Magical, definitely."

"Have you called on me to compliment me to death?" Willow quipped.

"Ah, no. Well, not entirely. If you weren't aware, I'm something of a messenger for Eustace, while being captain of the town guard, what little guard there is. As such, after dropping you off here with Bonnie and Lester, I made my way directly to Eustace, who was extremely eager to hear of the account. Now, Eustace isn't a man of the people as much as I am, but he's got something I don't: books. Lots and lots of books, all squirreled away in that mansion of his. And they're not all storybooks, either. Some of them are about mages."

Willow didn't like where this was going.

"There were old books, most of them were old, but a few were more recent, written in the last fifty years or so. They gave historical accounts of the raising of the city walls centuries before, and of the Arcana that each city was built around. As well as a more mundane accounting of the various paraphernalia of a mage. He asked me to ask you something."

She really didn't like this direction.

"You came without a staff, which is understandable as you'd been robbed beforehand. It said that a mage's staff can be a powerful inscribed weapon. Is that true?"

"It could be," Willow said, remembering the staff used by Clara in the warbeast battle centuries before. "But mages now don't carry such implements, at least not within the city walls. As I heard, open warfare between the cities died out ages ago with the signing of the treaty. After that, war mages were a rare species. Much better to specialize in something like architecture. Lethal spells aren't particularly taught at the Arcanum, at least as far as I was aware."

Gerald nodded. "Which brings me to my second question. Do you have an identification signet?"

This was what Willow had been afraid of. Every mage who graduated the Arcanum was gifted a heavily inscribed disc of bronze, proving their identity and their status as a graduate. It was the only thing that could prove such credentials between the city-states, with how frosty their relations were even now.

"I don't," Willow said, glancing away and towards the ground. The night had grown darker, making the road treacherous underfoot. She trod carefully, not wanting to go down in front of Gerald or injure herself.

"Was it stolen in the attack?" Gerald asked.

Willow took a breath and let it out slowly. No more lies. That was what she'd promised herself—a life without lies, either from herself or to herself.

"I never received one," Willow said. "I never graduated the Arcanum. I dropped out after... well, after an incident. A couple months later, the warbeast attacked."

Gerald nodded like he'd expected as much. "Why didn't you stay in Durum after? Was the city..."

"Intact, as far as I've been told," Willow said, though her throat grew thick with emotions she didn't want to think about. Annabelle had been the one to tell her how Durum fared, but she'd been known to embellish the truth when it suited her. Willow swallowed thickly. "I left because... that warbeast, it came for me."

This elicited a full-throated laugh from Gerald, and Willow stopped to watch as he leaned back, laughing into the night.

"Ah, Willow, I haven't had a good belly laugh like that in a long while," he said. "But you put too much on yourself, anyone can see. You're riddled with guilt. Warbeasts don't attack people. They're a force of nature. They attack cities and are attacked in turn by those cities. A single mage, no matter how powerful, would be invisible to them. Would certainly not be enough to attract one to siege a city."

"I'd like to think so..." Willow said.

"You don't need to think so," he said, stopping and turning to her.

They'd stopped beside a largish, single-floor building that spilled raucous laughter into the street through the cracked front door. The smells of tallow smoke and strong beer wafted out as well. It brought back memories, strong memories, from her time with the woodsmen. A powerful thirst gripped her.

"What is this?" Willow asked, deliberately turning away to eye the building. He seemed to get the message because he sobered up immediately and fixed her with a serious stare.

"This is an invitation," Gerald said, gesturing to the building. "I know you're different than the last mage. Eustace knows, from his books, that what you did wasn't much like any magic you'd find in the Arcana. But I came to tell you that we don't care. He doesn't care, I don't care, and everyone who's had their livelihoods restored because of that tunnel of yours doesn't care either. You shoulder the weight of the world, Willow, but you can lay that burden down. And if you want to lay it down here, in Glint, well Eustace would be mighty proud of that. That's the message he tasked me with passing along. If you want to stay when Bonnie and Lester move on, then that's all right by him."

Willow's mouth hung open with shock. She could barely read Gerald's face in the faint glow from the tavern front, but what she *did* see spoke to his utter sincerity.

"Or, you could depart with them. Or leave into the mountains with that Annabelle you came in with." His grimace showed what he thought of that last idea. "Whatever you choose, he wants it made known that you'll be welcome again here."

"I don't..." Willow said, then shook her head, her thoughts abuzz like an angry swarm of war wasps. "Thank you, for passing on the message. I'm still not sure what to do."

"My advice?" Gerald asked, and after a second, Willow nodded. "Come and have a drink with us."

He gestured to the tavern, and Willow found her feet moving quite without her head's reckoning. Her hand went out, touching the splintery wooden door as she breathed in that old tavern smell. She closed her eyes, banishing the memory of the destroyed woodsmen and a city whose fate she could only guess at, and opened the door wide enough to go inside.

The tavern erupted in applause.

* * *

The hot dark is smothering in its intensity. Willow finds herself whipped by a maelstrom and crouches down for whatever shelter she can find low to the ground. The earth is sparse grass on hard sand. She grabs the grass for what anchor it can provide and desperately searches for some feature in the pitch black.

In front, about three fingers above the horizon, a faint red disc hovers in the air. Is it the sun or the moon? It doesn't emit any light, at least not enough to brighten the world around her, only enough to make its presence known. An almost completely useless satellite.

She sweeps around for features but finds nothing until a hiss cuts through the roaring gale at her back. She spins around, still clutching the ground, and finds those two large red eyes pinning her down. They are oblong, like almonds, with slit pupils fixing her in a murderous stare.

"What are you!?" she shouts into the storm, and the creature rushes forwards again, fast footfalls rocking the ground beneath her knees. She sweeps her cloak—part of the dream this time—around her just before the world rocks to the side, and a voice cuts through the night.

"Mage?"

* * *

Willow opened her eyes and sunlight flooded in like a needle to the brain. She groaned and tasted the vile aftertaste of too many beers and an unfortunate number of crackers on her jerky-dried tongue. Willow shaded her eyes and glanced around, immediately finding herself in the back of the third wagon again, her robe draped over her.

With another groan, she sat up slowly and took in the too-bright world. Glint carried on much as it had done the previous day, completely unaware of the terrible pounding on her head and the way the sunlight speared her eyes. At the foot of the wagon was a young boy with a terrified look on his face.

"Y-Yes?" Willow asked. "Has something happened?"

"Uh, no," the young boy stammered and stepped back. His eyes fell to his fingers, which immediately began fidgeting. "I, um..."

She knew two things right away: this boy wasn't supposed to be here at this moment, and he wasn't too afraid of her to risk waking a mage. Whatever had happened last night had changed things for her in this little town.

The memories came slowly back, like thick treacle slipping down a board. She remembered being welcomed into the tavern with roaring applause, being hoisted on someone's shoulders at some point in the night after her second pint, and drunkenly explaining to a devoted circle of listeners her most painful secret—that she'd survived the Wasting, but came out of it paralyzed and a freak of nature.

"Oh no," Willow groaned, placing her head gently in her hands. The movement made the world rock around her dangerously, threatening to spill what little remained in her stomach from the night before. "Oh... no..."

"I can, um, come back later," the little boy said, backing away slowly.

"No," Willow said, though she didn't dare shake her head. "No, what is it?"

"Well." The little boy looked sheepish. She noticed he was in a checkered button-up shirt and brown trousers. He looked as though he'd been dressed up for something special. School, perhaps. "I was wondering, if it would be alright... Could you make one of those lights? Could I have one?"

The magelights? What hadn't she told the men in the tavern last night? And this little kid already knew all about it? What time was it?

"Yes," Willow forced herself to say, although she most definitely wasn't feeling up to the task. She sat more fully up and searched around for a flask of water—none was at hand. So instead, she drew a long, steadying breath, and intoned the simple concepts and formed the simple shapes that would produce one of the hardened lights.

The task was done in thirty seconds, and she held out the light for the little boy. He approached, eyes wide and staring at the dim light, and reached out with shaky fingers to take it.

"Keep it indoors," she warned. "Or it'll float away."

The boy nodded earnestly, then turned and bolted. As Willow followed his escape, she saw Bonnie reach out and grab the kid by the scruff of his neck. She said something quick and clipped into his ear.

"Thank you, Mage Willow!" the boy turned and shouted back. Then Bonnie let the kid run on down the road towards the center of town. Willow closed her eyes and rested her aching head on her hand as she attempted to gather herself to face the day.

Bonnie's footsteps were unmistakable now, and Willow knew when she approached the wagon. Willow opened her eyes a fraction and saw a waterskin held out in the older woman's hand.

With a grunt, Willow accepted the skin and drained a quarter of the contents before her stomach threatened to send everything back the way it came. Willow pressed her lips together hard, willing everything to stay put. Luckily for her, it did.

"Guh," she gasped and handed the skin back. "Thank you."

"I heard you had quite the night," Bonnie said.

"You send that lad over to ask me for a light?" Willow asked with a smile on her lips.

"He came over to ask all on his own. I might've given him some encouragement."

Willow smiled but didn't dare laugh for the headache that threatened to smash her world to pieces. Besides, there were more pressing matters at hand than the magical lights, which she predicted would soon invade the town.

"Did I do or say anything I'll regret last night?" Willow asked cautiously.

There was the briefest hesitation before Bonnie said, "Noooo."

Willow squinted again against the bright November sun. "What did I do?"

"Nothing," Bonnie said. "But... Well, I didn't know before. About the Wasting."

Willow wiped her hand down her face. How could she have been so stupid? "And that I'm a freak," Willow finished.

"Now you stop that," Bonnie snapped.

It was said with such force that it took Willow quite aback, and she opened her eyes as if she were about to stave off an actual attack.

"Nobody in there thinks any less of you for what you said. Some doubt it, no question there. The Wasting's just as bad here as anywhere else, but quite a few more believed it. After seeing what you did with the tunnel, they'll believe anything you say. You say you survived the Wasting, and came out of it with mysterious abilities the likes of which no one has seen before? Well, that's no surprise to any around here. They've never seen anyone quite like you, that's for sure."

Willow closed her eyes, mollified. "Okay, thanks," she said. "Thanks for that."

After a moment, Bonnie continued. "But I did mean to get you up. Someone's looking for you."

"Who?" Willow asked, but just at that moment, she heard quick footsteps approaching. She knew from that labored walk just who had been stalking the streets around town, trying to find out where her charge had gone.

She held back a groan. This was absolutely not the person she wanted to be talking to right now.

"Willow!" Annabelle spat.

Willow rubbed her forehead, attempting to banish the headache and for the most part not succeeding. Bonnie gave her a look that said, *should I stay?* and Willow gave the slightest shake of her head. Bonnie nodded and hopped down from the wagon wheel, striding off a short ways to begin unfurling tarps from over her wares.

"Where in the hell have you been?" Annabelle hissed. "I've been looking for you all..." She sniffed. "Are you drunk? Again?"

"No," Willow said, somewhat defensively. "I *was* drunk last night. Now I'm hungover."

"Pull yourself together, child. We're leaving."

Sure enough, when Willow squinted against the piercing sunlight, she saw that Annabelle had a pack on her back and was shouldering a second one as well. They were both loaded up with supplies and looked to weigh at least thirty or forty pounds each. No wonder Annabelle was in such a bad mood, lugging those things around.

"Where?" Willow asked, feigning forgetfulness to stall for time.

"The mountains," Annabelle hissed. "Asche."

"Your mentor," Willow said. "Carl's mentor."

"That's right."

Willow set her teeth and pulled herself slightly more upright. Prying her eyes open, she looked straight into Annabelle's.

"No."

Annabelle sneered. "What do you mean, *no*? Where else would you go?" When Willow didn't offer an answer, Annabelle looked around in disbelief. "Here?" she spat with incredulity. "This... no account backwater?"

"Here," Willow confirmed. "I've done something for them. They said—"

"*They said, they said.* Wake up, you petulant child! How long until they throw you out on your ass? How long until they discover you? The real you? How long until someone finds out what you did in Durum?"

That stung, whether she meant what happened with Carl or what happened at the city gate. Willow held onto Bonnie's words and just barely managed to keep from shrinking back.

"No," she said again. "Annabelle, I will not go with you to Asche. I will not go to your master. These people want me. They might even need me. I can do good here. I know it. You and Carl, you're fighting a war that doesn't have to be fought. You're itching for a battle that can pass us by. Thank you for everything. Thank you for healing me. But I will not go on to Asche. If you want, you can go that way yourself."

Their heated argument had drawn a little crowd, and from the glares, they all appeared on Willow's side.

Annabelle stepped back, traces of a sneer still evident on her face. She shook her head slightly, shoulders going slack. The fire seemed to go out of her eyes. "I can never go back," she said under her breath. "Not without you."

That shocked Willow—to discover that, through all her bluster and fury, Annabelle was held at the end of a noose the same as her. She wouldn't be able to return to her home, from which she'd been separated for so long, unless she arrived with her charge in tow. But of course, that had been why Annabelle had healed her, hadn't it? To spruce her up for her arrival at Asche.

Through the churning in her gut, Willow shook her head, steeling her resolve. "I'm sorry. But I won't go."

"We'll see." Annabelle scowled, then turned and stumbled through the crowd, receiving a shove somewhere in the mix that nearly pushed her off balance. She looked back for the offender but was met with a steely wall of silence. It almost caused Willow grief to see Annabelle abused, but Annabelle scoffed and trudged off towards Frank's.

Willow sighed. No chance now that she'd be welcome in their rooms. She'd just have to figure out alternate accommodations. It wasn't like she hadn't slept rough before.

CHAPTER 13

"I'm delighted to hear it!" Eustace beamed, spreading his arms wide and stepping forwards cautiously.

Willow, naturally shy, gave a small nod, and he encircled her with a gentle hug, clearly having been told by Gerald to be careful when touching her. Obviously the two men shared much information between them.

"If you're going to stay," Eustace continued after breaking off the embrace. "You'll need a residence."

"I was going to bunk in the back of Bonnie and Lester's—"

"Oh no, no, no," Eustace said, shaking his head back and forth so vigorously that she thought it might flop right off his thin neck. "That won't do. Bonnie and Lester, well, they're a special case. Won't take lodgings, those two. They prefer to stay close to their stock, and I can't say I blame them with the line of work they're in. But there's no need for you to sleep in the rough the way they do. Unless you prefer it?"

"Um... what did you have in mind?"

"If I may be so bold—a room in this very mansion. There are five bedrooms, though I've only ever used one myself. There used to be seven. But then I had one converted to a library and the other to an extension of the kitchen. One hell of a job, I'll tell you, breaking the wall between, but well done. You'd be pressed to see the original separator—what am I doing, going on about the kitchen? Yes, you can stay here, if it pleases you. I'm sure we'll have much to discuss. And meals will be provided, of course, until we set you up with a place of your own."

Willow was shocked at this bold offer. "I really don't know what to say."

"You could say yes?" Eustace offered, hopefully.

"Yes, then yes," Willow said and smiled. "I accept."

"Splendid. How I hoped for this the moment Gerald brought news of your arrival. With a mage on the town's payroll—fee is something we should discuss, of course, and you'll find our coffers dreadfully thin compared to a large city-state like Durum or Raly. But for the somewhat limited lifestyle we provide, I can assure you that your fee will be plenty. I can just envision all of the projects we can accomplish together! The bridge for starters, of course. Not that we don't trust your tunnel, but you yourself warned against its eventual collapse. And we really need a bridge for those higher convoys. And the warehouse! Yes, that should be first, the warehouse. Oh, where are those plans?"

Willow couldn't help but smile at Eustace's excited rushing about as he checked drawers and countertops for whatever papers he was gathering up. She looked out of the windows of Eustace's office, which offered a view of the mountains to the west, and thought she was doing the right thing. Going into those mountains with Annabelle was something she wouldn't do unless there was no other choice. No, not to be served up like a tasty morsel to her mentor. Here, she could live a life apart from everything that had happened before.

"—lack of an identification signet," Eustace said, which derailed Willow completely from her musing.

"What?"

"Oh! Gerald told me about the signet and your time at the Arcanum. No need to worry, of course, but I suppose your coursework might not be complete?"

"Yes. Unfortunately, it is not complete," Willow confirmed, a worm of dread settling in her stomach. But Eustace's smile didn't waver in the slightest.

"Well, hopefully I can help there. Come through with me into the library, if you please."

She followed the thin mayor out of his office, down the hall two doors, and to a larger room that had had its door removed at some point in the past. She could see where a latch had been morticed, but the crowning hadn't been re-carved to suit its new doorless state.

Beyond lay a room absolutely covered in books. Every wall was a bookshelf, save three cutouts for windows to let the light in. There were four small tables with a single chair each and an oil lamp, each piled with books that hadn't been put away. Willow didn't see how they could be put away, as the shelves looked entirely stuffed.

"Excuse the mess. I tell Dorothy not to touch a thing that's on these tables. I'm dreadful at keeping my place, you see, and I peruse several topics at once. Yes, let's come over here. Ah, here's what I'm looking for."

Eustace directed her to the left, pointing at a shelf about waist-level, mounted to the wall through which they'd come. He gingerly eased out a two-inch-thick tome, bound with stretched brown hide, and held it out to her.

Willow took it and immediately gaped at the title. *Introductory Principles to Architectural Magic Vol. 1* was embossed on the front in gold leaf, which led her to reassess the text's value. On the one hand, magic was clearly used to create the tome, which reduced the price. On the other, she'd never seen an Arcanum textbook outside of the city—besides the introductory volume owned by many hopeful would-be students before gaining admission to the school.

"Where did you get this?" Willow whispered, awed.

She cracked the volume to the middle and saw a page covered in mathematical equations and tables, which seemed to concern the compression strength of lengths of cut wood of various species. Flipping a random number of pages forwards, she found the familiar spell-form shorthand that had been present in the textbooks she'd sold when she left the Arcanum. The spells listed were complex and concerned the joining of several materials together of different types. It seemed that there was a slightly different spell for each combination: steel and wood, ceramic and bone, and many other types as well.

"Bonnie and Lester, if you'd believe it," Eustace answered. "About five years ago, they came through with a half dozen tomes from the Arcanum. It seems that an enterprising mage who settled in a town about a hundred and fifty miles south had decided to sell his old schoolbooks, but found himself without the buyers necessary in his adopted home. They took on the product, knowing my predilections for especially rare works."

"Have they been useful for you?" Willow asked. She'd begun scanning the shelves and found several other Arcanum textbooks concerning subjects as wide-ranging as botany and astrology. All save for the introductory work to enchanting, she'd never seen these before, as they were texts for advanced subject classes.

"Not as much as I would wish, unfortunately," Eustace said, with such regret that Willow turned to regard him. He looked at the books wistfully. "My own aptitude for magic is quite awful. I can light a taper easily enough, but anything more complex just slips my attention. I'm more liable to make a mess of things than anyone else. Though, that doesn't mean I don't enjoy dipping into what I've been missing. And I have to say that even the mundane aspects of that text there are quite useful, at least in the engineering of buildings. I had no idea scholars at the Arcanum knew so much about the physics of standing structures."

"Oh, they're all chock full of knowledge," Willow remarked.

His comments had brought her back to an unfortunate truth about the Arcanum—its desperate grasp on knowledge and power. What kept the city-states separate and powerful were jealously guarding their secrets, and she was surprised that Eustace had been able to get his hands on this many Arcanum texts in the first place. Sure, a city-state might send a specialist out to one of these small towns if they'd be paid enough for a project, but that specialist wouldn't be inclined to share the secrets of their trade. It was one reason mages were so highly sought after, even though almost everyone could perform basic magic.

"I hope I don't presume, but I thought this text might be helpful to you in your next endeavor. Perhaps the equations within would even help you determine more accurately the due date, as it were, of your tunnel?"

"Yes, I think so," Willow said, her attention again on the tome in her hands.

"Keep it. You have more use for it than I ever had. Perhaps a quick perusal while your room is being spruced up?" Eustace motioned to one of the desks.

Willow smiled in amusement and gently took the seat, opening the book in her lap as the table was too crowded to allow a space.

"Excellent, I'll just go and tell Dorothy to ready your room."

And he was off, leaving Willow alone with the library, the sunlight, and a book in her hands. With strange familiarity, she opened the text to its first page and began to read, as if she were in class once again.

* * *

All in all, the book didn't end up being that instructive after all.

Oh, there were plenty of tables and arcane formulas for stress and construction angles, which would be very helpful to even mundane architects. But what had disappointed her most of all was the general uselessness of the spells themselves.

There were spells for sticking different materials together, for supporting joins of various angles, and for slowly raising or lowering structures an inch at a time. There were spells for lightening large rocks so teams of men could lift and place them in stone walls. Other spells guided the course of mortar between the rocks so that very little spilled out. All of these spells were useful to a normal mage, there was no doubt about it.

But they weren't useful for her.

The reason being that the extremely specific use cases of the spells and their finicky casting procedures were all to allow a single mage to roll several off in a row, leaving a team of laborers to finish the rest of the job with manual labor. They'd been engineered to take as little essence as possible, trading versatility and longevity for low casting cost. By sticking wood to steel, supporting several forty-five-degree angles, and magically hinging a frame's feet to the earth, a mage could ensure a team of laborers could raise a frame—and sink it in the exact spot it needed to go—with no chance of breaking the wood joints previously cut.

In the text, there was no accounting for a mage like Willow, who could do all that without even the team of laborers. Therefore, when Gerald came to get her and escort her to the warehouse construction site, Willow left the tome behind.

It was noon, and the sun's rays were so strong it was almost warm in the low wind. The site was close enough, so she and Gerald walked. This somehow seemed to elicit even more glances and pointing hands than when they'd ridden the horse out of town.

"Is the tunnel…" she asked.

"Still strong," Gerald confirmed. "We've got the timber moved through. Without your tunnel, it would've taken weeks to move that much material over either the northern or southern bridge. If they still exist."

"I'm glad to have been of help," Willow said. "What's left?"

"*What's left*, she said," Gerald chortled. "Just building the bridge. Not much, perhaps, to you, but the raising of a bridge is a tedious and precise task. It needs to stand up to the constant rush of the river, and it needs to last for years. Even with the pilings still in place, it'll take a few months to connect the two sides of the river over the water. Even then, your passage will provide a valuable relief if, or when, traffic to Glint picks up again. I don't suppose you could raise more gold, could you?"

"To be honest, I have no idea how the mage prior performed the task," Willow said, then began to muse. "I suppose they could've used a scrying spell to identify the locations of all existing lodes, then perhaps a powerful psychokinetic pull? No, that would require too much essence. Perhaps a simple geologic shift? Just enough for the flowing river to access the lodes? Yes, that would be easiest. Let the water do all of the work."

She looked up at Gerald beside her to find him grinning down at her. Willow immediately felt self-conscious but responded with pride rather than shame.

"What?" she said, offended. "Do I amuse you?"

"Yes," Gerald said through his smile. "Look at this from my perspective. Here you are, a diminutive woman, no offense, who apparently has a magic so special she thinks she's the target of warbeasts far and wide. But you don't act like it, oh no. You act like someone's standing over you with a stick about to hit you at any moment. But in just one afternoon you perk right up. I wonder what caused it?"

It wasn't hard for Willow to guess.

"I spoke… severely to Annabelle," she said. "My nurse wanted us to continue on to the mountains. I wanted to stay. Words were exchanged."

"Well, I'm glad," Gerald said, chin held high as they approached what was clearly the site in question. "We'd have been sorry to lose you." And he gestured at the plot of land.

It was a medium-sized lot, perhaps a half-acre, twice as long as it was wide. There were piles of cut lumber stored under tarpaulins to protect them from the sun and rain. Sixteen long posts were anchored in the ground, four at the front and back and six along the sides, counting the corners twice. The warehouse would be large indeed, taking up most of the area of the plot, and she couldn't guess what they'd store in such a large building.

A heavyset man, short but solid with thick arms and an even thicker midsection, approached and gave Willow a once-over.

"You must be the mage. Willow, right?"

"I am," Willow said. "Eustace told me you might like some help?"

The man grunted in dismissal. "He likes to stick his nose in things he doesn't understand," the man, who must have been the foreman, said. "Thinks he can speed things up by throwing more men or… mages, at things. I told him, I said, 'I've already got twice the crew I need for the job.' But what does he say? He's gonna send a mage over to see what she can do. Well, see what you can, I suppose."

If Willow was being honest with herself, she agreed with the man. She knew little about architecture, and apart from recognizing the posts as the beginnings of a large building, she had little knowledge of what the next steps would be or how to go about them. Magic was useless without knowing what the project entailed, she realized.

"Do you have a set of plans?" she asked. "It might help to know what the next steps are in the process."

The man grunted again, swinging his head to the side and setting off to a table under a small, stretched canvas. She followed dutifully behind and found a thin canvas sheet weighted down on its four corners over the table. The man removed two of the weights and carefully rolled the canvas back.

Beneath the protective covering was a series of precise drawings that laid out the warehouse in exacting detail. Every length of wood was labeled, every angle specified, and the margins were chock-full of notations spelling out exceptions and details on the larger plan. Willow reverently turned back the top sheet and found even more sheets underneath, one for each side of the warehouse and each specifying their own sets of supports, doors, and windows.

"This is not what I expected," Willow said, realizing that even if she'd brought the tome, its information on compressive strength would have little use here. "You've got everything already planned out."

"Any engineer worth his salt does," the man said from beside her. He rolled the protective canvas sheet over the plans again, weighing the lot down with metal discs. She couldn't imagine the worth of the sheets, containing as much detailed planning as they did.

"I'm not sure what you need me for."

"I'm not sure either," he said back, hands on his hips. "Can you offer anything we don't already have with a work crew twice the size it should be? Damn Eustace and his rush!"

The foreman's cursing took her off guard, but Willow quickly regained her composure and looked the man, who was about as tall as her, in the eye. "I can offer this."

She held out her staff parallel to the ground and let go. It hung there, immobile, and the foreman's eyes widened. She caught a quick intake of breath from Gerald as well, but when she looked, he'd already carefully composed his face to something approaching nonchalance.

The foreman reached out, looked at her, and when she nodded assent, placed his hand on the staff. She felt him push down on the wood, then jerk it quickly side to side. Finally, he leaned forwards and put all his weight on it, lifting both feet off the ground for a moment before coming back to earth. The whole time the staff didn't move so much as a quarter inch.

"You can provide a single support like this?" the foreman said, amazement clear in his voice.

Willow raised her eyebrow.

"More?"

"Depending on the weight, I can provide up to two hundred."

The foreman's mouth dropped open, and he glanced back down at the staff, then up again. "Can you move it?"

"Within a certain radius of myself," she said.

"Is it just the staff, or…"

"It can be anything, I think," Willow said, suddenly unsure. "I suppose the effect might be less strong with unfamiliar materials."

The foreman gestured business-like over to the site, and Willow followed dutifully. There were a dozen men joining beams of lumber in an intricate pattern, which Willow just recognized as the front and back frames for the warehouse. And even then, she only knew it by glancing at the other end of the lot, where the back frame had already been completed.

"Raising the frames is a difficult and precise task," the foreman explained. "We do it in stages, and we mount a winch between the opposing structural posts to assist as well. As much as I complain, for a job as big as this, well, it'll require the full dozen men. What do you think?"

At her approach, the men fitting the smaller pieces together on the ground in the laid-out pattern had looked up. They stopped their work entirely, shamelessly staring at her. She imagined she cut quite a figure with the mage's cloak flapping in the chill breeze, and she tried her best to ignore the attention. Instead of starting at the front with the incomplete frame, Willow crossed the warehouse to the back, knelt down, and placed a hand on the frame that lay complete on the ground a few feet from the support posts.

Willow closed her eyes and let her consciousness expand into the frame, following the grain of the wood. She found natural endings at the joints, but pushing her awareness through to the connecting mate-rial eventually gave her a complete picture of the frame.

Fifty-six separate pieces of wood of varying lengths, from ten feet down to six inches. Most of the joints were sturdy, though a couple were iffy, and held tight by some kind of solid adhesive, probably a hide glue if she had to guess. She couldn't guess what the entire thing might weigh, though she knew it was massive, outstripping her own weight by an order of magnitude. That's as close as she could get to estimating—how it related to her natural body, through which her psychokinesis had flowed her entire life.

Strangely, she found it easier to move when her mind was focused on the frame. She was able to lift herself off the ground without having to give a second thought to keeping her latent powers from butting in against her developing muscles.

The foreman stood behind her and off to one side.

"I can lift it," Willow said.

"The whole thing?" the foreman confirmed. Willow nodded. "Now?"

She nodded again.

"Boys, get over here," the foreman yelled, gesturing wildly with his arm.

The crew ran from one end of the warehouse until they sur-rounded her and the foreman, at which point the diminutive man began barking orders to form up the crew and fasten the frame to the support pillars. Most of the men looked confused at the impending task change, but a few glanced quickly at Willow before running off to switch out their tools for ones more suited for the new task.

Within five minutes, the crew was formed up and divided evenly between the two end-posts, all quiet with expectant anticipation.

"Alright," the foreman said. "We're ready now. What do you need?"

Willow shook her head slightly. "Nothing."

As easily as if she were raising her arm, she likewise raised the completed frame, hinging at the bottom until it was fully upright. A few of the laborers stepped back in fear, but most watched in wide-eyed wonder. When raised, the frame was still a few inches away from the support posts, and she scooted the whole upright thing forwards slightly until it just touched the wooden beams.

"Fasten!" the foreman shouted.

Quick as a flash, the frame was lashed to the pillars in five places, negating Willow's need to hold it upright for any longer. She relaxed her hold and felt her consciousness retreat back into herself, becoming once again just the size of her body.

As the laborers got to work pounding rough nails between the posts and frame, the foreman took her aside, walking her to the center of the prospective warehouse.

"That was incredible," he said, sounding slightly out of breath. "I never thought I'd see something like that. It never even occurred to me."

Willow didn't know how to respond, so she didn't.

"Can you do the same with the front?" he asked, gesturing to the half-complete frame lying on the ground.

"I can," she said. "I can hold the pieces together as well while I raise it."

The foreman shook his head. "No need. Perhaps it's unnecessary, but I'd prefer my men to do their work the way they're used to—on the ground. Once the joints are fastened, I'll call for your aid again. That should be sometime tomorrow if my estimates are right. The back frame's put us back on the schedule for the front but moved us significantly ahead overall."

Willow nodded. "I'll be available at your leisure," she said, smiling. The stocky foreman stuck out his hand, and she gave as firm a shake as she could manage but knew that he was holding back from the limp way he shook.

Gerald had been watching the whole thing, leaning against one of the front posts with his arms crossed on his chest. He pushed off as Willow approached him.

"Impressive piece of work," he said, and Willow shrugged. "I didn't see you do any of the..." And he mimed the movements to create a spell-form. "Is this your special sauce?"

"It is," she admitted. "Among other things. I can use the basic spell psychokinesis without spell-form or concepts, and I can control a great many simultaneous castings of the spell."

Gerald nodded. "That's how you lived after the Wasting, right?"

Willow ducked her head in embarrassment. She still couldn't believe the alcohol had made her open up so much. "Yes, that's right."

He shook his head. "Incredible. I suppose he'll send word when he needs your assistance again?"

"That's what he said."

"Then I'll take you back to the mayor's," he said, turning away from the worksite and heading down the road. Willow followed and realized that she felt something she hadn't in a very long time. She felt useful.

And she felt wanted.

CHAPTER 14

Willow opens her eyes to a blistering wind and knows immediately that she is back in the dream. She is laid out on a scoured hillside in the pitch dark and slowly rises to her knees, feeling around for the thing she hopes to find.

She touches a length of hot, hard wood in the grass and clenches the staff between her hands. Her cloak envelops her body, and she uses the staff to pull herself up by fastening it in midair with her psychokinesis. It surprises her that she can do magic in this dream, though these visions have been growing more realistic night after night.

Willow can't remember how she's gotten there or what she had done recently in the waking world, but she knows she's being hunted. It only takes a moment for her to find the pinpricks of red light in the distance, though she knows their true size is much larger than they appear. The creature is coming for her, and she holds her staff out like a protective talisman.

And why shouldn't it be? This is a dream, after all, and she's seen another's dream. One of war. And is she not in a war much like that one? A creature stalks her in the hills, and she is a mage.

Let us see what the beast thinks of true magic. She begins weaving a spell of pure dream magic.

The creature thunders through the dark towards her. By incorporating the essence of dream into her spell, she finds it takes to the reality of the dream much more readily than even her psychokinesis, which is sluggish. She finds her powers boosted even beyond reality and slams the butt of the staff into the blasted hill as the creature comes within a hundred feet.

Light and coolness blast out in a wave, cresting over the hill and washing down the landscape, rippling over the creature that has stalked her for so many nights. The white light casts everything in pale tones, but she sees clearly enough what her enemy is.

A salamander, but one of enormous proportions. It is wrapped in a mantle of dark flame, the essence of nightmare and fire, and it hisses in fury at her spell of revelation. It forces itself forwards, towards her shining staff—the source of the cool, white light. As it moves, its mantle sloughs off like thick skin.

That it is so hindered by her dream spell amuses Willow, and she wonders at what other powers she holds in the land of nod. She whips the staff around her head, each pass lengthening it as a blade of pure force and light, until it is so long that, with an overhand chop, she slashes it down onto the creature's head.

Willow giggles at the strange way the salamander looks at her with its cloven head, blinking first one eye, then the other. Thus is dream logic, that it is able to survive at all, though its mantle is fully stripped away, revealing blistered and bleeding patches of hide unlike that of a normal salamander. The natural salamander is protected from its own fire essence. If that was so, then what is this?

The salamander looks deep into her eyes, searching her before it gutters out completely and vanishes. The sphere of light with her at its center begins collapsing, and she intuitively understands that the dream world is decohering around her.

If the dream will be over so soon, then let it. She has no qualms with leaving this nightmare.

The world collapses, and she passes into unknowing.

* * *

Willow woke with a quick intake of breath. Still tangled in the dream, she wasn't sure right away where she was and thought for a moment that she would find herself on the blasted hillside once again. But the dark that encompassed her was cold, and she was enveloped, not in her robe, but in a whole series of padded sheets. Her cheeks were slightly chilled from where they stuck out of the covers, but the rest of her was quite warm.

The mayor's mansion, of course. She'd gone to sleep here after turning down Gerald's suggestion of another night at the tavern. Truly, she couldn't handle too many in a row. In all the weeks since her departure from Durum and the woodsmen, she'd apparently lost her tolerance for alcohol.

She looked in the direction where she remembered the windows were, but only the faintest touch of orange outlined the glass. It was almost entirely pitch-black outside, but the orange would herald the coming morning. The nightmare and its strange conclusion left her feeling not tired at all. She hurriedly cast a magelight and threw off the covers, getting dressed in her newly laundered traveling outfit and robe. Her staff, familiar after the events of the dream, lay against the wall, and it came to her when she opened her hand.

There was no reason to lie in bed when the world that awaited her outside held such promise. She navigated the darkened maze of halls by magelight and memory until she found herself at the doors, which she quietly unbolted and stepped through to be greeted by an even harder chill in the morning air.

Willow pulled her robe tight about her and looked east, but the sky had barely started to become pale in that direction. She turned west, and just at that moment, a rooster crowed. To the west was an ominous orange glow that hurt the eyes to look at, though it wasn't very bright.

"There, that's Willow," a voice whispered from across the street.

After a moment of letting her eyes readjust to the darkness, she saw a small group of townspeople clustered under the eaves of the blacksmith shop. The blacksmith, a barrel-chested man simply named Jack, stood among them. At that moment, he didn't look nearly as intimidating as he had in the tavern when he'd passed her tankard after tankard of ale.

Willow quickly crossed the road, her staff clicking on the hardpan with every other step, and the group opened slightly to admit her into its tight circle. She cast a wary glance westward.

"What is it?" she asked, not knowing if the light or something else was what concerned the group. The eastern half of the group dared to glance up and see the light again, but the westward half didn't deign to turn their heads towards the source.

"We were hoping you could tell us," Jack said in a small voice.

"A forest fire?" Willow ventured. "What kind of tree grows in those mountains?"

"None that looks like that when burned," Jack responded as the light briefly flared in intensity before settling down to its former brightness. The sun was lightening the east, but just then, the majority of the light was coming from the strange new source in the west.

Willow raised her head and sniffed the air, breathing deeply. The wind was going the wrong direction, but it wasn't only the mundane air she smelled. The ethereal winds sometimes ran contrary to the mundane wind, and on that undercurrent, she caught the scent of concepted essence.

"There's something out there," she ventured, not wanting to say more than she knew. "I don't know if it's that." She motioned towards the light.

Its flashes were somehow taking on forms that were horrific to behold, even though they were just flashes of light and nothing more.

"No, it has to be," she mused. "It must be magic to look like that."

"There's a pass to the north," a frightened woman said. "It goes through the ruins. But I've been up for two hours now, and I can say truly that this thing didn't come through the north. It came straight over that hill there, no pass at all. Whatever it is, it don't need a road it seems."

Willow tightened her expression, realizing that she wasn't as alone as she was used to being. Every hesitation, each ounce of fear, was being carefully tracked by the small group as a bellwether to discover how terrified they should be. She sniffed the air again and gripped her staff tighter between her hands.

"Someone needs to wake the mayor," she said. "And the guard. Someone should find Gerald."

Half the small group disappeared immediately to dash down the street and back into the mayor's house. That left Willow with Jack and a few others, feeding off of each other's fear. She didn't dare look into the light again because she knew that if she did, what she saw would frighten her even more than she'd shown before.

And these people, for better or worse, were looking to her.

* * *

"How certain are you that this is no natural fire?" Gerald asked.

Thirty minutes had passed since Willow woke, and it seemed that the entire town was up and about. People were rushing around, gathering essentials into whatever vehicles they could scrounge up. A general evacuation order hadn't been issued yet, but things weren't looking good.

"Fairly certain," Willow said.

Between her outstretched hands was a visual distortion about three feet wide, which she was currently aiming at the approaching pillar of smoke and flame. Viewed from most directions, all you would see would be a highly distorted perspective of whatever was on the other side, but from Willow's vantage point, it magnified whatever she was looking at. There was a fair bit of distortion to the spell, but it served its main purpose.

The pillar, a black smear against the sky highlighted by the rising sun, had a base comprised entirely of licking, roaring flames. It was hard to see anything within that inferno through the illusions that danced around the base. Within the smoke she saw Carl, Leopold's body, and the crawling thing that had attacked Durum.

With gritted teeth and a cold sweat standing out on her arms and back, she glanced away from the view. With a psychokinetic tendril, she flipped to the next page of the text she'd looted, with permission, from Eustace's library. This text was on general surveying, but the ocular spell could be modified in many different ways, some of which involved reading currents in the etheric wind.

Willow split her focus and began a second spell while maintaining a steady current of essence to the first. The oculus should really be cast by multiple surveyors, but she was the only mage in attendance at the moment—if you didn't count Annabelle, and she didn't. She'd caught sight of her former nurse hanging around the edges of the group, fully loaded down and ready to flee.

Well, Annabelle might be ready to abandon this town to its fate, but she wasn't.

The next layer of the oculus was ready, and she stretched it over the base spell like a particularly thin and stretchy scraped hide. This filtered and enhanced the magnified view of the oculus, specifically rendering concentrations of essence visible in a whole range of colors.

The base of the approaching pillar grew even more unruly. Gouts and spurts of bright ruby-red licked out to catch the grass aflame, while tendrils of deepest amethyst reached into the column of smoke, warping its shapes into the fears of any viewers. The text coded the first false color as fire essence and the second as nightmare essence, which was a particularly nasty subtype of dream essence.

The combination did not escape Willow's notice, and she searched the scorching pillar's base against the disturbing images flashing therein. But the flames never let up enough to reveal the source of the disturbance.

"Very certain," Willow amended, registering the essential values indicated by the relative brightness of the spurting maelstrom against the thin etheric current. "It's a warbeast."

Gerald swallowed so hard she heard his throat click, and she let the oculus collapse before turning to look at him. He was making an attempt to gaze at the pillar but failed after only a moment and was forced to look her in the eyes again.

"It's coming for me," Willow realized with a sigh, her lip curling in something between anger and despair. "It's coming to get me."

"There was one before," he vacillated, but she shook her head with a sad little smile.

"I've seen this one," she said, putting words to the fear she'd had since she first glimpsed the pillar.

"You have? Where?" Gerald gasped, his eyes wide in amazement—probably at the misunderstanding that she'd seen it close up and lived to tell the tale.

"In my dreams," she admitted. "Just last night. It's coming for me. It's tracking me."

He couldn't argue anymore and slowly nodded his head. In the end, even he had to agree.

It was over.

So quickly, too. So soon after she thought of Glint as the beginning of a new life. This monstrosity was hunting her, and others would as well, just like the crawling thing that had been sent to Durum. Carl and Annabelle's master wanted her presence in Asche, and it appeared as if he wouldn't stop sending the warbeasts until she came to him.

Willow turned from Gerald and took up her staff and book, walking with a heavy heart to Eustace. He was fidgeting, glancing every now and then at the pillar, but unsure of what order he should issue. Though he was in charge, it was clear that he was well out of his depth.

"Willow?" he asked, a million questions rolled into one utterance.

"It's alive," she cut to the chase. "It's a warbeast, and it's coming here."

"We have to evacuate," Eustace said, setting his jaw. Now that the decision had been made, he was ready for action, for what needed doing, and he turned, searching for Gerald.

"Maybe," Willow interrupted. "But maybe not. I'll go out to meet it. If I start out now, you'll have plenty of time to evacuate the town if I should fail."

"Meet..." Gerald said, his brow creasing in a question. "What are you talking about, Willow? You have to come with us. When the beast comes through, I can't imagine anything will be left in the wake of that thing. And certainly nothing worth living in. We'll need to relocate, rebuild. We need you."

Willow shook her head. "I can't come with you. It's coming for *me*. I'm sorry, Eustace. I thought... I didn't know they would keep coming for me. I didn't know I would lead one here to your town."

Eustace took another quick glance at the pillar, then returned to Willow. He opened his mouth to contradict her—she saw the beginning of the effort in his face—then realization poured over him.

"You said Durum suffered a warbeast attack," he whispered, not wanting anyone else to overhear. Willow nodded. "It followed you?"

"No, this is a different one," Willow whispered.

She shoved the book into his hands and tore herself from the conversation. She took a step away and had to fight hard to stop a sob from bubbling up.

"If I fail," she choked. "I don't know where it will go. It might not go through the town. I just don't... I don't know anything. I'm sorry."

She bit her lip and walked fast through the anxiously gathered townsfolk, who all turned at her passage. Gerald was shouting behind her to the town, giving instructions. It didn't matter what he said, not now. Now, she was no more a member of the town than she'd been a week ago. The whiplash stung worse than the loss alone could have.

Willow was almost to the end of the main road, leading west to the edge of town, before she realized she was being followed. She turned back and ground her teeth, seething with embarrassment and anger.

"If you want to tell me *I told you so*, now would be a good time," she snapped. "I'm not sure you're going to get another chance."

"No, Willow," Annabelle said with resignation in her voice. She hefted a pack, one of two, off her back and tossed it at Willow's feet.

Willow bent and hauled the pack up, lightly tying the straps around her shoulders—in case she should have to abandon it quickly in the coming battle.

"Did you know this was coming?" she asked, not expecting an answer. To her surprise, Annabelle shook her head. "How many more will he send?" she asked.

"As many as it takes," Annabelle said. "You've piqued his interest, and that's a very dangerous move to make."

Willow nodded and set off again, becloaked, pack strapped on, and staff in hand. Annabelle followed a half-dozen paces behind. For a moment, Willow thought how strange it was to be leaving Glint on her own two feet, considering the state in which she'd entered.

* * *

It took perhaps half an hour of walking through the long grass away from Glint, but the pillar of smoke and nightmare was going at a similarly slow pace, so they met about two miles away from the most outlying buildings at the end of the town's main road. At five hundred feet, Willow untied the pack from her shoulders and shoved it into Annabelle's arms.

"You'd better get out of here," she said. Annabelle nodded and took several steps back but stopped.

"That won't be far enough," Willow warned.

"If you can't destroy this creature," Annabelle said, "I don't think a few hundred feet is going to save me. Or Glint, for that matter."

Willow tried to keep her disgust tamped down at the woman's casual acceptance of her mentor's cruelty and turned back to the task at hand. The pillar was fifty feet wide at the base, and flames licked up into the lower reaches, distorted into horrors from the coursing nightmare essence. At the base, almost invisible within the incandescence, was a very familiar salamander of massive proportions.

She wove a sphere of essence, less a spell than an extension of her will, and directed it upwards until it just touched her lips. She took a deep breath and lunged forwards, taking the sphere into her mouth and swallowing in a single motion until it was lodged deep in her throat. With the lungful of air and squirming essence held within, she barked out a single word.

"Stop!"

The command blasted out like an explosion and rippled the grass as it crashed into the essential wind, changing its direction for a moment to channel her intent. The salamander raised its head several feet and fixed her with an inhuman stare. At that distance, she could make out blistering sores on its skin, the same as in the dream.

She didn't know if it would work but thought it might get the warbeast's attention. Well beyond her wildest expectations, the base of the pillar began to shrink to an incandescent core surrounded by a thick wall of smoke from the charred grass. The salamander emerged from the wall of smoke, and only the places where its paws fell burst into flame. Even the nightmare images in the smoke had settled down to merely a disturbed writhing of half-shapes.

Willow walked towards the salamander cautiously, her staff held in front of her as if it could possibly deflect any attack from such a creature. The salamander, for its part, stood stock still amid the smoking grass and flickering images. Willow tried her best to not look directly at the twisting wisps of smoke as she approached.

The heat grew too much to bear, and she had to stop twenty feet out. She hoped her voice would carry.

"Can you understand me?" Willow shouted.

In her history of magic class, there had been accounts of warbeasts who possessed near-human levels of intelligence. Something about the way they were created elevated their natures to be closer to that of man, though their forms almost always became twisted beyond recognition. It was a long shot, anyway, and almost immediately, she felt foolish for speaking to the warbeast.

"I can," came its reply, and its voice shook her bones with its thick baritone. The etheric winds changed direction again, blowing from the salamander and its incredible reserve of essence, which it was taking pains to suppress.

Well, communications had been established. Now to the difficult part.

"Are you the same salamander from my dreams?" she shouted.

"Yes," the ground vibrated with its response.

"Why have you come here?"

"To destroy you," it replied.

Well, that was simple enough.

"I don't want to fight you," she yelled. "Must we do battle?"

"I am commanded thus," the salamander rumbled. "Though I do not wish it."

Oh, well that was interesting.

"I don't understand. Are you being controlled?"

"All of my kind are under the Master's control," the salamander growled. "All of my life, I have known only the womb and his command. There was a time, yes, there was a dream, once, of a stream. Of running water. But that was long ago. Long, long ago. In the womb, I became as you see, a twisted chimera. Yet my abuser's word pushes me onwards, always commanding me. I am obligated to follow his will or suffer a most gruesome death."

"And you've been ordered to destroy me," Willow said. The Master, she realized, must be Annabelle and Carl's mentor. So it was true, what she'd said—he really was growing warbeasts to send after her.

"I would resist if I could," the salamander said, its voice like a low peal of thunder. "I did not know who I was tasked to kill. Not until I saw you did I understand."

"*Who*?" Willow repeated. "What do you mean?"

"I have not long left to live, my queen, before the Master's imperative drives me insane and I am forced beyond my will to attack, but I will explain what I can. In your dreams, I hunted you, though within them I could not discern your nature. Only upon this plain, so far from that imagined stream of long ago, do I see the truth. I have been sent to assassinate my rightful lord. If you have any mercy in your heart, I ask one boon of you."

There was so much packed in there that Willow had trouble wrapping her head around it all. Queen? Why did this warbeast keep referring to her as its queen? It seemed quite adamant on the subject, though she knew no reason it should be.

In the end, she fell back on continuing the conversation rather than picking at any of the underlying logic with questions. The salamander appeared to grow more agitated with each passing moment, and she suspected its self-imposed peace wouldn't last much longer.

"I don't understand why you call me queen. I don't understand many things, though you seem to harbor me no ill will. Please, ask your boon."

"Kill me," the salamander choked with a cough like a small bomb. "Do not let the Master force me to attack you. Spare my dignity. My life is pain. I feel the shreds of my sanity slipping away as we speak. Send me into oblivion, to that sweet stream of my dreams."

The request took Willow by such surprise that her mouth gaped open. The salamander fidgeted, struggling against itself, and as each second passed, its control over its innate fire and nightmare essences lessened. Gouts of flame erupted in the grass surrounding the warbeast, twisting into nightmarish shapes as they ascended into pillars of smoke.

"I…" Willow said in a small voice.

How could she do what the salamander asked, even after it had stalked her in her nightmares? It was conscious. Alive. It spoke—was intelligent. To kill it… would be like killing a person. How could it ask this of her?

"I…"

"Please!" the salamander roared, its voice blowing around her like a wave. It slammed its head into the ground. The heavily charred grass around its body burst into flame at once, all but shrouding it completely in the nightmare dancing figures of Carl and the crawling warbeast.

Had that other one been conscious, too? *Please, gods*, she thought, *let it have not been.*

The salamander roared and began to scramble forwards. There was half a word in that roar, drowned out by its encroaching insanity, and Willow involuntarily took a step back from the furious warbeast. But it held itself back, at least for a moment, and even though it curdled her stomach, Willow made her decision.

Willow lifted her staff between her hands, laying it out flat, and dropped her arms. It stayed hovering in midair and slowly turned like a compass needle towards the warbeast. The salamander choked and roared, its mouth wide, opening onto its pink, smooth gullet.

With a thought, Willow sent the staff hurtling forwards, through the salamander's head. It stood, frozen for a moment, then slumped down onto the ground, where it began to be consumed by its own fires.

The nightmares blew away on the wind.

LEOPOLD'S INTERLUDE 3

When the party of soldiers, plus two academics, finally cleared the thick stand of trees, Leopold had no confusion about where they would go next on their trail. Two miles to the west was a broad and curving river that went over a small waterfall, but the waterfall looked all wrong. First of all, the water jumped up right before dropping down again. Second, he could spot the telltale sparkle of barrier magic even from so far away.

Dean Weatherby clearly agreed. He pointed the way to the piece of standing magic, and the company made a shallow dogleg left to head straight to it. As they approached, Leopold saw pilings driven into the river to the right of the barrier and stacked lumber on either side of its banks. It appeared that the bridge had been washed out sometime in the past, and reconstruction was already underway.

Leopold smiled at the barrier, which resolved into a sunken, hyperbolic tunnel as they approached. It was about ten feet high in the interior, with flared ends running from one side of the river to the other. Though he couldn't be absolutely sure, the magic *felt* like Willow's to him.

The company stopped about twenty feet shy of the strange structure, and the dean approached alone, retrieving a copper apparatus from within the folds of his cloak. Curious, Leopold jogged to catch up, and no one stopped him.

As Leopold admired the complex geometry of the hyperboloid, Dean Weatherby got to work attaching several leads and plates to the interior surface, which surprisingly adhered to the pure-magic barrier.

He grunted in surprise.

"What is it?" Leopold asked, then caught himself at his presumptuous tone. This was the dean of the Arcanum he was speaking to. "Sir?"

"This essence concentration..." Dean Weatherby said, then shook his head and collapsed the apparatus. He stood and pressed a palm against the barrier, just below the first runnels of water coursing overhead.

"Is it high?"

"It's nearly off the device's capacity," he said, offering the folded artifact for inspection. It looked a little like a brass spider with extremely long legs and a dodecahedron for a head. A few of the legs ended in plates and copper tape, which the dean had adhered to the barrier.

"What does that do?"

"The effluometer measures the steady sublimation of essence which occurs from any concentrated source. That could be a spell in mid-cast or even a barrier such as this—all sources of concentrated essence will eventually boil away into the etheric currents. From the rate of sublimation, we can estimate the concentration of essence and the duration of the spell before it breaks down completely. This barrier... it would have taken at least a dozen mages to construct a structure of this size, to say nothing of the containment shell layered on top. With that shell reinforcing the structural magic within—like a layer of hardened steel welded to a core of softer, more flexible metal—the structural magic will last much longer than it should. The device couldn't get a clear reading, but if I had to guess... I'd say this will still be here in fifty years, at least."

"Fifty..." Leopold breathed.

There was no magic in Durum that had lasted anywhere near as long. Sure, there were inscribed artifacts. But those functioned on an entirely different system, using the physical material of the artifact as their anchors and only releasing their imbued spells at the moment they were triggered. But even artifacts would rarely last so long. Only artifacts of great power, or those stored in special suspension cabinets, could last longer than a decade at the outside, to say nothing of raw magic.

Dean Weatherby put the effluometer away in his cloak and motioned to the guard behind them. Leopold moved to the side and touched the tunnel wall as the company passed to his back. The magic was completely smooth and vibrated a little at the roaring water that arched overhead. He remembered what the dean had said about the hardened containment spell over the softer core of architectural magic and smiled.

Where are you, my love? he wondered. To touch something she'd made, no matter how long ago, made his heart ache. She'd gone through here, maybe even spoken to some of the townspeople. He'd have to discover what state she'd been in when she passed. How she was getting along. If Willow was capable of magic like this, Leopold found it increasingly unlikely that Annabelle was forcing her on this journey. He knew in his heart that she was still running away from Durum and what she'd done at the gate.

Running from him.

That thought brought his spirits down, and he followed the tail end of the company through the melancholy underwater tunnel. By the time he'd walked up the shallow bank on the other side and back into the sunlight, Leopold noticed three horsemen had ridden out to meet them. The dean was conversing with the three, with Rolf at his side. After a few exchanged words, the two simply walked on, leading the company towards the town. Leopold was lost in his own thoughts as he came alongside the three riders.

"You wouldn't happen to have seen—" he began, shading his eyes to look up at who he presumed to be the leader. But the man's face brought him up short.

It wasn't that he seemed violent or angry or even distrustful. It was that he didn't seem anything at all—his face was completely blank, and he was staring out into the distance. With a quick glance, Leopold confirmed that there was nothing to capture the three horse-men's attention so much and took a few steps closer.

"Hello?" he tried, but received no response. When he took another step forwards, the lead horse, a chestnut mare, snorted and took an unsteady step back. The man on her back swayed alarmingly but managed to not fall off.

Leopold sniffed and caught the faint whiff of concepted essence. Control, illusion, subjugation. These three men were under some form of mind control, though Leopold didn't know what specific spell it might be, as they had never been taught, being alarmingly illegal to use. Who had cast this spell on the men? Had they ridden out this way to meet the company, or could it have been...

It was a short walk, a mile and a half, to the outskirts of town, where the townsfolk shied away from the column of obvious soldiers. A single man remained in the center of the street when all others had fled, a short man with a skinny neck and an excitable disposition. He kept glancing over his shoulder at the three riders who'd been sent off to meet them, still sitting on their horses at the near end of the underwater tunnel.

The dean was in conversation with the man, and Leopold caught the tail end of it as he walked past the column to the front.

"Perhaps I do recall such a person. A woman, thin, you say? Dark brown hair? Yes, she came through less than a week ago and bought some provisions. She mentioned turning south. Yes, I do believe it was south. She was going to skirt the mountains and head towards Breakneck. She was looking for work, I believe."

"Thank you, Mayor, for your assistance." Dean Weatherby glanced back, finding Leopold, who he gestured up with a wave of his hand. "And this at the edge of town? This scorch?"

"Some creature from the mountains," the mayor said, a slight stammer in his voice. Was he nervous? "It crawled most of the way here; we were ready to evacuate. Then it fell down dead. Sometimes things come from the mountains, you understand, but very rarely are they as large."

"I understand. My associate and I will inspect the creature, and my men will reprovision themselves at your fine general store," Dean Weatherby said with a hint of a sneer on his face.

"Certainly," the mayor said, his eyes darting between the dean and the column of soldiers. "We would be happy to supply you. It was Durum, you say, you come from?"

"That's right," the dean said. "Good day."

He walked past the mayor, down the road to the edge of the town, and towards the burned path that led from the mountains. Leopold felt confused by the highly charged atmosphere the dean had left in his wake. He hurried to catch up to him, being uncomfortable spending any more time in the mayor's presence, though he was unsure why.

It was a thirty-minute trek through tall, matted grass to reach the forward edge of the scorch and the large, blackened thing that lay there. The dean prodded its enormous foreleg with the end of his staff, and it collapsed in on itself, a shell of burned carbon.

"It's a salamander," Leopold gaped, pushing his glasses up. "I didn't know they grew to this size."

"They don't," the dean said, crouching above its enormous,

shovel-like head. "This is no ordinary salamander, but one nurtured in an essence womb."

"Essence womb?" Leopold repeated, feeling like a particularly dull student.

"You wouldn't know anything about them," the dean sighed, prodding the blackened char of the salamander's head. "They're used to grow warbeasts."

Leopold gasped quite involuntarily. "This was a warbeast?"

The dean nodded, then sniffed hard at the air. "Fire essence, of course, being the salamander's natural affinity. And something else. It smells... perverted."

"Dream?" Leopold suggested, taking a sniff himself.

"Nightmare," Dean Weatherby provided. "Dream twisted with the addition of several contaminant essences. Another field of study we don't pursue at the Arcanum."

"It's a close thing that it died before reaching the town. I know the Hound was putrefying, but do warbeasts usually die before reaching their targets?"

"This one did not die from the transformation," the dean said, indicating the salamander's head. There, at the tip of his staff, was a hole pierced through the dark carbon, about two inches wide. "It was killed."

"The mayor didn't mention anything about Willow doing battle with a warbeast," Leopold said.

"I suspect there were a great many things the mayor didn't mention," the dean replied, turning to look over Leopold's shoulder. When he turned, he saw the main body of the company well on their way from the town towards them. An outrider, who proved to be Rolf, tackled the distance in half the time at a dead run.

With barely a labored breath, Rolf made his report when he reached the dean. Leopold was just within earshot.

"There was another woman with the girl. They went north, to the ruins. The woman inquired of the store clerk about the pass just beyond the ruins, which leads west. They're heading to Asche."

The dean nodded as if he'd suspected such all along. "Then it's north we go," he said. "Unless I'm very mistaken, we're gaining on them." He said this last with a small smile.

When Leopold found Bryan's face in the column of soldiers as they marched by, the man averted his gaze in what looked alarmingly like shame. Leopold looked back at the small town they'd passed through with horror. No one was on the streets watching the column go.

What had the dean's men done while he had so successfully distracted Leopold?

Chapter 15

It took most of the day to trek from Glint into the outskirts of the ruins, during which time not a single outrider from Glint was sent to stop them. If Willow needed any further confirmation that her abilities scared people when she truly showed her power, then this was it. Even as enthusiastic as Eustace and the foreman had been about her powers, they clearly recognized the danger of keeping her anywhere nearby. Of course, Willow did, too. That's why she left Glint after slaying the suffering salamander.

Long tracks of cracked black rock appeared from under the matted grass. Eventually, the tracks were wide enough that the grass could hardly encroach except in the many and varied cracks that ran through the substance. It looked a little like stone. But when she stooped to inspect it closer, the substance appeared to be made of many different rocks glued together with some kind of semisolid material. In the midday sun, it had softened just enough to become slightly sticky.

The clear, cold blue sky seemed to suck their heat away as they followed the track—which had clearly been a road in centuries past—towards the heart of the ruins. There, Annabelle had said in one of her rare comments that morning, they would find a shattered highway, which would lead them deep into the mountains. To hear her tell it, the ancient city builders had made their way clear into the confusing maze of peaks and hollows. A way they would follow until they reached Asche.

The wide black road branched off at intervals, though little of those smaller branchings remained. After passing enough of them, though, Willow began to assemble patterns and features of the ruins, coming to a startling revelation.

"There used to be houses here," she blurted as they passed another turn-off leading to a crumbling slab of uniform dark gray rock. It was what people in Bridgewater called poured stone—a technology from the ancients since lost.

"What did you expect?" Annabelle said in exasperation, as if she were annoyed at Willow's even daring to speak. "This was a city once. Of course people would live here."

Willow whirled on Annabelle, who was following close behind, making the woman stumble to a stop in her tracks. She felt her rage boil up inside, contorting her face into something ugly and cruel.

"I will not be spoken to in such a manner," Willow barked. "I don't know what is wrong with you and why you hate me so much, but you will stop this sniping. Or, with the gods as my witness, I *will* leave you behind. Do you understand?"

"You need me to find Asche, not even mentioning—"

"I don't care," Willow interrupted. "Do you think I need directions when I can follow the trail of warbeasts sent to destroy me? Make no mistake, Annabelle, I can make this journey on my own. I thank you for all you have done before, but you can leave for all I care."

Annabelle stared at Willow with lips tightly pursed, as if she wished she could say something in return but didn't dare to open her mouth. She didn't nod, but the lack of a sharp retort was as good as assent in Willow's book, and she turned around and continued to the city.

Truly, she'd gotten used to the idea of not needing Annabelle, of being respected for her abilities and not feared. That it had all turned out badly in the end wasn't on her. It wasn't. It was partly Annabelle's fault, partly Carl's fault, but mostly their mentor's, who was sending the war-beasts to test her. If not for the constant stream of threats, she would've been able to stay in Glint and find a way to be useful for the small town. Maybe one day, when all of this was over, she might be able to do such a thing. She could never return to Durum, she knew, and didn't want to return to Bridgewater either. The memories were too painful.

Annabelle followed in sullen silence while Willow led the way into the city, past the first remains of standing structures. On the out-skirts, little remained of the houses that once existed in those turn-offs—besides the poured stone slabs they sat on. But as they drew nearer the colossal broken shards in the distance, more of the struc-tures endured. Some corners of the poured stone still stood, or blocks of it with hollow centers, marking larger plots—some with excava-tions underneath, like impossibly large cellars. More than a few of the buildings were constructed with the poured stone, shot through with rusted iron bars. It was a sight that Willow was familiar with from the surroundings of Bridgewater.

Soon enough, larger structures began to loom around them. A giant poured stone monolith rose proudly against the ruins surround-ing it. It was wider at the top and narrower at the bottom, like a giant capital *Y* with the top fork filled in, but it gave no context as to its pur-pose or reason for existence. Surely the ancients must have had a reason for constructing their buildings so large and out of liquid stone, but Willow couldn't fathom it. Why build so high with an un-known material when stone and wood were perfectly usable? Why create such a sprawl of ruins when the city-states had existed for cen-turies behind their circular walls?

The road upon which they walked split into two parallel lanes that continued forwards, separated by a raised mound of decayed brick surrounding wild-grown plants. Willow walked over and touched the leaves of a particularly large kind of plant she'd never seen before.

"Why did they do it?" Willow asked, rubbing the leaf between her fingers. "Why any of this? And what happened to them? What could destroy such a powerful race of man?"

"Are you talking to yourself, or do you actually want to know?" Annabelle asked from behind her.

Willow sighed to get a hold of her mounting annoyance, then answered.

"Do you know?" Willow asked.

"Yes," Annabelle said. "In Asche, we've preserved the records of the times long past. In so many other places, they're discounted, flung away like tall tales. Not especially realistic tall tales, but they were true. It's just that we can't imagine their world because the world we live in now destroyed it. The reason their stories don't seem real is that they were unmade by our own."

"How so?" Willow looked back, amazed that Annabelle was opening up at all with this. Maybe being yelled at had been good for her.

"The ancients lived in a world without magic," Annabelle began. "But they had a sort of magic all their own. With this magic, they could make lights and move carriages without horses, and a million other miracles we can't conceive of. Their magic was in their materials, in the advanced engineering they had access to. They pulled fuel from the ground, some kind of liquid fuel like fat oil, and burned it to create power. Then they distributed that power with their magic lines.

"But it all came to an end when our world came crashing down onto theirs. It isn't clear why real magic erupted, but it did, and all of a sudden as well. Within fifty years, their old magic stopped working altogether. Something about the two magics made them incompatible, with our magic winning out in the war. Then the ruins, which used to be cities without walls, began to be attacked by magical creatures. That's when society formed into city-states to survive."

"Did anyone make the creatures?" Willow asked. "The ones who attacked the cities?"

"No one knows," Annabelle said, shrugging. "But in those early days? I think they didn't know how to make warbeasts then. I think the magic that came into us also came into some of the other animals, too. Now we have magic, and so do a few animals, which we call magical creatures. Others, like the warbeasts, are created with magic and don't count."

"They teach you all this in Asche?" Willow asked.

"I had a mentor who was particularly interested in the technology of the old world." Annabelle's face was stone still, like she didn't trust her own emotions about the dangerous man. "We certainly know more about the old world than you do in your city-states, but he knew even more. That's the root of his power, melding the two magics together."

"I thought they couldn't be mixed," Willow said. "That our magic destroys the old one?"

"They had different types of magic then," Annabelle said. "Different sciences. Only their magic of power was disrupted so completely. Many of their other magics relied on it but could still be brought to life in carefully controlled circumstances."

"Is that why Asche was *destroyed* in the wars?" Willow asked, quoting the word with her fingers.

"It's why you're taught that. Asche is dangerous to the power structures that exist as they do in the other city-states. That's why they tried so hard to wipe the city from the face of the earth. But they failed."

Willow couldn't imagine the power Asche must have access to if it could withstand directed warbeast attacks from all the other local city-states. It must be terrible to use. Perhaps, she thought, it was better that they were taught that Asche had been destroyed. Perhaps that kind of knowledge should stay hidden along with its supposedly destroyed city.

But then again, that was exactly why Durum had been so unprepared for the creature Asche had sent.

They walked in a more companionable silence into the interior of the city, where the shards she'd seen on the horizon resolved into the shattered remains of structures that seemed to scrape the sky. All around was the evidence of their destruction: the debris of poured stone falling from such a fantastic height, leaving craters on the road below. Entire sections of poured stone wall lay across their path, around which they had to climb and scramble.

Willow found it difficult not to stumble among the scattered remains as she gawked at the colossal ruins surrounding them. From the rectangular slots in their walls, she could imagine windows and doors, which led her to imagine more . People walking the streets, horses pulling carriages—or even those horseless carriages Annabelle had spoken of. Hundreds, or even thousands, of people living and working within those titanic buildings. How they could stand to work so high, she had no idea. How the buildings even supported their own weight without magic was impossible for her to imagine.

A faint, wet wind blew from a crossstreet to the left as they reached a particularly large intersection of roads. Looking left, into the wind, Willow spotted dark clouds on the horizon above the loping mountaintops. There was movement out there, the faint shapes of trees rustling in that wind, and Willow didn't like the look of it at all.

"A storm's coming," she called back to Annabelle. "Looks like we're headed right into it."

If she figured right, it was coming from the west, and the crossroad seemed to lead directly between two of the mountains. Probably, that meant it was the road they were to take.

Annabelle came around the corner and surveyed the storm, then gave a curt nod, as if the storm was just a bit of an annoyance and not a potentially dangerous development. Willow didn't know all of what was in the bags they'd packed, but she was willing to bet the bags themselves weren't waterproof. The only spell she knew for shedding rain wasn't mobile at all, which meant they'd have to sit tight when they hunkered down.

"We have to keep moving," Annabelle said. "We'll make camp when the storm hits us."

Willow looked around at the buildings, which were so high they blocked out the sun above. She didn't want to be anywhere inside the maze when the rain began sheeting down. From how derelict and weathered they appeared, she was sure the structures would suffer further degradation from even a slight wind. It was a miracle they hadn't all toppled by now.

Willow knew she and Annabelle had to make the best time they could.

CHAPTER 16

The storm arrived with the suddenness and fury of one being hit by a runaway horse cart. Willow believed that had she and Annabelle been in any other place in the city, they might not have found a ruin that provided shelter soon enough. As it was, they were both soaked to the bone and leaning into the gusting wind when they stumbled into the relatively dry first floor of one of those shattered relics. This one reached at least fifty feet in height before ending in a series of staggered shards and bent wire.

Willow collapsed to her knees, taking deep, heavy breaths as she slowly regained her composure. Annabelle had wandered farther through the crumbling detritus to slump down beside a pillar of poured stone, which was half-decayed and crumbled where her shoulder rubbed against it.

The storm blasted against the edifice, and Willow heard the shattered stone on floors above topple and crack against the wide, abandoned levels of the ruin. Much further into the first floor, the space was blocked by cave-ins and grew dark strangely quickly. It was like being in a deep cave, though one with many entrances and at risk of collapsing at any moment.

The cloak was soddened and heavy, so Willow undid the clasp and let it drop off her shoulders, instantly shedding a good ten to fifteen pounds of weight in the process. The heavily embroidered fabric slumped in a semicircle at her feet. Though she was exhausted from their headlong rush through the driving rain and blasting wind, she spread it out over the stones to give the cloak a chance to dry.

With that out of the way, Willow let herself slump to the ground, looking out through the many crevices and holes in the outer wall at the gusting storm outside. The rain was coming down so hard and thick that the building just across the road, less than fifty feet away, was completely hidden by the whiteout. Willow had never seen a storm of such fury in her life, though she was quite a long ways away from home now. Perhaps this was what the storms were like closer to the mountains. If so, she wasn't surprised that the bridge at Glint had washed away. Instead, she was a bit worried about how they'd survive the trip through the mountains, even if they had the ruined ancient road to follow.

Though the building on the other side of the road was hidden, the road itself was mostly visible. Willow sat entranced as she watched a hole in the ground begin to disgorge gouts of shooting water, as if a high-pressure essence pump was starting up somewhere under all that rubble. It spurted with such power that chunks of the black semi-solid rock around the hole blasted away with every gush, widening the hole second by second.

Suddenly, a four-legged form sprang past the man-sized crack through which Willow was watching the street. She jerked in surprise at the movement, and before she could gain her feet, three other sprinting figures passed by. What were they? What could they be?

She was exhausted from their run against the wind to the large ruin they were now holed up in, but she gathered herself and hobbled as quickly as she could to the crack. There, she stuck her head out into the storm. The force of the wind gathered her hair and whipped it forwards with such force it was as if someone was pulling at her. But try as she might, she couldn't see anything in the driving rain in the direction the loping figures had run.

Willow was just about to pull herself back in when, with a glance at the other side of the street, she saw movement once again. From this vantage point, she could see just the base of the ruin on the other side of the road. As she watched, something dark and as large as a horse scuttled up the sheer wall, like a giant spider.

The sight made her recoil. She jerked her head back inside the ruin, thinking horrible thoughts about what might be crawling up the side of *this* edifice at that very moment.

It wasn't natural; that much was obvious. No spider got that big, no matter what the storybooks said. That left only one option: a magical creature, though one she'd never heard of before. And the running things that had passed by the ruin—creatures that looked so much like overlarge dogs—had to be some kind of magical creature as well, though with so much rain and wind, it was hard to smell their essence. She couldn't even guess what it might be, so flooded the etheric winds were with the storm.

Willow was just about to turn back to sit beside her pack and cloak when a dark figure flopped out of the hole in the road with the latest gout of water. But this wasn't a magical creature or even a mundane one. It was a person, very obviously a person, even from twenty feet away. Before she could stop herself, Willow was running out into the storm.

"What are you doing!?" Annabelle said, her scream amplified by the cavernous ruin. But Willow was already running as fast as she could, leaning sideways against the wind and trying to keep her feet. A misstep sent her tumbling over, the wind flipping her once before she regained a lower center of gravity.

She crawled to the sodden shape and, so close, heard a wet coughing coming from them.

"Are you okay?" she screamed into the storm.

At three feet apart, she saw that the figure was that of a pale woman dressed all in black, perhaps five years her senior. The woman whipped her head around in surprise, then turned back to look at the hole. The look on her face said everything.

"Is there anyone else down there?" Willow yelled.

"Yes!" the woman screamed and began to crawl back towards the hole.

Willow gritted her teeth and searched her memory. She knew there was a spell for this; she'd learned it in her first semester, though she'd never had the essence to cast it.

Carefully, she stood again, leaning into the wind, and began to exude essence down through her arms as she wove her hands in the spherical spell-form. She intoned concepts for force and water, stability and fluidity, and with those flowing together in the form between her fingers, she flung them out at the gushing hole.

The spell flew over the sodden woman's shoulder. It hit the just-receding water at the surface of the hole, blowing outward with the force of essence Willow had put into it. The black-clad woman was within the spell's range when it activated. Immediately, her hair and clothing were stripped of water as every significant source of liquid was pushed back away from the spell's locus.

Willow struggled past the spell's spherical barrier, about fifteen feet wide, as the magic worked to wring her out like an old dishtowel. Her own outfit's extra water was dumped unceremoniously at her feet, not crossing the line of the spell. She struggled onwards to the edge of the hole beside the woman, as the spell did barely anything at all against the force of wind buffeting them.

"What just happened?" the woman yelled.

"Bubble-shield," Willow said by way of explanation. "Where are the others?"

"In the tunnels," the woman shouted. "I don't know how far up. I don't know how far I was swept. They're trapped. The door won't open to let them in."

Willow didn't know what door the woman was referring to, but she deduced that if they reached the trapped group, there would be another way out of the flooding tunnel. There would have to be, because there was no way they were getting out the way they were about to go in.

"Can you jump down?" Willow yelled, pointing into the tunnel. When the woman looked, she seemed amazed that the tunnel below them was mostly dry all the way to the curved floor. There was a terrible echoing, rushing sound coming from the hole, but Willow would deal with that when the time came.

The woman nodded and, before Willow could say another word, she gathered her dark outfit together at the hem and jumped down into the hole, plummeting eight feet and landing with surprising grace on the smooth, curved brick wall. Willow much more carefully lowered herself down until she was hanging by her fingertips, at which point she felt the woman's hands on her thighs, and she let go.

The woman in black kept Willow from falling into what would clearly have been her death. Not three feet away, a little over halfway across the underground tunnel, rushed a wall of water barely kept back by the bubble-shield spell. In fact, the spell was struggling so much that she could almost hear it groaning with the effort of holding the water back.

"This way?" Willow pointed into the surging current, speaking at a much more reasonable volume. Even though the stormwater was rushing past them in a solid wall, it was still quieter within the tunnel than in the maelstrom above. The woman nodded, and Willow quickly assembled the spell-form and concepts for another bubble-shield, which she cast at the leading edge of the dangerously quivering original shield.

Two things happened at once. The new bubble-shield spell expanded, pushing an almighty volume of water ahead of them back and away, and the original bubble-shield failed at the same time. Luckily for them, they were completely within the radius of the new bubble-shield. But unluckily, the raging torrent blocked most of the light from the daytime storm above.

"Shit, fuck!" Willow muttered, trying to clear her head and form her hands quickly for a small magelight. When that was cast, she thrust it into the hands of the black-clad woman. "Hold this," she said, and the woman's face lit up in awe as she cradled the solid magelight.

Willow hurriedly sped through the casting of another bubble-shield. She could already hear the new bubble straining against the impossible weight of water rushing against it.

With a hip check, Willow pushed the woman as far forwards as she could until she was sure they would both be within the radius of the new spell. Then she cast it at the rearmost left wall of the bubble, into the current.

Willow's ears popped, and the old spell failed at the same moment the new one sprang open. She took a breath and found it difficult, then discovered why with horror.

"We've vapor-locked ourselves," Willow gasped against the thin air. "There's no new air... and we just lost half the air we had before..."

The woman in black was gasping too, holding the solid magelight to her breast hard enough that Willow thought she might crack it. Willow led her forwards by the shoulders until she stood at the front of the bubble, towards the current, which illuminated the tunnel ahead to a distance of perhaps twenty feet.

A head poked out from behind a corner in the distance, around the silvery surface of trapped air, and Willow felt the slightest twinge of relief. The woman in black hadn't been swept far from where she'd been sheltering. Of course she hadn't. The impacts alone would have killed her. The rest of her party was still there, just two more casts away. If they could survive.

"I have to cast twice more," Willow said, feeling faint, her words coming out in a whisper. The woman's eyes went wide with fear, but she swallowed and nodded her head. *Tough girl,* Willow thought, starting in on the form again.

She had to whisper the concepts. There was so little air in their little world, but she didn't need to push the woman forwards to get her to stand alongside the front wall of water. Hoping for a smaller bubble to keep the air pressure from halving again, Willow cast the spell ahead and gritted her teeth.

The difference wasn't as extreme as the last time, but the air in her lungs still blew out, though she hadn't exhaled. Her eyes watered, and her ears ached, then popped. The woman stumbled as she tried moving forwards, just five feet from the twin wall of water that contained her party. The young boy started screaming, reaching out towards her, and was held back by an adult.

Willow couldn't muster the air to verbally concept, though she moved her lips and imagined the words she wanted. The world was fading, though whether that was from the magelight losing essence or her own low oxygen level, she had no idea. One more cast was all she had left in her. She spun the spell-form, mouthed the concepts, and launched it towards where the woman in black had collapsed to her hands and knees, the magelight lighting her from above.

The spell blew outward, the breath in Willow's lungs escaped for a final time, and Willow fell to her knees. Then there came the enormous crash of a door being flung open. The last thing she heard before she fell face-first onto the smooth brick floor of the tunnel was a hurricane rush.

CHAPTER 17

Murmurs in the dark. Then came a faint buzzing, and a golden light washed down onto Willow's face. With a gasp, she opened her eyes.

She was surrounded by about a dozen men and women. Willow darted her eyes around, but she didn't see the woman in black she'd rescued—not until a whimpering cry made her crane her head left. There, she saw the woman holding the little child she'd glimpsed through the low-pressure bubble, shushing him and smoothing his hair. He had to be at least five, though he was crying like he was much younger. The woman in black had tears streaking down her face, too.

Something caught in Willow's throat. She sat up and coughed hard, then finally regained her composure. When she had, the woman in black was kneeling in front of her, the little boy smashing his face into her side.

"You saved my life," the woman said. Now that Willow could see her face clearly, there were lines between her nose and cheeks. She looked older, maybe in her mid-thirties, but dressed in the same all-black that the others in the small corridor wore. "Thank you."

"No—no problem," Willow wheezed, then was caught off guard by another cough.

After the experience in the bubble, she felt like she couldn't ever get enough air again. If she went the rest of her life without having to hold her breath, it would be too soon.

"Where are we?" Willow asked, looking around.

The door they'd come through was to her right. She was facing a curved wall with another at her back, and the corridor continued to her left, lit with tiny magelights on a string. *What a funny way to mount them,* she thought.

"In the underground tunnels," the woman said, and the boy, who could only be her son, sniffled. "You're living above?"

"Just passing through," Willow answered, getting unsteadily to her feet. When she staggered, supporting hands shot out and kept her steady. She nodded for the assist, and the hands withdrew.

"From Asche?" the woman asked, an edge to her voice that warned of imminent danger.

Willow raked her eyes across the small group, but none of them had any weapons. She thought her chances were fairly good if they decided to jump her, so she answered with the truth.

"From Glint," she said, and a few of the group nodded in recognition. "We're heading to Asche, through the mountains."

The woman's lips compressed into a tight line, but it didn't look like she was going to share her thoughts about the journey just yet. Willow decided to take the lead.

"I'm Willow," she said.

"Diantha," the woman introduced herself. "Tomas," she nodded down to the little boy.

"Do you... live down here?" Willow asked.

Diantha nodded and looked down the tunnel into the dark, lit only dimly by the string lights.

"We do," she said. "I've never seen a storm this bad before. We weren't expecting the sewers to flood so quickly. And when they did, we were trapped, unable to open the door against the pressure. We all owe you our lives."

Willow waved it away. "I'm traveling with someone else. A woman. She's taking shelter in the ruins above. I have to get back to her."

Gazes shifted between members of the group, though Diantha's eyes didn't leave her own.

"There are other ways to the surface," she said. "I wouldn't suggest going back the way we came."

"No, I can't imagine that would be safe," Willow smiled, finally feeling herself enough to gain control over the muscles in her face. "But there are other ways up? We were sheltered beside the road to Asche."

"The highway," a man in the group added, and Diantha nodded.

"We can get you up again," she said. "And if there's anything left of the ruin you were sheltering in, you may find her yet. As long as you don't tarry."

"The storm—" Willow said, but Diantha shook her head.

"The beasts," she corrected and stood. The rest of the group followed suit, and it became immediately obvious that she was something of a leader in the small band. She gently put her hand on Willow's back and pushed her alongside, down the corridor.

"What beasts?" Willow asked. They moved to the front of the group, past the strung magelights illuminating their way.

"Creatures above," Diantha said. Tomas was sticking close to her leg, but as far as possible from Willow. She tried to smile at the boy, but he only buried his face against his mother's thigh. "Dangerous animals. They nest and hunt in the ruins of the city. It's a death sentence to walk the streets at night, and in the day, it isn't much better. Perhaps you only survived because of the storm."

"Perhaps," Willow said. "I saw things running in the storm. They were... big. Animals I've never seen before." Diantha nodded. "They're not normal, are they?"

"What is normal?" Diantha asked. "Normal for you, or normal for me? For you, perhaps, there are not beasts that will reach down and snatch you from your allies, spinning you in a cocoon to devour at its leisure. For me, there are no beasts you would consider fit to keep as a companion, though I've heard of the practice in other lands. There are only us and the creatures above."

"Magical creatures," Willow breathed. "The city is infested with them?"

"I know the term, but no. These are no mere zephyrs and salamanders. These are unnatural monsters, sired by the passing titans generations ago during the height of the city wars. They copulated in the shattered city, and the remains of those atrocities are left still."

"I had no idea that was possible," Willow said, astonished.

She'd never heard of the warbeasts being able to reproduce. But once she put her mind to it, she realized that everything she knew about warbeasts came from city reports, which were the last stop for the creatures. Once they arrived, they'd do little more than attack and slowly grow insane. Of course they would behave like animals on their way from the lands in which they were created to their targets. She should have realized it sooner.

The group fell into silence as they walked through the semi-dark tunnel. In the conversational lull, Willow looked up to inspect the string of magelights, truly an interesting piece of artifice, but straight away she realized there was something off about it. She slowed, then stopped as she peered intently at a single magelight, reaching out to touch it.

She hissed and drew back as the solid surface of the magelight burned her fingertip. But that wasn't right, was it? Because this wasn't a magelight at all. It didn't have the smell of magic in any way. And if she peered close enough, she could see a thin wire suspended in the center of the light, which glowed orange with heat.

"What in the world is this thing?" she asked, not expecting an answer.

"You've never seen anything like it before?" Diantha asked. Willow shook her head, then paused, remembering the machine Annabelle had shown her back in Durum before the attack. It had had a light like this, hadn't it?

"Maybe. Once," she speculated.

"You're a magic-user?" one of the men in the group asked, and Diantha shot him a warning glare.

Willow turned around to meet the chastened man's eyes. "I am," she agreed. "But this isn't magic, is it?"

"Electricity," Diantha said, just as all of the lights on the string dimmed in concert. Diantha glanced down the tunnel. "We need to hurry," she said. "We were expected half an hour ago."

After that, they set out at a fast trot, and there was little chance to chat more, but Willow had so many questions. What was electricity? How did it make the little glass balls shine like magelight? And the way the man had called her a *magic-user*—it was as if that were a rare status. In the world she knew, everyone could cast a few utilitarian spells, such as ones to untie knots or light a candle. Using magic wasn't strange, but it didn't make you a mage.

The corridor abruptly ended ahead, and before Willow could prepare herself, she was swept out with the rest of the group into a much larger space. The walls ran straight up and down but were curved around as if the room was a big circle. The curved room was much wider than the corridor. It could just as easily be a cylinder with a solid center rather than a curved room, given how the curvature of the back and forward walls matched.

There were dozens more people in the room. Before she knew it, Diantha was pulling her along over a floor made of perforated metal. Willow could see through the flooring to other floors which contained even more people, all illuminated by the strange non-magic electricity.

What was going on here? What was this place?

"Alexandros!" Diantha called out, Tomas now walking beside her and her hand tightly gripping Willow's traveling clothes at the shoulder. "Alexandros, goddammit, where are you?"

"Diantha!"

A muscular man, perhaps six feet tall, burst from a side room and rushed forwards, gathering Diantha and Tomas into a crushing hug. Tomas squealed, "Daddy!"

"When you didn't return..." The man, who must be Alexandros, choked up at the thought. "We couldn't send out a search. The storm..."

"You couldn't have," Diantha said, pressing her forehead against his for an intimate moment. He clasped the back of her neck with his hand.

"We have a guest," Diantha said, pulling back and motioning towards Willow with her head. "A traveler—from the surface. She has a companion left topside that she's eager to get back to."

Alexandros seemed to switch modes on a dime, pulling himself up and holding out his hand.

"Alexandros Fotos," he said, his big hand nearly crushing hers.

"Willow Tremont," she responded.

"I was swept away, and Willow saved me," Diantha added. "She used *magic* to do it."

The way Diantha emphasized the word made the hairs on Willow's arms stand on end, and she realized that the calculus of busting her way out had shifted dramatically. There were so many people around her, subtly watching their interaction, that she wasn't sure at all anymore if she'd make it out alive. She needed to find out what magic meant to these people, since it clearly didn't mean the same thing that it did to her.

"I don't care how you did it," Alexandros said. "You saved my wife from the flood. I and the creche owe you a great debt of gratitude."

"The creche?" Willow asked, looking up and around. There didn't appear to be another floor above them—the ceiling was smooth poured stone—but from her new vantage point, she saw the beginning of a metal staircase sloping down to the floor below. It looked so rickety and thin that she wouldn't trust her life to it unless she absolutely had to. "You live here? In these ruins?"

Alexandros laughed. "Ruins!"

"Alexandros is the elected chief of the creche for the next two hundred days," Diantha added.

The lights, which were strung all around the circular room, flickered again.

Alexandros's face went hard. "You're a magic-user," he said. "Are you doing this?"

"This?" Willow asked.

He motioned around. "The lights. Are you casting any magic right now?"

"No," Willow said definitively. None of her telekinetic spells was active, of that she was sure, though how that should affect... Her eyes went wide. "This is the magic of the old world? This... electricity?"

"That's one way to say it," Alexandros said, a smirk barely twitching on his chiseled face. "You're absolutely sure?"

"Absolutely."

"Diantha," he said, then turned on his heel, marching straight back into the room from which he'd run.

Diantha and Tomas followed, as did Willow after a moment's hesitation. She wasn't sure if she'd been invited, but she was intensely curious. She also had to get back topside before something happened to Annabelle, especially with all of the deformed magical creatures running about.

The room was the size of a small classroom and full of strange equipment she'd never seen before. More lights than just the string overhead illuminated the darkness—various dials and glowing embers, which she imagined ran on the electricity of the old world. Where did they get it? Did they generate it within their bodies like most humans did essence? Or was it something else?

"Minus four-point-two," a young man said, speaking into a strange artifact positioned on a short post on the desk in front of his mouth. He was pressing something to his ear and writing down numbers on a sheet of paper under three columns. Each column had numbers such as the one he'd called out.

"Four-point-three," a woman shouted from just beside Alexandros.

"Four-point-three," the young man corrected, nodded to no one in particular, and wrote a few more numbers down. Alexandros tapped the speaker on the shoulder, and he looked up without startling.

"What's the data looking like?" Alexandros asked.

"Map!" the speaker yelled, and an even younger boy, perhaps fifteen, scurried over with a long, shiny roll. The man with the headset cleared the table beside him of the note paper, took up a pair of calipers, and motioned to the table. The runner rolled out what was clearly a map, though the substance on which it was traced was unlike anything Willow had ever seen. It was stiff and shiny like ice, but flexible as well.

The speaker perused the map until he'd found what he wanted—though Willow couldn't make heads or tails of the projection. Then he bent down with the note paper and calipers. He checked the paper, adjusted the calipers, and drew a series of faint circles on the map around what seemed to be randomly chosen positions. He did this twice more, the three circles converging on a point farther *left* on the map, in the middle of what looked at second glance to be a mountain range.

"Shit," Alexandros spat and looked at Diantha. "Something's coming. Something big."

"A warbeast?" Willow asked.

Alexandros wheeled on her, pinning her shoulders with his massive hands. "You know what's happening? If you do, we need all the help you can give us."

Suddenly uncertain, Willow vacillated. "I'm not sure. It's just... I've seen one recently. How do you know something's coming?"

Alexandros looked hard into Willow's face, then roughly guided her over to the station manned by the woman who'd shouted the corrected number at the man with the headset. She was peering down at a device but looked up as they approached.

"Meg, explain the detector quickly to our friend here," he ordered.

The woman looked once at Willow before pushing her to the side. "Don't touch it. It'll lose calibration. This is our essence detector. It functions on the principle that essence and electrical energy are diametrically opposed, which means that the more essence there is in the air, the faster electrical effects will fade." She motioned to the device, and by leaning over, Willow saw that there were indeed two strips of thin metal held side by side. "These two strips of metal hanging on the wire will repel each other when statically charged. When that charge interacts with essence, it breaks down, causing the strips to come closer together. We measure the difference over time and can, in a fairly crude way, measure the amount of essence saturating the world above."

She then jerked her head towards Alexandros. "Good enough?"

"As you were," he nodded.

She called out another number to the man with the headset, who continued jotting them down.

"We gather reports from two other sentinel locations," Alexandros said, leading Willow a few steps away, then pinning her once again. She noticed that much of the activity in the room had quieted with all eyes on the two of them. "By triangulating the three locations, we can determine the probable course of incoming essential threats— or warbeasts, as they were called in the old days."

"It's coming through the mountains," Willow realized from the unrolled map. "It's coming from Asche, isn't it?"

"It looks about that way," he replied. "Asheville has produced more than its fair share of warbeasts recently, though all have bypassed the city. This one looks like it's coming straight for us, though. Any idea why that is?"

Willow swallowed hard and nodded. "It's coming for me," she said, which surprised even the burly Alexandros. "They're sending them... to test me."

"To test you?" he asked.

"I have to defeat them," Willow said. "Their leader is testing me as I approach. That storm, it's part of the warbeast, isn't it?"

"Probably," Alexandros said, lifting his hands from her shoulders.

Willow realized what she'd become again, twice within two days: a target. "Get me topside," she said. "I might be able to... well, if I can't do anything about it, I might be able to lead it away."

"Clarice!" Alexandros yelled, and up came a thin, quick woman who hadn't been there a moment before.

By the gods, was she fast!

"Lead Willow here to northwest stairs 3," he said. "And if anything should happen to her along the way... make sure her body leaves the creche. Do you understand? She must not be here when the essential threat arrives."

Clarice nodded, her dark, chin-length hair bobbing. Without saying a word, she grabbed Willow's hand and pulled her out of the small room and down the curved corridor. The residents of the creche parted in fear before her, and she had to work hard to keep their terror from infecting her. *I am a person*, she worked hard to remind herself. *I am worthy of love. I am not a weapon.*

They exited the curved creche faster than Willow had thought possible, though Clarice was hell on wheels even when tugging her along. They zigzagged down halls and around blind turns so fast that Willow would have no idea how to get back even if she wanted to. As they went further on, the air took on a heavy, wet odor, and the lights on the string above began to flicker.

"We're close," Willow gasped as she ran along behind Clarice. "I can feel it coming."

Suddenly, they were at a perforated metal staircase, and Clarice was pulling her up as fast as she could, nearly yanking Willow over with the ferocity of her speed.

They climbed that way for perhaps thirty feet, then Clarice came to a dead stop at a metal door with a central spinning wheel. The lights just beside the door were barely lit and flickered terribly. The door itself vibrated with the ferocity of the storm just outside.

Clarice put her hands on the wheel, but before yanking it around, she turned and looked Willow full in the face. She had large, dark eyes that seemed to see Willow, just for a moment, for who she really was.

"Good luck," she said, then spun the wheel and savagely slammed herself into the door.

It opened a bare inch before faltering, but that was enough space for so much water to shoot in that it soaked fully one half of Willow's magically dried traveling clothes. Willow lent her strength to Clarice, and they pushed the door open another inch, but the buffeting wind took that progress away from them as quickly as they'd gained it.

Willow closed her eyes and took a deep breath, feeling the door, feeling the metal and poured stone around her. It wasn't stone, she realized then, but some kind of mix of hardened ash and sand. It had never been stone, which she should've known from the way it crumbled so much faster than stones that happened to be around ruins like this. The people of the old world were no less incredible for her discovery.

The maelstrom pushed against the door, nearly shutting it before Willow let herself flow into the door and hold its place. The string lights immediately went out all the way down the metal stairs, and Clarice let out a gasp of fear, backing away. Alone, Willow bent down to resist the terrible wind and rain as the door opened with the force of her imbued psychokinesis. She staggered through and quickly looked back, but Clarice was nowhere to be seen. Then she slammed the door and turned the wheel via her last tenuous grasp on the metal portal before ducking into a corner and quickly surveying where she'd come out.

She was in a ruin, which was clear enough, and towards the middle of it. There was still enough light to see because many of the outer walls had been completely demolished, leaving little between her and the swirling hurricane winds. There were pillars set at even intervals along the wide, flat floor, and just across from the corner where she was taking cover was a set of poured stone stairs enclosed in a much larger pillar.

Body low to the ground, Willow sprinted from beside the metal door to the enclosed staircase, and even so was nearly blown off course by the terrible wind. It mostly abated when she entered the small vertical space, but the whistling of the wind past the doors up and down the ruin was almost unbearably loud.

Willow lurched forwards and, catching herself on a metal railing, looked up. There was a gap between the spiraling sections of stairs, which allowed her to see perhaps a hundred feet high before there were no more floors to see. She counted ten switchbacks before the clouds of rain intruded into the staircase and guessed that she might emerge a hundred feet high if she climbed them all.

High enough to battle with something that was of air and water essence, which now clearly filled her nose. A strategic spot to make a last stand, if there was one to be made.

She began climbing.

It wasn't as difficult as she'd thought it would be, though without a doubt, her legs were running low on energy already. Despite cascading with cold rainwater, the stairs were remarkably even, which allowed her to make better time than she'd expected. Within ten minutes, she had reached the top of the hollow, poured stone pillar, where no more stairs ascended, as the rest of the pillar had crumbled away higher up.

There was a doorway here, same as on every level, though this one's lintel had crumbled away until it met the rain-soaked ceiling. The wind gusted savagely as Willow exited the sheltering staircase. She immediately fell to the ground, frantically clutching handfuls of the crumbling stone for anything to hold onto. She began to slide on the drenched, wind-streaked floor before her hand caught a protruding metal spine, and she grabbed onto it as if her life depended on it.

Well, she might fare better being swept off the ruin and not fighting the warbeast, but it would be a toss-up either way.

Willow cast about and found the ragged edge where the ruin had crumbled unevenly, leaving most of the west side of the building on the street below. There was a pillar beside the crumbled edge, and, gathering her strength, she crawled slowly towards it as the wind tried to tear her from her precarious perch. She found the strangest of handholds—using the technology of the old world as if it were no more than crags in a rock wall. She clung to bundles of wire and strange ornaments of metal embedded in the poured stone. Eventually, she made it across the gap to the pillar, against which she stood while the wind clawed her back and forth.

Only once she'd dug her fingers into a secure hold on the pillar did she dare to look out into the savage maelstrom. Visibility was poor, very poor, but from the scent in the air, the warbeast wasn't far off. She'd made a good decision in gaining higher ground. If it came down the street between buildings, she could lob chunks of concrete at it if it wouldn't listen to reason.

What were the chances of that? The salamander had been ready to parley, but the crawling thing at Durum hadn't been. Were they all conscious to a certain extent and just needed to be snapped out of their fury? Or were some driven so insane by the essence wombs—as the salamander had called them—that they wouldn't respond to communication?

It was a question without an obvious answer. And it was the most important question in the world to her now. Because how could she be expected to survive an attack from a warbeast that created such a storm surrounding it? Though her teeth chattered and her fingers were going numb in the ice cold rain, she leaned out to scan the street below, expecting it to come into visibility at any moment.

Only a sudden increase in the scent of wind and water essence jerked her up from her mistake. It was here. It was coming fast. But it wasn't on the street.

It was flying.

CHAPTER 18

It was more horrifying than she'd expected, and she'd seen two warbeasts already from Asche.

The creature had enormous wings that it beat to generate hurricane winds and pelting rain, a body the size of a small house, and a head almost as large as Willow herself. It had clearly once been a roc—a giant eagle that would sometimes steal off with a lamb once or twice a year, but which was harmless otherwise—but it had been enlarged and empowered beyond its nature. The standard roc was a magical creature that had some amount of wind essence in its body to allow it to lift heavy loads. But this one had been imbued with much more wind essence than normal, and water essence as well.

It was, if she had to name it, a storm roc.

The roc hovered just at the limits of sight, about two hundred feet away and just fifty feet higher than Willow's own perch in the skyscraper. Its eyes flashed in the deluge, and she knew it was looking for her before proceeding. She had the advantage of being much smaller than the roc and hidden by the ruins as well.

She'd throw that advantage away. She needed to. Again, she shunted essence into a small ball, gave it a concept of magnification and pressure, and then swallowed it in a single bite. It lodged in her throat around her vocal cords, and she had a final thought before she spoke.

Please let it be like the salamander.

"Speak!"

The roc's head swiveled at her command, finally sighting her among the debris of the old world. The wind gusted towards it as it inhaled.

I wonder what it will say.

It screamed. The blast was so loud it was like a physical force, and Willow went down to her knees, leaning against the pillar with her hands clasped over her ears. But she could still hear the storm, though her sight was blurry. She hadn't broken her eardrums again, thankfully.

When she got her head together again, Willow realized two things. That was not an effort to communicate. And the storm roc was barreling towards her through the near whiteout, its wingtips scraping gouts of poured stone from the ruins on either side, its beak wide open.

Willow turned and leaped away from the pillar just as the roc passed, smashing the poured stone structure into a deadly spray of rubble and taking a good two feet of crumbling floor with it. She got to her feet, drenched in chalky slurry, and felt the ground buckle as the poured stone broke apart beneath her. Without a moment to think, she took off parallel to the ragged edge, trying to gain as much distance from the site of the attack as possible. There was a terrible grinding, and the floor where she'd been standing pulverized and crashed down to the level below in a pale landslide.

Searching the sky, she ran to another pillar on the edge and craned her neck out. There! She saw the roc flying up and around, coming in for another attack.

"Please!" she shrieked, not bothering with the inhaled essence. "We don't have to fight!"

The roc screamed again, and Willow just managed to duck behind the pillar when the wave of sound pounded the ruin around her. Stone slurry writhed in standing waves, and pools of rainwater flashed into a low mist. If the roc hit her with that scream from close enough, she wouldn't have a chance.

Willow took a running leap to change pillars just as the roc crashed into the building. It ground into the exposed, poured stone floors with its talons and dashed the pillar she'd just been hiding behind into a cascade of drenched debris with its iron-hard beak. She couldn't help but scream in fright at the giant bird's sudden appearance, which alerted it immediately to her new location.

Gripping the side of the tower with its talons, it inhaled again. The gale momentarily funneled towards it, and Willow wished more than anything that she had her staff with her. With her staff, she could batter the bird from a distance. With no other options, she cast around and found a fist-sized chunk of stone that had fallen from the ceiling. She hauled it up and held it out towards the roc, trying for a fast imbuing.

The wind and rain stilled as the roc finished preparing its scream, and Willow launched the rock as hard as she could towards the bird. With how little time she'd had to connect with the chunk, it wasn't fast, but the stone was heavy, and she'd lucked out in her trajectory. It disintegrated in a spray of grit against the roc's beak, causing the bird to lose cohesion on its wind essence attack, which spluttered out through its beak in a whimper.

If a bird could glare in hatred, the roc was doing it now. Though she could see only one of its eyes, it had her locked in a death stare. Evidently, it thought the screaming attack was not worth trying again. Instead, it began working its way into the tower towards her using its feet and beak, cracking the ruin to pieces all along the way.

"Shit, shit!" Willow panted as she scrambled on the slick stone and rubble, going down to all fours and quickly regaining her feet to shoot off again. Not fast enough, though, because the roc darted its head into the building and snapped its beak shut right on top of her. Willow screamed and dropped to the ground.

But she wasn't dead. She looked up and saw that a pillar had been behind her at the time, and the roc was currently trying to gnaw through it to cut her in half. Its open beak was suspended right in front of her, its breath hot and wet on her face. She ducked and slid out from under the razor-sharp implement, but not before sending a stream of ice-concepted essence straight down the bird's gullet.

The pillar disintegrated, and the roc screamed in pain and anger, smashing its head against the ceiling and floor, trying to crush her by blind flailing. Willow sprinted away as quickly as she could, and from behind her, she heard the grinding, ripping sound of the roc moving. She turned back when she got to the open corner of the ruin, but the creature wasn't there anymore.

Willow only had a single heartbeat of terror at losing the roc before it emerged from the whiteout to her side, crashing into the ruin and crushing both the floor she was standing on and the one below. The poured stone canted down at a dangerous angle, and Willow immediately dropped to her hands and knees, scrabbling for a handhold, but she was already sliding too fast. Her eyes went wide as she searched the rapidly moving shattered stone for a crack big enough, but by the time she saw each one, they were already out of reach. She didn't dare look behind at how much space was left before the drop-off.

Then, as suddenly as the roc's attack, she was no longer sliding on the canted floor but flying through the wind and water. Willow sucked in air once, twice, her eyes bugging out before she shrieked in terror. She was plummeting between ruins, over a hundred feet high. She wheeled her arms and legs, but that did little good. The roc screamed above, blasting stone shrapnel out from the shattered facade. Whether in anger or triumph, Willow couldn't tell.

Even as she fell, Willow sought some way to save herself. *If I had my cloak,* the thought flashed through her head, and she imagined soaring on the wind like the roc. But it was down below somewhere, in whatever ruin Annabelle was in. There was no way—

But she felt it. She sensed the cloak and her staff, their positions faint but clear in her mind. They were less than a hundred and fifty feet down the street, and Annabelle must be too. In fact, they were moving. Was Annabelle carrying them? Had she run into the maelstrom at the sounds of the roc's attack? She was insane!

Willow reached out to the cloak and, miraculously, felt her bond with the material bloom in her awareness. She yanked hard, and the cloak rocketed out of the street through the wind and rain towards her falling body. Willow gritted her teeth and searched for its dark form but saw nothing in the rushing storm. She was navigating by feel alone.

The sodden cloak hit her like a very soft horse cart, which was still enough to take her breath away. She tumbled, tangled up in the cloak, towards her final encounter with the ground. Unless she could do something to stop it.

The nice thing about having such a connection with the cloak was that it was very much a part of her body, and at no point in her life had her arms or legs ever been so tangled up that she hadn't known exactly how to unravel them. The cloak sprang open. Willow hung on with all of her might to the reinforced seam at the neck, and it grew stiff and spread wide, like a great wing. The ground, which had been rushing up at a lethal speed, seemed to slacken off a bit.

There was no way around it—this was going to hurt. Thirty feet. Twenty feet... She had seconds left before impact. At the last moment, she closed the cloak around her body and stiffened it into a series of ripples and whorls to hopefully take the worst of the shock.

The impact drove the breath from her body, and she bounced twice before rolling to a rest, but she was alive. By the gods, she'd survived a fall of over a hundred feet. She easily made the cloak unravel itself and fasten to her neck and shoulders again as she looked about her in amazement.

She was alive!

Only the reek of essence saved her in time. Willow looked up at the dive-bombing roc just as it let out a blast of sound. Willow raised the edge of the cloak, and it took the rippling sound wave like a physical blow. Even so, the muffled screech drove her to her knees and made her go cross-eyed. She shook her head and stumbled to a stand.

The roc was coming around and hadn't yet seen that she was still alive. Willow knew she had seconds left to manage some kind of defense. As much as she'd had qualms about destroying the salamander, this was something different. This was a fight to the death.

Willow knelt and pressed her hands against the ground. She'd landed on the road, made of a two-inch layer of cracked black rock, with a layer of gravel sandwiched between it and the earth below. Seeping her mind into the road, she felt its inherent toughness and weight. It was less than rock, but more than clay. With telekinetic reinforcement, it might even be strong.

The roc turned and let out a shriek when it saw her kneeling on the road, still alive. It dropped forty feet to fly just above the asphaltum, its great wings beating tornadoes that slammed into the ruins on either side as it charged Willow.

The pendant Carl had given her grew hot in the hollow of her throat as she seeped her mind further and further into the rock, as far as it would go. The roc had cleared the nearest group of buildings and was barreling towards her, its eyes blazing with something like hatred. It reared back and thrust its sword-like talons out to eviscerate her.

Willow raised her hands, and the road rock cracked and shattered for ten feet around her, flying together into a rough spherical barrier. The beating storm grew faint, then disappeared entirely as the interior of the sphere quickly became pitch black. A few stray pieces of road slammed into the outer shell of the protective bubble, then there was silence for a long second.

The shell was rocked by a massive impact, and only through her connection with the rocks themselves did Willow see the devastation of that single attack. The warbeast had scored three grooves, each several inches deep, into the rock chrysalis—one so deep that a faint sliver of storm light punctured the pitch darkness.

Willow swept her hands out, and the rough sphere collapsed away from her into a ring of rubble. She quickly searched around and found the roc climbing high into the sky, circling again for another attack. It was showing its broad back and wings to her, making a perfect cross-shaped target.

She inhaled, gathering the essence in her body into her chest. She pushed it down her left arm, then brought it back around again.

The creature furrows the destroyed warded tunnel as it claws towards her, screaming with lightning leaping off its back. Its face is almost human.

No, Willow thought, faltering for just a moment before she pushed the essence through to her right hand. The pendant grew warmer still as she cycled it back through her chest.

Carl's eyes grow wide and meet hers as she realizes, too late, that she has no control over the spell in her fingers. He doesn't even turn away as it erupts.

"Stop," Willow whispered, and the essence unraveled and blew away in an unconcepted rush from her left hand. "I can't do this,"

Willow said as she watched the roc come fully around for its next attack run. "I can't."

But she remembered the salamander and how it had begged her, as its claimed queen, for death. Warm tears cut through the cold, driving rain as she watched the roc come screaming towards her. The long, sad history of the creature unfolded in her mind. How it must have been captured and imprisoned in an essence womb, persuaded magically or psychologically to undergo this mission, and then lost its mind. It wasn't a creature to battle. It was a creature to pity.

Without moving a muscle, the black ring of rocks shot off from around Willow and towards the roc. It saw the coming storm of death too late, veering to the left, but that only gave the swarm a greater target. The cloud of deadly rubble slammed into the roc from below. With a ragged scream, it crashed into the side of a ruin and then rolled end over end to a stop on the broken road.

The storm cleared almost immediately. Annabelle found Willow sobbing in the street before the roc's corpse.

LEOPOLD'S INTERLUDE 4

"On your left," Dean Weatherby shouted as he blasted one of the scurrying toothy things with the end of his staff. Leopold turned and saw by the firelight that two of the creatures had teamed up to pounce on him at the same time.

"Freezing chill, freezing chill!" Leopold cried, just as the creatures leaped.

The concept wasn't fully imbued into the spell-form yet, but there was no time left. Leopold slammed down with his hands, and a wave of frost caught the leaping lizards and drove them into the grass. Where they hit the ground, the fronds shattered like glass, but the lizards were only dazed.

"Fuck," Leopold said and rushed forwards with his dagger. He stabbed each lizard through the head before they regained their senses, and his knife ran with sparking blood.

"Aaaaargh," one of the guards shouted as he was overrun by at least five of the foul beasts. Two other guards turned and began laying into the heap, but not before the conglomeration scattered, leaving behind a shrunken and desiccated body. The corpse reached up with one trembling arm to his comrades, then collapsed.

Vampire lizards. The name was so much less terrifying than the lizards had proven to be. Dean Weatherby had warned them that they might encounter roving groups of the things, but they hadn't been prepared for an attack like this. To be fair, the dean had said they'd never attack a group this large.

"Enough!" the dean shouted, pointing his staff into the grass.

The three coiled shafts unfurled, and from within came a light so bright that Leopold had to shield his eyes. A wave of heat washed over Leopold's face, and through squinted eyes, he saw a beam of yellow light lance out into the grass. Wherever it hit a vampire lizard, they burned white-hot like magnesium.

Dean Weatherby laid about with his lance of light, igniting the lizards and burning the grass all around them. Now Leopold had to save himself from the inferno, but that was a task much simpler than dodging the lizards. He quickly cast a spray of water and doused the grass behind him and at the feet of the guards nearest him.

Within a couple of minutes, the attack was over. Whether the dean had driven the lizards off or exterminated them all, it was impossible to tell. At no point had it been clear how many lizards had ganged up on them when they awoke to the first guard screaming. The horde just seemed to keep on coming.

They'd made camp for the night just outside the giant ruins. It seemed like folly now—would they have been safer in the ancient streets than out here in the tall grass? But the smell of putrescence carried on the wind from the city prompted the dean to raise camp a full hour earlier than normal.

Leopold went around helping where he could. He was no good with magical healing, but he could right the tents that had been upended and stomp out coals. The guards were hard at work dragging human bodies away from the camp. Outside the ring of light, they were beheaded, just in case the old wives' tales were true.

In all, they'd lost five men and two tents to the lizards and the dean's ray of light. Nobody slept the rest of the night, and when they started off into the city once the sun rose, they were irritable and chafing at each other.

It wasn't long until they found the source of the stink from the day before.

Leopold knew he'd be summoned to the front, so he arrived of his own accord. The dean was crouched down beside the head of a roc, but one much larger than any he'd ever seen. The dean ruffled its feathers as he touched it here and there.

"Festooned with tumors," the dean said.

Leopold pointed to one of several deep craters in its body. "Is that what killed it?"

The dean reached into the bloody hole and retrieved, along with some pulverized tissue, a chunk of black rock.

"Do you recognize this?" he asked.

Leopold shook his head.

"Asphaltum," the dean said, pointing back to the thirteen remaining men of the company. "From the road."

"It hit the road?" Leopold asked.

The dean stood up but kept hold of the chunk of black rock. "I think the road hit it," he said as he made his way back to the company.

Sure enough, just a little farther along, they found a nearly perfect circle of missing road. Leopold grabbed a chunk of the asphaltum and inspected it. Yes, it did look like what the dean had recovered from the roc.

"I'm reminded of a zephyr," the dean said from behind Leopold, which caused the young man to jump.

"What?" he murmured reflexively.

Dean Weatherby motioned down at the road. "This hasn't been melted or frozen or even phased—as if passing directly through solid matter. It was disturbed by psychokinesis alone. There's a creature that has such an ability: the zephyr. It's a small thing really, only the size of an acorn, but it's surrounded by a psychokinetic storm that resembles a whirlwind. That serves to keep its body safe and allows it to husk the grains on which it feeds."

"Do you think a zephyr did this?" Leopold asked. He couldn't imagine a creature he'd meet on the plain taking down a roc that size. What could he even do against something like that?

"No," the dean said, tossing the bloody chunk back into the circle. "But something like it."

It wasn't hard to take the hint. Leopold had seen Willow do things he couldn't explain. Like on the day they'd found her wandering the streets when she cracked a plate on the table that should've been out of reach. The day she killed Professor Brandeweiss. He'd suspected her psychokinesis might be able to extend past her body after that. But she'd never talked about it, and he didn't ask.

The dean was telling him, none too subtly, that he already knew about this, and probably more.

"Hmm," Leopold said. He walked on, nursing his slight limp.

There was that question again in the back of his head: what did the dean really want with Willow? Why was the company following her when she appeared to be heading deeper and deeper into the unknown lands west of Durum? And what would happen when they caught up with her?

CHAPTER 19

There is something, Willow thought, as she and Annabelle followed the remnants of the highway between the mountains, *about this place. Something almost comfortable.*

It wasn't like the forests on the piedmont, that was for sure. At any moment, they could've been jumped by a host of magical creatures, including such horrors as skinbears. They'd never been safe there, not even in the wooden structures of the small, abandoned town. Not from their own kind, at least.

But here in the mountains, there was something that soothed her. Something about the way the trees swayed in the chill November wind. It was as if there were no fell eyes watching them. Nothing sizing them up for a meal. It was just a forest, as the forests around Bridgewater had been. They hadn't been big enough for anything as dangerous as a skinbear to live in, so they were safe for lumber. The only things that frequented those trees were the tree sprites.

Annabelle didn't seem to have gotten the message, though, because she was twitchier than ever. Even though they were able to follow the remnants of the ancient road cutting through the valleys and in between hollers—a construction feat Willow was unable to imagine possible without magic—Annabelle still watched the treeline warily. It was as if she expected an attack at any moment. Honestly, it was putting Willow on edge just a little to see how spooked she was.

"Relax," Willow said when Annabelle had turned full circle for a roving sweep of their surroundings for the umpteenth time that morning.

The nurse turned and scowled at Willow with an expression that held a fair amount of derision. "Don't tell me to relax," she snapped. "You may be able to kill a warbeast with rocks, but there are those of us who would be just as dead if we got jumped by a particularly large squonk."

"Those things don't jump people," Willow said, though she wasn't sure if she was remembering her bestiary correctly. If she recalled, the squonk was more likely to dissolve into water than it was to attack.

"Whatever," Annabelle said dismissively.

The other woman was sulking, strung along with high anxiety for too long a time with no recourse. They'd been walking the highway for three days, and only within the last few hours had the road begun to crumble away. Soon there would be little left to follow besides the ancient cuts into the mountain, and the path would grow wild and dangerous. Willow had little doubt it was the massive, artificial structure of the road that spooked magical creatures from their vicinity.

The sun was high enough in the sky that even its feeble rays were able to pass into the holler through which they were walking. The trees atop the surrounding ridges were illuminated with the faint gray sheen of frost, and Willow was quickly made aware of how cold it had gotten the night before.

"Let's stop for lunch," Willow said.

Annabelle, in front, turned around again to scan the area. Willow, annoyed, went to rummaging through her pack. She quickly came up empty, even though she'd nearly upended the bag in the process.

"Do you have any provisions left?" Willow asked when Annabelle finally decided the location was safe enough and began to unpack the cookware.

"I ran out of provisions yesterday," Annabelle grumbled. "Are you out now too? You should have kept better track."

Willow bit off a sharp reply and spent another minute questing around elbow-deep in her pack before she gave up. Her stomach rumbled as she fought to keep her anger in check.

"I'll find something," she ground out, getting to her feet again with the aid of her staff.

Annabelle looked like she wanted to say something in response, but she shut her mouth quickly enough. If Annabelle didn't want her going out to hunt, then she shouldn't be making cracks about how she was so much weaker than Willow.

Without another word between the two, Willow climbed off the road and up onto a short, sheer rock wall that had been carved by the ancient road builders. It only went about eight feet up before the mountain's natural slope took over. Willow clumsily clambered over the lip and into the knee-deep orange piles of leaves. Looking down, Willow could just make out Annabelle setting up the cooking triangle.

"Shit," Willow said to herself, then began to trudge up the mountainside.

Since her final surgery, Willow hadn't needed as many calories or as much essence as she used to. In fact, back in Glint, she'd subsisted on a couple of meals of entirely mundane food, not cooked from magical creatures at all. Without her body needing constant psychokinesis to move, it was much easier to keep herself alive nutrition-wise. Of course, that said nothing for how easy it would actually be to find something to hunt. Before, she'd acted as a veritable beacon for magical creatures, and they were never too far away. But that same feeling which had calmed her before asserted itself on her mind.

She was alone out here in the woods. Or mostly alone, anyway.

There was a lot of space between the tree trunks as Willow climbed, and she thought they were probably oaks, the same as back in Bridgewater. She looked up into the crowns of the trees, searching for the telltale *X* of a tree sprite's legs, and it was a little bit before she finally saw one perched up high. A tree sprite wasn't nutritional in any way, being entirely made up of chitin and essence, and thus was no good for hunting. But the sight of the familiar sprite, both from her life before Durum and right at the end with the woodsmen, gave her comfort.

She'd begun to breathe heavily as she ascended higher and farther from the clearly man-made road—hopefully far enough that she'd be able to find something to hunt—when she first smelled it. The scent was mostly familiar, the smell of forest and insect essence that the tree sprites produced, but there was something more as well. Something... human.

Willow cast about with her eyes, but as far as she could tell, she was alone on the mountainside. No magical creatures, no mundane creatures, and certainly no other humans. But there was that smell, something definitely human mixed in with the essence of the sprites. If there were people out here and she couldn't see them, then they had to be hiding from her.

"Come out," she called among the wide-set trees, clutching her staff tight to her chest, but nothing happened. She backed up until she hit a tree trunk and was spooked by what she thought was the sound of something skittering up the trunk behind her. But when she looked, there was nothing there.

The forest was too empty, she realized. Much too empty, as if it had been cleared out. It was like a dead zone, save for the tree sprites in the waving treetops above. Maybe there were other animals nestled in the deep leaf litter, but something about the feel of the place told her that there weren't. It was like the plains, where there was nothing larger than a vole for miles around. Nothing any good for eating.

She'd thought it would be easy to find food in the mountains. With plenty of places to hide in the trees and hills, there should have been lots of creatures, both magical and mundane, but there just weren't. This went against every instinct in her body. She couldn't shake the feeling that *something* had cleared the animals out, but she couldn't think of what. If it had been people, then they would've used fire. Or, if they'd hunted the mountain clear, there would have been signs of their passage. If it had been a warbeast, it would be obvious where it had passed from the trail of destruction.

But there was nothing.

Willow started to get spooked and turned around the tree trunk to head back down to the road. Maybe there was something in the river beside the highway's remains. Perhaps a fish or two that Willow could snatch up out of the water. She hadn't particularly wanted fish, but that was neither here nor there. They had to eat, and that was all there was to it.

All the way down, Willow felt eyes on her back, but when she turned there was nothing there. And she couldn't rid herself of that smell either, the mixed scent of tree sprite and human. But there was no one in the woods, she tried to convince herself. No one and nothing. Clearly she was alone.

That's what she thought all the way up until she found the bear. Its light brown fur blended in with the leaf litter so well that she almost stumbled over the creature, causing her to backpedal wildly and thrust her staff forwards to shield herself from the beast's unstoppable charge. But the charge never came. After letting out an embarrassing yelp at the bear's discovery, she inched forwards and prodded the bear with the end of her staff.

Why she did such a thing, she had no clue, which she only realized between the first and second prods. If this bear was hibernating—for an unknown reason right in the middle of the forest, but let's leave that aside—then she might wake it. After hesitating and prodding the bear a second time to no avail, she realized the truth. She'd intuitively understood upon finding the creature that it was dead, not asleep.

Leaves fluttered down around her with the bitter gusts above as she circled the corpse to find its head, which was laid gently upon the springy leaf litter. Its eyes were closed, and up close, the smell of the bear was great, though she could sense no hint of corruption or decay. It was recently dead, but for what reason wasn't clear. Setting aside her staff, she wormed her fingers into its fur to roll the bear over onto its side.

There, on the flank that had been hidden by the leaf litter, was a small dark hole, through which almost no blood had spilled. It hardly looked like a hunting injury, though that was surely what it was, because when Willow stuck her finger into the gore, she was able to reach all the way up to her knuckle without encountering intact bone. From the position of the wound right beside the bear's heart, whatever had struck the bear—an arrow, most likely—had killed it instantly.

Again, she looked around, but the smell of human had lessened, as had the scent of tree sprites. Perhaps there had been hunters in these woods, and they'd lost their quarry. It felt a little like stealing, but she and Annabelle needed every pound of the bear they could jerk and preserve for the long trek through the mountains.

With a breath out, she wormed her mind into the bear, through her tightened fingers in its fur. Her pendant grew warm at her throat as she passed more of herself into the bear, enough that, finally, when she rose to her feet, the bear rose with her.

She thought with levity about what Annabelle would say when the nurse saw her emerge out of the woods with the several-hundred-pound corpse floating alongside her. It seemed like it was worth a laugh, at least one, before the grim work of butchering the creature began. Even that thought wasn't enough to dampen her spirits as she began to trudge down the mountain.

But a thought stopped her cold. Her eyes went to the bear, then to the place where it had lain down and died.

There had been no leaves on the bear's coat, even though the leaves were falling intermittently. How long could it have lain there before she found it? Not an hour. A half hour? That seemed unlikely, given the size of the corpse.

A minute? A few seconds? Had it lain down and died while her back was to the large oak? But there had been no blood trail, hardly any blood at all. She checked again and, yes, there was no arrow shaft as well.

That reminded her too much of the arrows in the walls of the cabin. What Annabelle had told her were the arrows of elves. Again, Willow looked around, then up into the trees. There were no tree sprites in the canopy now. There was nothing, and she caught no scent of man or sprite on the wind.

The thought of an elf searching for its quarry, a creature powerful enough to destroy a prey this size and finding her there… alone… in the woods… sent a shiver up her spine. She turned back down the mountain and began to trot, a dangerous proposition with the ground hidden by the leaves and the bear floating along beside her, but she wanted out.

She didn't want to spend another second in those unnaturally desolate woods. Woods that seemed like they'd been cleared, with a dead animal that seemed like it had been left. Intentionally.

For her.

CHAPTER 20

Willow caught the scent of woodsmoke on the driving, chilly wind and stopped just before they began their ascent up the next forested, rolling mountain from the holler. Annabelle went on a few paces more before turning back.

"We have to keep going."

"There's someone here," Willow said. "There's a fire."

"We'll light a fire when we stop," Annabelle said. She'd cast both of them portable heat cores, which kept them warm under their cloaks, but Willow was having none of it.

"We need to find out if anything is waiting for us up there," she said, pointing with her chin towards the forested peaks. Willow could only imagine what might be hiding in those hollers, and she didn't want to be surprised. They'd only gotten by so well over the last weeks because of the plains and their uninterrupted sight lines.

"You don't want to talk to these people," Annabelle said, coming back. "They're country folk. Twisted and weird."

"They're folk, though," Willow confirmed.

She hadn't been sure if a magical beast might be able to cut and light a fire up until now, but Annabelle had verified it. Willow set off to the right, up a steep hillside beside the rocky highway they followed. Annabelle stayed back on the dark rock for a few minutes as Willow climbed, then joined her in the ascent. It was much easier than Willow thought, given that she had her psychokinetically stabilized staff.

Annabelle had no such aid and scrambled in the wind-blasted dust behind her.

When they reached the ridge above, Willow caught sight of a thin streamer of smoke rising from a stand of trees not too far off. Annabelle came huffing up behind.

"This is a waste of time," Annabelle said. "You'll not find anything out from these people that you don't already know. They're miscreants."

"Why do you hate them so much?" Willow asked.

Annabelle looked over to the streamer drifting on the wind and spat on the ground. The move shocked Willow.

"They're pigfuckers," Annabelle said.

"They... have sex with pigs?"

"No, that's just what we call them. If they did, that wouldn't be so bad. Nobody's business, really, but their own. These people fuck magical creatures in those woods. They mate with them and produce cursed offspring, which blur the gods-scribed lines between man and animal. They're a violation of natural law."

Willow started towards the stand of trees. "You never showed this side of yourself back in Durum."

"That's because there weren't abominations like this back there."

"There was the warbeast," Willow countered, bristling at the word. After what she'd discovered during their journey, the term seemed cruel and calculated to turn a thinking being into a tool.

"It showed its true colors. It never spoke in the human tongue—"

"It was insane with pain," Willow snapped.

"That's just what the creatures want you to think," Annabelle said. "They're just hopped-up animals like the rest of them. They can speak, but they only play at humanity."

The screening copse of trees was thin, and they'd only passed a few steps into the pines before they saw the little cabin. Melodic sounds came from within. Someone was playing a guitar or something that sounded like it.

Willow walked up to the door and raised her staff.

"Willow," Annabelle warned, but Willow knocked wood against wood three times, then stepped back.

The song immediately stopped.

She heard shuffling within as chilled winter air blasted her ears raw and threatened to tear her cloak from her body. She held the folds of fabric closer together around the little core of heat.

The door opened, revealing a stooped man with a wild mane of graying hair. He was dressed strangely for the season, with only a white blouse and a pair of short trousers. He looked at the two of them, then leaned out and peered around.

"You're here, then," he said, seeming satisfied that there were no others in the trees.

"Were you expecting us?" Willow asked.

The man waved them in and disappeared into the small wooden hut. Willow hesitated a moment, considering her circumstances and what she was about to walk into. The man seemed to be expecting her, which put her ill at ease, but from Annabelle's reaction, he was clearly not allied with her mentor. And they were so close to Asche now. If nothing else, she wanted to get an outside perspective, something to temper the solitary viewpoint of Asche she'd been fed during their journey. And though he was dressed strangely, Willow didn't smell highly concentrated essence about the structure. It didn't seem like he could possibly harm them.

She didn't look back to see what Annabelle thought but pushed her way into the humid interior. She turned, holding the door for

Annabelle as the other woman made up her mind and headed in as well. Willow shut the door and latched it with a cord-and-hook she found at eye level.

The most enticing aroma permeated the shack—something savory stewing in a black cauldron held over the fireplace on a swiveling iron arm. Bryan and Margaret had had inscripted heating elements on their iron stove—she hadn't seen a fireplace cooking setup since leaving Bridgewater. The sight brought back memories she wasn't entirely prepared for.

Willow swallowed the lump in her throat and pushed away thoughts of her distant home.

"We didn't mean to interrupt your dinner," she said to the man across the small house as she surveyed the interior. Between them was a table just big enough for one, a single chair, and a small loom hanging up on the wall. Every square inch of wall space seemed to be reserved for the multitudinous iron tools that hung there, many of which Willow recognized from her life out in the country.

"I expected you a bit later," the man said as he turned with a bowl of soup in his hands. "But it's plenty good as it is. Please, sit."

He laid the bowl down on the table in front of Willow, then scooted the chair in beside her. Willow lost her nerve and glanced at Annabelle, who only rolled her eyes. She gingerly took the seat just to spite her.

The man returned with another bowl, filled it, and sat on the floor beside the table. He began noisily slurping the stew. After weeks of eating only what they could catch and, more often than not, burned by their still rudimentary attempts at field cooking, the stew smelled like a gift from heaven. Willow cautiously dipped her spoon and took a sip.

It tasted just as good as it smelled.

The soup was so good she didn't notice until a few minutes into eating that there wasn't a trace of essence in it. Whatever meat he'd added to the brew wasn't from a magical creature. That was fine by Willow—they'd slaughtered a rabbit haloed in a nimbus of frost the day before, which had filled Willow enough even though its meat hadn't been that plentiful. With a surplus of essence coming in through eating magical creatures, she'd found her appetite strangely depressed to an almost ordinary level.

Dinner proceeded silently, save for the slurps of their host. Willow supposed she should slurp, too, but years of manners forbade her from following his lead. Annabelle resisted as well. This gave Willow the mental space to catalog the room.

There were a bevy of tools for woodcutting and slaughtering on the walls, but none for farming or processing grain. She supposed this man must either trade for flour or go without, a thought that Willow couldn't comprehend. Without bread, what was there? Meat, perhaps, but she hadn't smelled a coop or pigpen as they approached. Did he hunt and scavenge everything he ate?

The man finished up first and watched Willow. As the minutes went on, she became more and more uncomfortable with his gaze. Annabelle observed this scene, standing on the other side of the table.

Once the single bowl was blessedly empty—Annabelle hadn't asked for anything, and the old man hadn't offered—Willow rose and looked for a tap but chided herself after a moment. Of course there wouldn't be any running water here—she was too used to city life in Durum. But there would probably be a stream close by where he'd wash the dishes.

The man rose as well.

"Where do you clean your—" Willow started, but the man took Willow's bowl. He disappeared out through the door into the cold, leaving them alone in the house.

Annabelle rose and dusted off her traveling cloak as if she didn't want even the smallest speck of dust from inside to remain on her.

"Satisfied? I'd suggest we leave before he returns. There's no telling what he's got in mind—"

"I'm going to stay," Willow decided. "He knew we were coming. Aren't you even a little curious why?"

Annabelle shrugged. "It wouldn't take a great genius to fool you. He was cooking for himself."

Willow looked over at the cauldron, which he'd swung out of the fireplace, letting the flames roar up the flue.

"No, I don't think he was," she said.

The man returned shortly after, pretty much as soon as Willow had noticed the strange guitar leaning up against the wall in the corner. It had a long neck and a circular body drawn tight with some kind of stretched hide. He cracked the door, came in, and followed Willow's gaze to the instrument.

"Excuse me, but we never introduced ourselves," Willow said, trying to bring a little civility to this extremely strange encounter. "I'm Willow Tremont. And this is Annabelle…"

It was then that she realized she didn't even know Annabelle's last name. Strange that they'd traveled so far together, and she didn't know it. Annabelle remained silent on the matter.

"Walter," the man said, then motioned to the floor before the fire. It was stone-flagged, but even through Willow's shoes, she felt the radiating warmth. As she sat down, she immediately felt like she might doze off soon if she wasn't careful. The man carefully picked up his instrument and sat down in front of her. Annabelle reluctantly joined them a little farther away from the fire.

"Walter," Willow said. "Did you know we were coming?"

Walter nodded his head. "Yup," he said, picking a few notes from the strings. They danced around the small house and died on the wooden walls. She'd never heard anything like it before.

"How? We haven't told anyone where we're going."

"If you listen hard enough out here, you're liable to hear a great many things. Take, for instance, the two stone golems waiting for you at the pass out yonder."

"Stone golems?" Willow asked. Walter nodded and strummed a chord.

"There's been a regular menagerie running through these hills over the last month, but the golems stopped and hunkered down in the boulders at the highway's edge. There's no way to go around them—too steep to the right, and the river to the left. You'll have to go right between them."

"Do you know—" Willow started, then swallowed. "Can they speak?"

"Oh yes, they can speak. They'll talk with about any critter that happens by, as I hear it."

Willow sighed. "Good. I hate—"

"Killin' 'em," he finished for her, and she nodded, shamefaced.

Was she that easy to read? If so, how was she possibly going to get through her interaction with Annabelle's mentor?

"You'll have to before you pass," he said. "But they'll know it's coming. They know who you are now—word's passed back up through the valley, probably all the way to Asche. They'll be expecting it if they're still themselves. So will the rest, I reckon."

"You're not surprised?" Willow asked. "People usually are when they see me battle one of them. Especially if they see me put one out of its misery."

"You're special to 'em," the man said. He began picking notes so softly that Willow could barely hear them. "They think you're their savior."

"I'm no savior," Willow said. "I'm a calamity. I couldn't stay in Durum—the warbeasts would just keep on coming. I'm a danger to everyone around me, and I can offer nothing but death to the creatures from Asche."

"They want it," Walter softly interjected. "Do you know how long a warbeast can live in misery? Centuries. Can you imagine being in pain for so long?"

Willow clenched fists that were no longer tender from atrophy. "Yes."

"If you think things are bad now," Walter said, plucking a little louder, "you're in for a surprise when you get to Asche. Just don't lose sight of yourself, Queen. Don't let what you see twist you. Remember who you are, to yourself and to them."

Willow stared at her clenched fists. It was too much, *too much* to be worshiped by the tortured, miserable creatures she was fated to destroy. And that wasn't even getting into the issue of how the title *Queen* had even gotten back to a man like Walter. But, perhaps that was what she was missing, what Annabelle had said before. Maybe he was a little bit more than just a man, and his *listening* involved communing with creatures that hadn't revealed themselves to her.

"That song," Willow whispered, still far away in thought, mesmerized by his fingers as they flew over the strings. "What is it?"

"Passed down by my memaw, from her memaw back as far as anyone can remember. I'll sing for a bit, then you can stay the night. You'll have to be on your guard once you enter the mountains, and this might be the last good sleep you get."

The notes rose in a fever pitch, then died down again to something that sounded almost like water running through a brook.

He sang.

"Almost heaven..."

LEOPOLD'S INTERLUDE 5

The sense that he was traveling with a nest of vipers eventually became impossible to ignore. Leopold had had suspicions as soon as they set out from Durum hot on Willow's trail, but with every day, he saw more signs.

Dean Weatherby's staff was much more than just a staff. It was a powerful and rare artifact the likes of which Leopold couldn't even imagine. Why did he need such a tool just to find and persuade a wayward student to come back home?

The guards were more than guards. As if what had happened in the little unnamed town wasn't enough, in the time since then, he'd seen signs of a coming battle they shouldn't be preparing for. Once or twice, he'd seen chain mail in the guards' packs that glowed—armor inscribed with powerful enchantments. He'd bet his right arm it was created to resist psychokinesis and a host of other similar spells. None of them could hope to survive being hit by the kind of spell Willow had unleashed through the broken gates of Durum, but they might survive the backsplash from being near one.

And there was Bryan. They never spoke of it, but the older man drew inward by the day. He had the confidence of the other guards, and whatever he was learning from them obviously gave him conflicted feelings.

There was only one thing Leopold could do: leave the company behind and set out on foot to catch Willow before they could. If he could somehow find her, he could warn her about what was coming. She might be able to prepare something to stop them, perhaps even something on the scale of the tunnel she'd left behind in Glint. Although there hadn't been any sign that she'd cast a spell since then. At least none of the impossible variety.

It was dangerous, but he had to do it. He lay in full gear in the small tent, and when there was a break between the circling guards, he took the chance. With only the clothes on his back, what rations he could carry in the small pack, and his still-hidden sphere of incomprehensible power from Willow, he set off into the night. The more intelligent magical creatures might know who he was by the power he carried, but the smaller ones didn't seem to care. He'd have to battle twice as hard to clear ground as he had with the company.

He'd do it, if it meant warning Willow.

He was half a mile from the company when he risked casting a small magelight, complete with a modification on-the-fly that would direct the beam mostly forwards. He hoped it would be enough that the guards wouldn't be able to see the sparking light in the distance as he weaved through the long grass choking the overgrown highway.

There was only one way to go from what he'd seen when daylight had revealed the landscape ahead, and he headed due west. A gap lay between two low mountains through which ran the remains of an ancient highway of asphaltum. He entered the pass in the pitch black and, for a moment, thought he caught the scent of wood smoke. But when he stopped to smell again, it was gone.

Maybe it was just a vague memory of home. How he wished he were home right now, or even back in Durum, where everything at least made sense. With Willow. How had things managed to go so wrong?

He was barely midway through the bordering pair of mountains at the pass when he heard a rustle to his right. He swung the narrow beam of light around at the same time he heard a *thunk*. There was a vampire lizard nailed to the ground with a featherless arrow. He searched from the direction the arrow had come, but there was no sign of the elf who'd shot the creature.

Was he still under their protection?

He made his way past twin heaps of white blasted rock that bordered the trail—perhaps once a milestone of sorts—and continued walking all through the night until the faint red haze of morning illuminated the clouds overhead. He was so deep in the mountain's shadow that the freezing night air numbed his hands.

He couldn't stop to sleep. Alone, he'd be faster than the company, but he wanted to gain as much time on them as he could to prepare Willow for what was coming. He couldn't imagine seeing her after what she'd done in Durum. To him, she was two people at once: the same old Willow, wracked with guilt at the unintended death of her professor, and some kind of nearly warbeast-level mage who was capable of leveling landscapes with the cast of a single spell. That they hadn't seen signs of spellwork of that magnitude since the town long ago made him wonder if those two forces were battling inside her as well. And if the first was winning.

Exhaustion dragged at his feet, but he kept on going as the clouds overhead grew light enough to illuminate the way. He extinguished his magelight and tried to put distance between himself and the company he knew would be following in his footsteps—tracking both him and Willow now that they knew he was gone.

He spotted a bundle in the middle of the ruined highway straight ahead. He slowed his pace until he stood above it. The package was wrapped in thick green leaves alien to these mountains. In fact, they didn't so much look like leaves at all, but more like green leather. Was it something Willow had discarded? Or a trap Annabelle had set? Not in the middle of the road, surely.

He crouched and, mindful that every second he stalled was a second he was losing to the approaching company, tugged at a thick cord of creeper that tied the bundle together.

When the leaf-leather unfurled, he couldn't believe his eyes. Food, and lots of it. Jerked meat, some kind of bread, and compressed blocks of what looked like vegetable matter. It was a gift, and it was meant for him. He scanned the treetops once more but saw no sign of his benefactors.

So he was still under the protection of the elves. Was it really that important to them that he reach Willow? He didn't spend time wondering why but hastily rewrapped everything but a strip of jerked meat and dumped the whole package into his small pack. He'd already wasted enough time as it was.

He was no tracker, as his flagging body kept reminding him, but thankfully, the signs of Willow's passage were hard to miss. Beside the road the next day, he found a heaped mound of earth. The ground on either side looked like it had been scooped out with giant shovels in a single stroke, and he supposed that was, in effect, what Willow had done. He didn't want to know what monstrosity she'd buried under there, but the others weren't so easy to miss. Later that day, he found the remains of some kind of giant insect splattered through the forest for at least a hundred feet to the right of the highway. Entire trunks had been stripped from the force of the passing entrails.

And there were more gifts. Food the second day, a staff on the third, made of some kind of smooth semi-transparent material. He'd have said it was gemstone if he hadn't seen the elves' exoskeletons in the clearing so long ago. Leopold hesitated to touch it at first, but it had been a gift, and he didn't know what would happen if he refused one from his benefactors.

The staff turned out to have some surprising side effects. Where it had been difficult to pass through the overgrown highway before, he now found it as easy as walking the paved streets of Durum. The vines and creepers seemed to part before his feet, and he always set foot on solid ground. Leopold inspected the staff again, but there were no inscriptions. Could it be part of whatever integral magic the elves used to pass through the forest so easily?

Magical creatures of all stripes had been making moves at him in the days and nights, but with the staff, they stopped completely. After six hours of no such attacks, he finally defused and let evaporate the ball of concussive force he'd held at the ready, trusting in the magic of the elves. If they were trying to help him, then he'd let them help.

A few days later, he found another gift in the road. A cloak and bag, although what effect they had, he had no idea. He exchanged the cloak given to him by the guards for the gift but stuffed the empty bag into his still serviceable one. It would have been a pain to transfer all of his food from one to another, and there was no reason to waste a bag he might need later when they were so easy to store.

* * *

Two days later, walking on the road and making excellent time, he felt a twinge in his back. He turned around and searched the hillsides on either side of the highway, then the stream at the bottom of the gully, but he couldn't find anyone watching him. He supposed the elves were probably there, but he hadn't seen one the entire journey since that first night.

He turned, and before he'd taken three steps, the twinge turned into a pressure that almost brought him to his knees. He tried to turn again, then the pressure increased tenfold, and he toppled face down on the broken asphaltum. It was like he was carrying a hundred-pound weight in his pack, but he couldn't move his arms and legs to shift it. He realized he'd been paralyzed. His chest rose and fell shallowly under the magical weight.

It took two days for the company to arrive. Two days of endless hours spent alternately worrying about Willow, and then himself. He was losing his lead minute by minute, but he couldn't move a muscle. Then there was his second most recurring worry that the elves' staff would fail, and he would be attacked by predators on the road. By the time Dean Weatherby and his troop marched up the broken road, he'd figured the trap out. The elves had known. They'd tried to help in their own way by offering replacements for the gear that had been tainted with sigils the dean had sewn into his clothing. But he'd kept the pack—stupid—thinking there was no reason to discard it. He didn't blame the elves for leaving him in the road. He should have known this would happen.

Dean Weatherby came at the front of the column just past twilight, and Leopold caught the soft sounds of the group breaking to make camp. The dean crouched down beside him, precariously close to his battered glasses, and tutted.

"You shouldn't have run off."

"You expected it," Leopold gasped in anger. After two days of no food and water, he felt faint, but he'd keep himself awake enough for this. "Why'd you trigger it? Leash too short? Amateur."

Leopold couldn't see the dean's face, but he felt the other man's anger crackle the air between them. The dean reached down and picked up Leopold's staff.

"Interesting. I wondered how you were doing it. Seems like the elves have taken a liking to you."

"You thought I'd already reached her," Leopold chuckled weakly, the edges of his vision darkening. "Not what you were expecting. You thought she'd stay to fight for me."

"We all have our little disappointments," he said, and Leopold saw him raise the foot of his staff.

"You wouldn't have stood a chance," Leopold sighed.

The staff came down hard on his temple.

CHAPTER 21

Asche was much different than Willow had expected. On the journey here, with her dozens of executions of sentient warbeasts, both sane and insane, she'd built up the idea of Asche as a sick and twisted simulacrum of a city. A place where terrible beings were born and where terrible things were done.

Both may have still been true, but it was much less the dark fortress that she'd been expecting. First of all, there was no wall surrounding the exiled city-state. At first, she'd thought the outlying houses and shops were just another small town as they passed through. But at the crest of a ridge, she saw the entire city laid out before her, and it was revealed to be more than a small town. Thousands of people bustled along streets paved in stone.

Second, the buildings were as Annabelle, who sullenly followed behind like a chastised child, had described. Many were constructed in architectural styles that seemed alien to Willow, but taken as a whole, the city had a strange sort of cohesion. As if it had come from another place or time.

The most surprising thing about the city-state was the presence of nonhuman creatures following docilely behind their owners. Great hounds, three times the size of any normal dog with bristling amethyst spines, hulked along carrying packs laden with produce. In an open-air smithy, she saw a salamander at least three feet long blowing gouts of flame into the coalbed where a nest of smaller salamanders writhed. The blacksmith—whose left arm, which was multisegmented and glossy, held the steel directly—didn't seem perturbed at the nearness of such a dangerous magical creature.

Perhaps it was because of the brass bands that encircled all their necks. The inscriptions glowed bright enough that she could see them in the daylight, flaring when the creatures dared to look Willow's way. She looked each of them in the eye, although few of the humans seemed to notice her. The creatures shot her furtive glances, which were immediately followed by jerked heads as their inscriptions glowed and reasserted control.

"So this is what he meant," Willow murmured, thinking back to Walter in his cabin. She hadn't understood him then, and she felt sick now. What else hadn't she understood about this place, about what she was walking into?

She followed the large main road towards the towering building at the end—the town hall where she'd finally meet this master of Professor Brandeweiss and Annabelle. The person who'd sent wave after wave of warbeasts to their deaths in single combat against her.

"You use the magical creatures. They're bound to you."

"As they should be," Annabelle replied firmly. "They're beasts of burden, nothing more."

The looks in their eyes told Willow that that wasn't true. These were no mere salamanders and rockhounds—their size alone betrayed the unspeakable things done to their ancestors. These were closer to warbeasts than their natural counterparts out in the forests and mountains. And she'd bet her staff they harbored intelligence that bordered on human.

Willow didn't acknowledge Annabelle's remark, instead keeping pace to the town hall at the center of the city. Everything she'd been taught about Asche should have shown it as a wasteland, but apparently that was all a lie. How much of what she'd learned in her history of magic lecture was propaganda? She felt her stomach roil with anxiety at just how much she didn't know. Would she be able to walk into this unknown confrontation and make up the difference with raw power?

She still thought so.

The doors of the hall loomed as she climbed the steps. They were made of fused stone, which shimmered in the sunlight, so different from the pale stone that made up Durum and the sandstone they'd used in Bridgewater. Perhaps this building really was left over from an era past, as Annabelle had suggested.

Willow expected a grand gallery as she pushed through the double-high doors—a battlefield where she would pit her wits and power against this master. But what she saw instead was a carpeted lobby illuminated by buzzing lights that ran along twin flanking lines of stone columns. As Willow walked in and past the columns, searching for any laid traps, she saw that the lights were actually luminescent insects hovering in midair. Why they didn't just use magelight or inscripted lights, she had no idea.

She heard Annabelle let out a sigh of relief behind her but didn't deign to inquire as to why. The woman had nearly completed her mission. Now it was Willow's chance to get what *she* came for. She took a deep breath and set off across the lobby.

There was what she could only describe as a secretary at the desk at the end of the hall. With a final glance for hidden assassins, Willow approached, preparing herself as best she could, and clicked her staff on the ground. The secretary, who'd been writing something down on a sheet of paper, looked up.

"Willow Tremont?" the woman asked.

Willow's eyes widened, and she broke out in a cold sweat. She had the near-inescapable urge to glance about the hall again for any traps. How long had they been expecting her? "Y-Yes," Willow stammered, then clicked her teeth shut, feeling foolish for showing weakness. "You knew I was coming?"

"I was told to expect you," the secretary said, rising from her chair. She was wearing a long dress and, one of her feet ended in, not a foot, but something vaguely insectile. "Right this way," she motioned. "The governor is expecting you."

With every other step, the insect foot clicked against stone under the carpeted runner. Though Annabelle seemed unaffected, Willow couldn't stop staring at it. Eventually, the secretary looked back and caught her.

"Prostheses like this aren't common where you come from then?" she asked, and Willow jerked her head up.

"Sorry," she said automatically, but the secretary waved the apology away.

"It's not strange here, no matter what you may think. I was in an accident as a child, but I'm not the only one. Some voluntarily get prostheses to enhance themselves, although having had no choice in the matter, I can't see myself giving up another limb."

"Could they not grow it back?" Willow asked.

"We have our own expertise," was the reply. "I'm sure if you'd ever been sick, you'd know that it takes a lot of accumulated knowledge to treat an illness."

That stopped Willow in her tracks.

Ever been… sick? She hadn't looked at herself in a mirror in probably a month, but she no longer limped, and her muscles didn't ache either. If she had to guess from that remark, her sunken cheeks had filled out as well. Only the buzzed side of her head, where hair was already regrowing to a stiff fuzz, indicated she'd ever been seriously injured.

And that's what she needed to remember now.

Willow gripped her staff hard as she forced herself to recall those buried memories. She had been hurt by these people, nearly killed, and had people she'd known and loved killed by them. And after it all, she was here. She'd survived and come out of the ordeal with unnatural powers unmatched by anything she knew.

Asche might have thrown her a few surprises, but she was going to make them relent. By the gods, if she had to tear this city out from under them, she would!

After going down a long hall with framed portraits lining the wooden walls, the woman knocked at a door intricately inlaid with filigreed silver. A muffled voice shouted in the affirmative, and she led the way through.

Beyond the door was an office with a high, multi-paned glass wall looking down the main street. Thick draperies bordered the window, and the floor was carpeted with a sumptuous rug. An elderly man stood from behind a hulking wooden desk that reminded her of the dean's and smiled.

"Thank you, Samantha, that will be all," he said. The woman nodded and left, closing the door behind her. He came around the desk to stand face-to-face with Willow.

"Willow Tremont," he said, his smile wide like he was a child at a candy store. "My oh my, how you've grown! I can almost feel it from here."

Willow's resolve faltered. Was this even the right man? Was the governor Annabelle and Carl's master? She'd been expecting some kind of climactic battle, not this octogenarian who looked like he could barely make it to the toilet five times a night.

"You know my name," Willow ventured. "What's yours?"

"Andrew Yates," he said, rolling up onto the balls of his feet in excitement. "Oh, how I've waited for this day!"

"How did you know I was coming?" Willow asked. Had Annabelle's master told him? Or had the hybrids, like they had with Walter?

"You had to come, did you not?" he said. "My tide of warbeasts made sure of that. You could have hidden behind the crumbling walls of Durum and attacked from there. But it was Annabelle's job to get you out, and it seems as if she succeeded."

Willow looked behind her, but Annabelle had shrunken away from the two of them and stood with her back pressed against the door, as if she wanted nothing more than to escape this room. The nurse's fear unnerved her, but that warning bell was well-swamped by what the old man had revealed.

Willow's stomach turned with rage and disgust.

So this *was* Annabelle and Carl's master. *This* was the creator of the warbeasts, every one of them. That humanoid thing that had threatened Durum, with its melting face and insane screeching, had almost destroyed everything she'd come to care for. It had killed Leopold.

Her fists clenched, and her molars ground together at the memory of his crushed corpse.

"You... you..." Willow could barely keep her mind on track with the rush of traumatic memories. "You have to stop making them."

"Oh, I've already stopped," he said, and the smile widened just a little further. "Why would I make any more? Oh no, no reason to do so."

Willow blinked in surprise, and words failed her. He'd already stopped? This wasn't going at all like she'd expected, and she felt as though she were way, way out of her depth. Why did he think he didn't need to make any more?

"But I killed them all."

"No, miss, you certainly did not," he said, the smile not wavering for a moment. "Did you come straight west? Or hook around to the south? I suppose you might have met the corvid if you'd come west.

The deathworm, I think, I sent to the south. Ah, there were so many. All for you, of course. I didn't know which way you'd come, so I had to cover all my bases, as the ancients used to say."

South? He'd sent warbeasts south? What had happened to them?

"Where are they?" she asked, feeling the blood drain from her face. "The ones you sent... to the south."

"Oh, they'll have arrived at Durum by now," he said. "Yes, certainly the first dozen or so. Leave your quarry no ground, as they say. Can't have you going back if you lost the stomach for it, could I?"

Durum. The city might have been destroyed by the thing with the purple nimbus if she hadn't killed it, and it was the *weakest* of the warbeasts she'd encountered! Some of the others had begged her for death, but over half had been too far gone to know what they were up against. Their battles were far beyond anything Durum could have matched.

"No," she spat and dropped her staff, reaching out to grab the man by the lapels of his strange blouse. It was padded with great *V*'s of fabric folded to either side. A convenient knot encircled his elderly neck. She considered pulling it tight and choking him with it. "It's... not... possible!"

Andrew laughed, a high laugh that was much like a child's, with no knowledge of good or evil. The laugh of a little boy who'd kicked over an anthill just because he could. It made her want to scream.

"I thought you'd be smarter than this," he said, shaking his head. "Oh well, you'll learn. I'll see to it."

Willow summoned up her psychokinesis and... nothing. Her eyes went wide as her staff refused to respond to her call. Something was blocking her, as if there were waves of essence crashing in against her own and canceling them out. The old man reached up and touched the side of her neck.

Something folded against her skin. It sealed with a burning heat on the other side of her throat. When she jerked back and reached up, she found she'd been collared.

"Good girl," Andrew said, not once removing his bright eyes from hers. "Now, **play dead**."

CHAPTER 22

Once again, Willow wove magic in the thick air between her hands. The idea that she'd be consciously casting spells again so soon after her self-imposed ban was ridiculous, except for the circumstances she found herself in.

"Void," she intoned, and the sphere of essence between her hands turned black like sackcloth. She added another layer to the spell, and another, spinning each in opposing directions and giving an ultimate destination.

Forwards.

The essence surrounding her in the small chamber reacted to her spell. It swirled around and fell into the void core as it made contact. The air was thick with the stuff, almost like a heavy mist, and it glowed like fog in daylight. From what Andrew had told her in one of his little lectures, only an essence concentration of over a hundred em per cubic inch would glow.

So what was she saturated with now? What was she breathing every moment of every day?

Willow completed the spell and stepped back quickly to the opposing wall of her chamber. She was trapped in a cube, one side a translucent gold barrier through which Andrew could inspect her progress. She'd woken in here minutes or hours after he'd given her the command to *play dead*, and found she was unable to break the collar around her neck.

The spell activated. The two outermost layers rotated at a speed she couldn't track with her eyes, and the sphere of void essence twisted with them into a thin stream. It hammered through the twin spinning cases and drilled into the golden barrier.

The entire spell lasted less than ten seconds before the core was exhausted. Its spinning encasements dispelled as the pressure between the essence surrounding it and the void disappeared. She knew it had failed. If it hadn't, the whole room on the other side of the barrier would have been obliterated.

Slow clapping echoed from the spaced silver plates that made up the walls of her prison. She peered through the thick essence to see that, at some point in the process, Andrew had appeared.

"Splendid work. Really, amazing stuff," he said, his smile wide and eyes bright. She'd come to think of them like wolf's eyes. She should have known when she met him—when he couldn't drop that rictus grin—that there was something wrong.

"I'm reading over two thousand em from that latest attempt. You haven't tired yourself out yet, have you?"

In response, Willow roared and spread the two hundred-plus limbs of psychokinetic power that surrounded her at all times. She focused on one silver panel in particular, tearing and ripping at the seams of her prison, but the metal wouldn't budge. The metal itself nullified her attacks when any spell came into contact with it, though it wasn't the same disturbing effect that Andrew's office had had on her. The golden barrier was the weak spot.

"Someone needs to control their temper," Andrew lightly chided.

Willow crossed the twenty-foot span of the cell in a flash until she was tearing at the barrier itself. Whoever had cast it had pumped it full of an impossible amount of essence for it to survive everything she'd thrown at it. That, or it was being fed by the same essence source that constantly streamed into her cell.

"That'll be quite enough," Andrew said, but Willow wouldn't obey.

She scratched at the collar on her throat, once again overcome with the idea that if she could just get it off, she could break free. With Andrew right there, it would be child's play to tear him apart. She sliced a finger on the metal.

"I said, **sit**."

The collar weighed a hundred pounds in an instant, but Willow was prepared for this cheap trick. She reinforced her legs with psychokinesis, adding her essential strength to her growing physical prowess. Her joints popped in protest, but they held.

"Stubborn today," he said with a frozen smile. "**Sit**."

The weight doubled, but she resisted. She straightened until she stood at her full height, eye to eye with the old man. She smiled back.

"**Sit**," he said for a third time, and the weight became almost unbearable.

She could feel her bones creaking dangerously and knew that if her psychokinesis slipped for even an instant, she would break every bone in her body. Her smile wavered.

"**Good girl**," Andrew said, just as she exhausted the last dregs of essence in her body.

She fell to a knee and began violently shaking, from fear more than anything. What if he hadn't called it off at the end? Was she really committed to letting herself be crushed by a smiling psychopath in a laboratory?

She exhaled slowly, all the air in her lungs even as they screamed for more. There was little to do in the cell but attempt to break free and think. And in that thinking, she'd devised a method to chart her non-consensual progress. She knew from her mother that an adult's lungs took in about three hundred and fifty cubic inches of air. Given that the essence saturation in the cell was at least a hundred em per cubic inch, the single breath she took, which barely brought her back to full capacity, suggested that her capacity might now be somewhere around thirty-five thousand em.

That was if Andrew was telling the truth about the em concentration in the air. If she was achieving perfect essence intake through her lungs... And if the idea of thirty-five thousand em wasn't insane to begin with.

"Hmm," Andrew said, tapping the plate beside her cell.

She couldn't see it, but she assumed there was one there because the other cells on this level of the laboratory had one. They were all empty, though. She supposed he hadn't been lying before when he said he'd given up creating warbeasts.

"You're proving to be much more expensive than I thought," he said, then shook his head. "But no matter, you'll be well worth it. Although I'm sure you'll be the death of some of my aether vaults."

He shook his head again, then kneeled to her level, his strange suit bowing out at the chest.

"Did you know that, at first, it wasn't called essence? They called it aether. I've taken up the term. I prefer it, but the ancients thought they'd discovered something they'd long dismissed. Luminiferous aether."

"I don't care," Willow breathed. She was exhausted physically, even though it was her psychokinesis that had taken the beating. The nearness of death had taken its toll on her yet again.

"Don't shirk your lessons," Andrew said with that rigid smile. "They called it luminiferous because, as I'm sure you're aware, it glows when gathered in sufficient concentrations. It was years before I was able to see the effect myself. This was back when I was still dean of the Durum Arcanum."

Willow jerked around to look at him, surprise evident on her face.

"Oh yes. You wouldn't know it, though. I was given the boot, so to say. The trustees and governors found my more enlightened ideas... objectionable. No reason to develop something ourselves if nature would do the trick for us."

"The warbeasts," Willow said, finally propping herself into a sitting position. "You were trying to create warbeasts again in violation of the pact."

"The pact? My dear, we never *stopped* growing warbeasts. And if you think Raly has either, you're fooling yourself. No, I daresay Durum, shining Durum, probably released a few of their own at the end. How I'd love to have seen it. The battles must have been extraordinary."

Willow clenched her teeth, trying not to remember everyone she'd left behind. Margaret and Benny. Bryan. Leopold, who was a cold corpse by now. How many waves of warbeast attacks could they have withstood? She knew the answer.

She blinked hard, hating the hot tears that coursed down her cheeks.

"I... hate you," she hissed with barely restrained rage, her breath hitching with a suppressed sob. "I hate you!"

"Thus spake man to his god," Andrew said.

"You are no god."

"Oh," and Andrew laughed. *Laughed!* "Maybe not to the others, but to you? I'm your god, Willow Tremont. From my hand flew the disease that made you what you are."

The swirling mist of essence in her cell froze, glowing particles suspended in midair. Andrew looked up at a panel and hummed to himself again.

"What did you say?"

"The Wasting. It's an invention of my own creation—in fact, the very idea that got me booted from Durum. I came to Asche, climbed the political ladder, and finally gained access to the resources I needed to complete my research. A disease that attacks the spinal column, rendering its infantile host paralyzed. The victim must gain superhuman magical abilities or die."

"You made it?" Willow choked out, not quite believing what she was hearing. "With magic?"

"Magic? No, my dear girl. With science! The ancients have lost more than we could ever know. But within their preserved ruins in Asche, I found laboratories and texts that taught me the forgotten art of genomic manipulation. It was easy once I had the equipment and the samples. Polio… it was a miracle they didn't destroy themselves sooner."

Willow scooted away from the transparent barrier. "No," she whispered, and the particles of essence began to swirl again. She shook her head. "No!"

"Very interesting," Andrew said to the panel, the trail of their conversation seemingly lost. "And good news! It appears you're coming along right on schedule. I'd hate to see you be unprepared for your big reunion."

"What—" Willow couldn't force herself to ask the rest of the question. Everything that came out of this man's mouth was poison, whether it was true or not. She had to recover from what he'd just revealed, or she'd lose her mind.

"My old colleague Dean Weatherby is on his way here to see you. I daresay the reunion will be one for the ages."

* * *

A door opened far away and footsteps approached. Willow managed to sit up and wipe her face free of most of the tears and snot before Annabelle appeared in front of the barrier.

"Willow," she said, her voice magnified by whatever inscription work was present in the silver plates.

Willow looked away.

"Willow, please," she said. She sounded on the verge of tears. "I didn't know. Please look at me."

"You brought me to him," she said tonelessly. "You knew he was going to do something."

"I thought he wanted... I thought he would make you some kind of soldier. Not this. Not a..."

Willow looked at her through the barrier. Annabelle seemed better now than she had on the road. She'd clearly had a shower and was being taken care of. Willow, on the other hand, received chunks of cooked meat portaled in from somewhere else that she had to eat with her hands. She hadn't had a bath in weeks.

"A warbeast," Willow said. "Tell me, did you know then? When that thing was attacking Durum? What it had been? Did you know it was once a person?"

Annabelle looked away. "I suspected," she said. "But it's been so long since I left Asche, and I never knew much about what he was doing down here."

"You knew enough, though, didn't you?" Willow said. "You suspected he'd done it when you saw me for the first time."

Annabelle sighed. "Yes," she said. "That's when I first put it together."

Willow scoffed. "Lucky. I wish I'd known enough then to stay far away from you. If I hadn't let you and Carl work me over..."

But wishes weren't horses, and she was being forced to grow now beyond her control. How long could she be in this essence womb before she began to change? How long before she lost her humanity?

And how long before she lost her mind?

"You were right, though," Willow said. "He did send that warbeast for me. I just didn't know then that if I had stayed, we could have fought them off. Maybe the cannons wouldn't have done anything, but I could have. And I'd still have the city."

Willow reached out, threading her fingers through the concentrated essence, feeling nothing. There was nothing left to feel. She was hollowed out.

"Did you know the dean is coming for me? With guards? And what will Andrew make me do, I wonder? Kill them?"

Annabelle shook her head. Willow lowered her arm, but the fog still curled and folded in on itself around the psychokinetic limb she'd left in midair.

"You're not here to get me out," Willow said. "So what are you here for? To apologize?"

Annabelle shuffled back.

"Not accepted," Willow said, and the other woman fled from the laboratory.

Leopold's Interlude 6

They kept Leopold in the back as the column moved through the mountains. His staff had been almost useless to the fifteen remaining men as they traversed the overgrown highway. Its magic only seemed to affect the wielder, who would swiftly leave the rest behind if they didn't check their progress. Leopold would have tried to make a break for it, would have left everything behind and stumbled into the frost alone and freezing, but for the manacles he wore.

They were mostly heavy iron and chafed his wrists. But he noticed bands of inscribed copper and, strangely enough, silver running through the insides of the cuffs. They reached halfway up his forearm and sapped his will and essence equally until he was nearly stupefied. He wondered if these manacles were meant for Willow.

What would they do to her when the column caught up?

Every night they suffered attacks, which Leopold was unable to assist in defending against. He wouldn't have if he'd had the ability. Instead, he would've run off, damn the danger. Their guards dropped like flies. First fifteen, then thirteen, then ten. When they reached the city after a particularly vicious attack by nearly invisible arboreal elves, there were eight guards left in their party.

Plus the dean and Leopold. Ten total.

The night before they entered the city—the one they'd glimpsed

The remaining guards unsnapped their leather armor to reveal inscribed brass chainmail underneath. The metal seemed to glow slightly, as Leopold had seen one night so long ago.

"You can leave your other weapons here," the dean mildly suggested. "The null rods will be the only things effective past this point, I'm afraid."

The guards each unbuckled their belts and slipped their scabbards from the leather strips. In their place, they applied the holstered null rods and re-buckled. Leopold caught Bryan shoving something wrapped in cloth into the back of his belt, where the dean wouldn't notice. He averted his eyes instantly. Whatever it was, it might help Willow and possibly himself.

"Alright," the dean said, tapping his staff on the ground. Rolf stood beside him, still with his sword strapped beside his null rod.

"Forwards," Rolf ordered, taking the lead.

Leopold stumbled along behind the company, dragged by the guard on the end. When they entered the darkness, the man drew the null rod from his holster and swiveled his head from side to side as his eyes adjusted to the dark. It was warmer inside the building and much darker.

When Leopold's eyes finally adjusted, he saw laid out before him not a sunken theater, but a smooth-floored great room. It looked as though it could seat almost a thousand, lit all around with bobbing lights. It was like the town hall in his own hometown, except ten times the size. He wondered if it was normally used for governmental functions when it wasn't being commandeered as some sort of showdown chamber.

"Corinth Weatherby, it's been a long time," a voice boomed out from all around them. The guards turned in confusion, with only the dean keeping his eyes straight ahead. Leopold followed his gaze to a large double door set in the other side of the hall.

"Not long enough," the dean called out, his voice magically amplified by a quickly whispered spell. "I thought we'd never see you again. I should've been so lucky."

"Lucky is what you are. What you all are. You are here to see the beginning of a new order. You have the honor to serve as the sacrifices that will carry my world through its birthing pains."

"You always talked too much. Shut up and come out! Unless you plan to bore us to death."

"Never," the voice said, then the doors at the other end of the building cracked. Out strode an elderly man with a giant smile plastered on his face, dragging a woman behind him on a leash. Without her limp and the sharp angles of her cheekbones, it took a moment for Leopold to recognize that the woman was Willow.

A low sound started in Leopold's throat, and he pushed through the syrupy effect of the manacles. The light from outside faded and blinked out as the doors behind them slammed shut. And still Leopold tried to scream. Eventually, through an infinite moment of effort, he shrieked.

"Willow!"

She was so far away across the great hall, but her eyes opened wide, and he felt the moment she locked eyes with his. Her mouth fell open.

"Leopold?"

"You've brought a snack, how thoughtful," the old man said with a grin. "What do you think is going to happen, Corinth? We battle for control of the wraith? Or are you planning to kill her before she reaches the threshold?"

The dean gripped his staff so hard his joints cracked.

"You will not make that monstrosity," the dean growled from behind clenched teeth. "And if you do, I'll be damned if you're the one in control of it."

"Ah, so it's the first, then," the old man mocked. "You'll take her back to Durum? You fool, Durum's gone."

Time ground to a halt. Durum gone? Leopold turned his head to find Bryan and saw that the man's face had gone ashen. What did the old man mean by *gone*?

"I know," the dean said, and a strained smile grew across his taut face. "I'll just have to take your little fiefdom, won't I?"

"Oh, to be young! Such ambition," the old man laughed. "Everyone wants to rule the world."

He pulled something from the breast of his jacket and gripped Willow around the neck from behind. Leopold had just enough time to realize the old man was holding a short dagger before he plunged it into Willow's back.

"Let the game begin."

CHAPTER 23

Willow felt a white-hot pain bloom in her back, and she tried to take a gasp of air—but she couldn't breathe. Her heart spasmed in her chest, and she knew it was beating against *something*. Andrew pulled her close to him.

"Carl did a wonderful job keeping you contained, but we don't need this anymore," he whispered into her ear, then pulled the silver amulet from her neck. The moment it was gone, her world expanded two, three, four times, and the pain of her mortal injury faded.

The flesh body collapsed to the ground, though little blood ran from the injury. It, the wraith, saw that the dagger which had been plunged into its flesh was inscribed and thin. And from the feel of the effect, it could tell the device was meant to keep it out of the body.

It was about to turn on its attacker, an old man, but six other bodies in the chamber drew rods of magic so intense they almost hurt to observe. The wraith knew instinctively that if those things touched it, they would do grievous injury.

A glowing circular gateway of white light opened in the air above.

The wraith paused, momentarily enraptured by the portal. The white light pouring through its borders promised peace and respite. As much as it wanted to ascend to the gateway, it couldn't. A thin tether suspended it between worlds, leading to the prone body of a woman on the floor.

It drew back to the present as a man in the center of the group raised his staff and pulled back like a javelin thrower. The tip unfurled into three spiraled prongs, and he hurled the device. As the staff flew, the single shaft unraveled, and the three constituent rods spun in the air as they latched onto the wraith. Binding themselves to it, they compressed the wraith to a smaller size, squeezing it into a spherical prison.

It raged at the violation, but the three rods had already sealed themselves around the back and were shrinking the wraith to a size akin to the man. It knew itself to be so much more than this, and it hated that man with his staff. It would give anything to destroy him.

There was a younger man with the group, a body without a black rod, manacled, and the wraith was aware as he gently touched a small sphere in his robe—a sphere that seemed vaguely familiar. He made a sign towards the wraith, and the sphere exploded in a blinding shaft of fire.

"No!" roared the man who'd thrown the staff, but the damage was done.

The wraith's stabber hurled himself to the ground, and the inferno blasted at the bands that contained the wraith's power. The bands melted in an instant, their inscriptions flowing together into a meaningless babble, and breaking the bonds became child's play.

The wraith expanded again, dwarfing all of the men in the room. The men tracked it as it grew to its full size, almost scraping the ceiling of the vast wooden chamber. One of the men drew a sword and rushed towards it.

It gripped the man, but something under his armor made him slippery. It tightened its hold on him, and the man stumbled. Harder still, and he went to one knee, then began scrabbling at the leather. Smoke billowed out from under his breastplate, lit from within by a faint red glow. The man screamed, and the wraith clamped down a final time.

Whatever had been protecting the man gave way, and he pulped like an overripe apple. One of the dangerous rods fell to the ground from his corpse, still sheathed. What a waste.

The six men wielding black rods ran towards the wraith and the mush that was once the man with the sword. It reached into the floorboards, seeping through their fibers, and jerked. The wood splintered before the oncoming charge.

The manacled man yelled something and threw himself into another man, sending them both to the ground. At some point, the young man's manacles had come undone, perhaps from the sheer density of essence in the air. No matter—if he took up a rod, the wraith would kill him.

With two hundred hands, it plucked shards of wood from the shattered floor and hurled them towards the attackers. Its hands might not be able to reach them without undue force, but the wood had an easy enough time peppering their bodies until they sprouted quills. The men fell on the spot, staining the stage with seeping blood.

The man who'd thrown the staff chanted, and the twist of his essence formed into the same wounding effect that the black rods held. The wraith gathered its full strength to smash down on the mage in mid-cast, when the previously manacled man came from behind and slid the pulped man's sword through the mage's chest. The man stuttered mid-cast, and the lance of death dispersed on ethereal winds. He fell to his knees.

The last man in scripted armor threw something at it, shining and twirling through the air. It flung a board from the stage towards the man, which bisected him easily, but his projectile was coming fast. The wraith reached up to intercept the missile, but too slow. The object entered its body and...

It wasn't a projectile. It was a cane. A metal cane. A cane her father had made her long ago when her body was wasted. A cane she'd used to defeat an impossible enemy.

A cane she thought lost forever.

Willow found herself, the cane hovering midair, staring down at Leopold through eyes that were not eyes. She had a thousand. And she had none. Her real eyes were back with her body, which was slowly bleeding out behind her. Andrew was still standing over it, watching the slaughter with glee.

Willow turned as much as she could. Really, she moved her attention past the numerous twists of essence hiding among the rafters, towards the old man and his rictus grin. That grin faltered for the first time.

He looked down at her body, and she instantly saw his next move. He dropped to his knees and reached for the inscribed dagger, no doubt to widen the wound and speed her demise, but she caught him with the cane. It passed through him as easily as it had the deathworm, and his body slumped to the floor in two pieces.

Then Leopold was there. Leopold! He was alive, *miraculously alive*, and he was kneeling beside her. He turned her onto her side, exposing the tip of the dagger through her breast.

"Oh gods, I don't know what to do," Leopold muttered. He touched the inscribed handle of the dagger, then pulled back. It was clear he was afraid of killing her faster.

The gateway called her, the tether weakening with every passing moment. But she couldn't leave him. She couldn't.

"Remove the dagger, Leopold," Willow said, the air itself her vocal cords. He looked up into the swirling sphere of essence, which was her ethereal form. What had Andrew called her? The wraith?

"You'll bleed out," he spoke to the cloud, eyes searching for any feature to fix on. But there was nothing human in there.

For the barest moment, she nearly commanded him to proceed anyway—the pull of the gate was so strong. "Annabelle!" she thundered instead.

Leopold ducked and covered his ears. She'd said it with every board of the theater, every post and nail, even the ones surrounding those knots of essence in the rafters. She'd have to deal with them eventually.

They waited, Leopold applying pressure around the twin puncture wounds, until Willow sensed a presence approaching the closed doors at the other end of the theater. The locked doors rattled ineffectually. Willow punched a hole in one of them, through which Annabelle slowly emerged.

"Oh," she gasped, looking around at the carnage.

Willow had been reborn in it, so the sight no longer bothered her, but she supposed another would be disgusted. She gripped Annabelle around the waist and hauled her across the room to land on her knees beside Leopold.

"You'll have to do the healing, I'm afraid," Willow said from above. Annabelle looked up for the first time, trying to focus on the luminous sphere.

"He did it, then," Annabelle breathed. "I don't know if I—"

"Not yet, he hasn't," Willow said. "My body isn't dead. If you are truly contrite, save me now. For him."

Annabelle glanced at Leopold, then bent down and examined the knife. She bit her lip and began weaving her hands in the spiral spell-form.

"Pull the knife on my command," Annabelle said to Leopold. He laid his hand on the handle and nodded. Willow watched with detached amusement. Who would've thought her boyfriend, back from the dead, would be working alongside her traitorous guide?

"Now," she said, and Leopold pulled the knife.

Immediately, Willow felt a connection open up that had been pinched by the knife and its inscriptions—the thread that tied her back to her body. Through the thread, she could sense she was very close to death. It felt familiar, as if from a half-remembered dream.

The glowing gateway overhead closed at the pulling of the knife, leaving behind not even a breath of essence to indicate its presence. Despair tugged at her with its disappearance, but she had made her decision.

Healing essence poured from Annabelle's hands into Willow's chest, coating the inside of the channel that ran through her heart. It pulsed with the imperative to *heal*. She felt flesh knitting back together, chambers and vessels sealing, and blood conjuring out of nothing. Leopold watched agog as the puncture wound in Willow's back closed up completely.

Annabelle rolled the body over onto its back and opened an eyelid. She bent down and laid her ear on the chest, then looked back up at the hovering, thirty-foot-wide sphere.

"Your body's alive. You can return now. I think."

Willow found that, for a long moment, she didn't want to. She was afraid. Afraid of seeing what she'd done through human eyes. Afraid of starting life again knowing what she was capable of. Of knowing that this almost limitless power coursed through her veins. Even after everything, she'd barely used a thousand em.

Slowly, Willow sank. The sphere contracted as she followed the thread which led back to her body. With proximity, sensation returned. She felt soreness in her chest, bruises blooming on her knees from where she'd hit the floor. Wetness on her cheeks, she didn't know what from. Had she been crying?

She followed the thread completely, and, as she entered her body, a bloody bar of metal with a wooden handle fell to the ground beside a corpse a dozen feet away. She opened her eyes.

When had Leopold taken her head in his hands? He was smiling. He was crying. She was crying, too, hot tears tracing lines to her ears.

"Hey," she choked out.

He leaned down and kissed her.

MORE BOOKS YOU MAY LIKE

Grimoires and Gunsmoke by S. Dudley

**When a dragon-blooded emperor reaches for godhood,
Earth reaches back—with bullets.**

The plan was simple: conquer a new realm, harvest its souls, and become a god.

But nothing about Ohio is simple.

Armed with grit, ingenuity, and a lot of guns, the scrappy humans of Earth prove they're not the kneeling type. In a clash of magic and modern firepower, alliances are forged, friendships are tested, and ambitions burn brighter than the skies over the Midwest.

Can humanity stand its ground, or will the emperor's quest for divinity grind them to dust?

Perfect for fans of epic battles, unlikely heroes, and a healthy dose of fantasy-meets-modern warfare.

Available now on Kindle Unlimited, Audible, and paperback!

Legend of the Runeforger by Possumtail

**Trapped in a robotic shell,
one man must reclaim a future he can't remember.**

In a distant future, Alexander scrapes by in a rundown repair shop while secretly searching for answers to his fragmented past. He has skills he can't explain and only foggy glimpses of who he used to be.

His solitary quest takes an unexpected turn when he crosses paths with a sharp-witted girl who awakens echoes of his lost humanity. Together, they navigate a galaxy full of stagnant technology, shifting loyalties, and corporate secrets, but Alexander's awakening has not gone unnoticed.

Powerful forces are closing in. Some want to control him. Others want him destroyed. With every step forward, he risks drawing the attention of enemies who see him as the key to something far greater than he understands.

Will he succumb to adversity or emerge from the crucible stronger than before?

Embark on an epic science-fiction adventure that explores identity, survival, and the price of progress across a fractured galaxy.

Available now on Kindle Unlimited, Audible, and paperback!

Demon Queen Wants to Paint by Amber Atlas

All she ever wanted was to paint.

After falling into the sea, Rosa awakens in a strange new world where demons, elves, and other fantastical creatures are real. Unfortunately, she has been reborn as a baby. And not just any baby, but the daughter of the Demon King himself.

Follow her journey as she learns to accept her new identity as Crown Princess Morrigan while navigating the dangers of demon society and the Underworld. After all, being discovered to have a human soul might be the least of her problems.

About the Series: *Demon Queen Wants to Paint* is a cozy reincarnation fantasy full of magic, charm, and quiet determination. Perfect for fans of slice-of-life isekai, slow-burn growth, and coming-of-age stories about finding joy, friendship, and your place in a world that doesn't quite fit.

Available now on Kindle Unlimited, Audible, and paperback!

Thank you for reading a MoonQuill original novel. More exciting stories can be found on at www.moonquill.com.

We would greatly appreciate it if you could take a moment to leave a review. Each one helps the author and supports their ability to continue writing fantastic books for everyone to enjoy!

Scan the QR code below to subscribe to our mailing list and be notified of new releases. You'll receive a few ebooks for free!

www.ingramcontent.com/pod-product-compliance
Lightning Source LLC
Chambersburg PA
CBHW020750310726
48969CB00002B/477